Chinese Spring

Also by Christopher New

The China Coast Trilogy:

Shanghai

A Change of Flag

The Chinese Box

and

The Kaminsky Cure

The Gage Street Courtesan

Goodbye Chairman Mao

A Small Place in the Desert

The Road to Maridur

CHRISTOPHER NEW

Chinese Spring

CONTRABAND

Published by Contraband
an imprint of Saraband,
Digital World Centre,
1 Lowry Plaza,
The Quays, Salford, M50 3UB

www.saraband.net

ISBN: 9781912235148
ebook: 9781912235155

1 3 5 7 9 8 6 4 2

Designed and typeset by EM&EN
Printed and bound in Great Britain by Clays Ltd, Elcograf S.p.A.

Chinese Spring

June 4th 1989

The noise of gunfire rose from all over the centre of Peking. It was unremitting. On the streets leading down to Tiananmen Square furious people stared in disbelief at the glow in the sky, listening to the sound of shots . . .

The bicycle rickshaws scooped up the injured, others were shunted onto bikes and pedalled to hospital. Many were carried away by frantic local residents. There was confusion and despair among those who could hardly credit that their own army was firing wildly at them. Many were bystanders, perhaps naive about the savagery of the situation. Indeed, it was hard at times to grasp that this army was launching into an unarmed civilian population as if charging into battle . . . A line of soldiers was strung out facing a huge crowd. The air was filled with shouts of 'Fascists! Stop killing!' . . . Young people were singing The Internationale *to a background of gunfire.*

1

June 4th 2012

The day he learnt he was dying, Dimitri Johnston went to Victoria Park in Hong Kong, to join a candlelight vigil for the people killed in Beijing twenty-three years before. He'd gone there with Mila every one of those years. He still remembered the first time, eight years before Britain handed Hong Kong back to China. For weeks the taxis all flew black pennants from their aerials – as had he and thousands of others – and the shock was like the stunned silence after a thunderclap.

By now the vigil had become a ritual, sometimes he thought an empty ritual – why remember the hundreds killed then, but not the untold millions killed a few years before? But he still went there all the same. Perhaps because those few were demanding reform – they weren't just passive victims sacrificed on the altar of their rulers' blind certainties and ruthless ambitions. Whatever the reason, he'd never forgotten that BBC correspondent's voice – what was her name? – quivering with suppressed indignation as she described the killings of that June night while the camera focussed on the shocked faces of the living and the limp bodies of the wounded and the dead.

But that was then and this was now and he'd just found out he was dying himself.

It was past seven when he left Dr Chan's consulting rooms and dusk had rinsed the last jaded light from the hazed and sultry summer sky. When Chan told him the results of the scan, Dimitri had felt a thud in his stomach and then a long churning emptiness. It had been some seconds before he could ask, 'How long?' and his voice had sounded faraway, not really his at all.

Now he was only numb, numb except for that faint insistent churning in the top of his stomach. He walked past the fountains in Statue Square and boarded a crowded tram, climbing the steep narrow winding stairs as he always did. *Rush hour,* a voice said inside his head, *but you're in no rush now and never will be again.*

How strange, the fountains plashed as they always plashed, the street lamps shone just as bright, the crowds bustled past just as busy, the people on the tram sat or stood as they always had. How strange, they couldn't see there was a dead man walking there among them – or standing, rather, clinging to the handrail just like themselves, the living. Well, if not dead, as good as.

The bell clanged, the tram lurched forward and he gazed at them all while his stomach quietly churned. Filipina maids volubly gossiping . . . Old women sighing over heavy shopping bags . . . Mothers holding children on their laps . . . Office-workers busy texting or sagging gratefully on the plastic seats, heads lolling, tired eyes closed. And an Indonesian maid standing near the front, demure and silent in her headscarf and ankle-length skirt. Gazed as if from a great distance, or through a thick glass wall that would never be broken. *You have no more part in all this,* the voice spoke in his head. *It will just go on without you.*

A young girl gestured to him, half-rising from her seat, as someone always did – he'd reached that age. He smiled and shook his head, as he always did. 'Thank you, but I like to stand,' he said in Cantonese. As if he was still strong as a horse and the cancer cells weren't madly multiplying inside him. He imagined them like seething maggots in a lump of raw meat – and what else was a human body if you peeled the skin away? *Stand while you still can,* the voice reminded him.

The girl raised her eyebrows as if to say, *Are you quite sure?* Then she smiled herself and, with a faint shrug, sat down again. Perhaps she was going to the vigil too. But then she'd have a better reason than he had; she'd still be here next year and the year after that and the year after that. She was Chinese, she'd have to live with China's authoritarian government, with corruption big and small, with petty injustice and gross, mild and harsh suppression. She'd probably have children one day who'd have to live with all that too . . . Yes, she'd have a reason, whereas he . . . Not any more. Besides, it never was his fight anyway, not as it was hers; he could only be an ally, a supporter, never mind he'd lived there all his life. British – even though his mother was a white Russian, a refugee from the Bolsheviks – a foreign devil, he could leave at any time and take Mila with him. Even now, when he was under sentence of death. But he'd never wanted to leave, he was born there, it was his home. The pain gripped him suddenly and he grimaced, imagining it was a crab now, nipping his gut with its huge claws. And so he should imagine it, he thought a second later; it was what the damned word meant. Only nipping, to let him know it was lurking there, waiting for its meal. And still that relentless stirring of quiet dread.

The tram jolted and ground past the glitzy malls, the grand hotels, that age-old sports ground – a soccer match under floodlights in all that humid heat – and then the humbler family shops, the hawkers and street-side restaurants. Huge double-decker buses growled past on one side, glistening limousines or dull red taxis cruised or crawled by on the other. *If you don't come back here in the next few months*, he heard that voice again, a sinister stranger whispering in his ear, *this may be the last time you ever see it.*

He could tell they were reaching Victoria Park just by the thickening crowd on the street, quietly shuffling through barriers towards the still distant vigil. Yes, quietly, as if heading towards church. It was always like that – no shouts, no noise, except from a few fringe demonstrators. Just a slow, orderly progression into the park. Tens of thousands were making their way there and it was as gravely quiet as a funeral procession. Well, that was almost what it was, a vigil for the dead.

Then he heard the far-off amplified voices of the speakers. He was late, the ceremony had begun. Now the Filipinas paused in their gossip, the demure Indonesian maid turned to look, the weary office-workers awoke or glanced up from their phones. Even the tired women with their heavy bags craned their necks to see, while children knelt on their mothers' laps. There weren't many police there, he saw. There never were. Or were they somewhere out of sight? The side-streets leading to the park, closed to traffic, were teeming with people heading towards the vigil.

When the tram stopped, it almost emptied. They were nearly all going there, he realised, except the Filipinas and the Indonesian girl, even an old man with a buckled back, limping along on a bamboo stick, and a woman with two young children in their smart school uniforms – a Catholic school, he recognised the badge. The girl who'd offered him her seat got out just ahead of him and smiled again when she saw he was going there too. A quiet, almost collusive smile. Narrow black jeans and a sleeveless white blouse. She walked on along Sugar Street with quick lithe steps, dodging and weaving through the quietly shuffling crowd. Probably a student. Ten or fifteen years ago, she could have been his student. But that was all past now. Soon everything would be. It was as though he was watching the world across a deep chasm now, an unbridgeable abyss that had suddenly opened at his feet.

Mila was waiting for him under the big old Flame of the Forest tree that grew near the entrance. He could pick her out from the crowd at once by the red band she wore round her head. There were people brushing past her, yet it was as if she stood completely alone, separated by some essential detachment that held her always apart. He remembered how she'd stood alone like that waiting for him near the border over forty years ago, a young woman then, when she'd just escaped from China during the Cultural Revolution. She'd swum across Deep Bay, braving the sharks, with an old tyre for a lifebuoy, and phoned him from a call box as soon as she'd reached land. She didn't even know then whether he was still there or not – or had she sensed it far away in China? But there she'd stood in the damp baggy shorts and T-shirt she'd swum in, calm and detached, waiting for her fate, waiting for him. And some part of her had remained detached, remote almost, even when she was closest to him. It was one of the things that had attracted him from the very first, that inviolable composure. And now he was going to leave her. A sudden throb of tears behind his eyes. He paused until he'd mastered them, then walked more slowly on. How could he tell her? How could he not?

She didn't speak, but her eyes questioned his and he could only wince a smile then glance away. Away at the tall buildings all round the park, towers of glittering lights, at the dark uneven hills beyond and between them, then back at the hundred thousand people, it must be – half a dozen soccer pitches' worth, anyway – already gathered there, each holding a flickering candle in a translucent white cone. And, leaning low over them as though to bless, the large golden face of the full moon. The Flame of the Forest's bright red flowers were blooming over its fresh green leaves, he noticed, and the smaller bauhinia nearby were delicately blossoming too.

'How's your back?' he got in before Mila could speak. Yes, he'd seen from the faint stiffness as she turned to him that her back must be hurting. Whenever he saw her move gingerly like that, he pictured the Red Guard zealots in Shanghai throwing her from the stage all those years ago because her father was a bourgeois intellectual and she'd been to colonial Hong Kong. He'd never known exactly what happened, she kept it all locked inside her. So he imagined it a hundred different ways. And yet, despite that stiffness, you could tell at a glance she'd been a dancer. A certain poise, you couldn't miss it.

She dismissed his question with a shake of her head as though a fly was buzzing round it. 'What did he say?' she asked.

He shrugged. 'Wasn't much to say.' His voice trembled faintly. He glanced quickly round, anything to deflect her, round at the myriad candles flickering in the dark. 'A lot of people here tonight.' His voice a tone higher than usual, false, strained. As there always were a lot of people, he thought. They never stopped. 'More than last year by the look of it.' What irony, the only place in China where people could demonstrate in their thousands against their own government – and it was a colonial park named after a foreign queen! Was that the legacy of empire? There could be worse. What did the Russians leave in Afghanistan but a few burnt-out tanks? What did the Americans leave in Iraq, what would they leave in Afghanistan, but the charred and twisted wreckage of a few helicopters? Here there was at least a place to gather and remember, to offer hope. Wasn't that a better legacy?

But how was it such thoughts came to him now, when he was standing on the edge of that dark abyss?

She was watching him, he felt it, with those questioning eyes. 'Shall we give it a miss today?'

Had she guessed at once? He shook his head. 'It may be the last time,' he said wryly, yet, again, with that faint quiver in his voice.

Her eyes closed for a moment. He imagined her registering *the last time*, considering each word one by one.

'Well, yes, they may not allow it much longer, I suppose,' she answered in her precise level learned English, each word a pebble dropping into clear water.

As if *that* was what he'd meant. But not allow it? This was Hong Kong, not Beijing! How could they stop it here? There'd be riots in the streets. But then Mila had been through the Cultural Revolution. She'd seen what they could do then and she thought they could still do anything if they chose. Besides, weren't there riots in the streets in Beijing twenty-three years ago, and still the army shot them? He imagined columns of tanks rolling over all this green, row after row of soldiers, as they did then down Chang'an Avenue and into Tiananmen Square. No, surely that couldn't happen in Hong Kong. But then – a little thump in his gut – even if it did, he wouldn't be there to see it. He was remote from it already, moving away from the Earth like a dying comet.

Mila took his arm, a thing she rarely did, and they went into the park. The two of them together. And that faint churning at the top of his stomach, that came along too. Would it always be there, till the very end?

Two or three men and a young girl were standing at the entrance, handing out candles. 'San-san should be here somewhere,' Mila said as she took two candles from the girl. 'She's just back from Shanghai.'

'You are from Shanghai?' the girl asked with a surprised smile. She spoke Cantonese, but with a mainlander's accent.

Mila shook her head.

They passed the gleaming white statue of the Goddess of Democracy, set against a replica of Tiananmen, and sat down some way from the stage, as far back as possible, where the crowd was thinner. A man sitting nearby turned to light Mila's candle with his own. She nodded and smiled, then turned to light Dimitri's. He glanced at her head bent over the flickering flame. Her hair was still jet black, but he knew she dyed it now, although she'd never said so and he'd never asked.

'So what did he say?' she asked, gazing down now at her own candle.

'Who?'

She looked sharply up at him now and there was no getting out of it. 'Chan, of course!' Her widened brown eyes regarded him steadily. 'What did he say?'

He glanced away at the distant stage. 'It's come back. Metastasised.' Again that tremor in his voice, that tremor like a sob. 'There's not much time.'

She was silent a moment. Now he imagined *not much time* sinking down like three leaden weights, down through the ocean of her mind, sinking till they rested with dull, grave thuds, one after another, on its dark, still floor.

'But what about treatment?' she asked quietly after some seconds. 'Didn't he say?'

He shrugged.

'Dimitri!'

He shrugged again. 'What's the point?'

'Is that why you didn't let me come with you? You didn't even want to ask?' Yes, even she could be hurt, angry.

'I didn't need to ask.' His voice was dull and heavy. 'He told me.' No, he hadn't let her come with him. Because he'd needed to be alone when he got the news, good or bad. To hear it without an audience, even Mila, watching how he took it. Now it was he who was gazing at his candle, as though it was his life's wavering flame that he was addressing, not her. 'He said there was some new chemo they could put me on, but it's still pretty experimental. Not sure I want to go through all that again just for a few months or whatever.'

'Whatever?'

'With all the side effects and so on. Some of which they haven't even found out about yet.'

'What do you mean, "whatever"? How long?'

'He didn't really know. Probably no one does.' He saw, behind and through the candle's flame, the veneer of professional gravity on Chan's smooth face, the fatal columns and rows of figures like minute tombstones on the graveyard print-out he was holding, the quiet, bland, comfortless walls of his office. Chan's voice had been only faintly consolatory. It was routine for him, after all, even if they had known each other for twenty years, ever since they were colleagues in the university.

'But of course you must try the chemo, Dimitri.' Her voice was quiet and composed again now, relieved but determined. 'You never know–'

'Ah there you are,' San-san's voice sounded behind them. 'Thought I'd never find you. I was just going to phone.' She laid her hand on Dimitri's shoulder, pressing him lightly down as he started to rise. Thank God, he wouldn't have to talk about it now, to argue with Mila. Not that they ever did argue anyway. It wasn't possible with her. Confrontation wasn't her way; she had subtler means.

'How was the concert?' he heard Mila ask. Her voice sounded only slightly forced.

But then the speeches began again on the stage; 'Later,'

San-san murmured as she sat down on the grass beside them. He lit her candle with his own. She was his son's wife, he thought as he glanced down at her slim, strong violinist's fingers clasping the fragile plastic cone. But he'd known her since she was a child, she was more like his own daughter, especially since her father died. *Died*, there it was again.

2

He listened and didn't listen to the speeches, numbed by that dense dark certainty like a black hole inside him. His eyes strayed to the giant characters *RESIST!* projected onto nearby buildings, while the crowd chanted, 'Never forget June 4!' and, 'Democracy will win!' What had that got to do with him now? It was only when they all stood to hold up their candles in silent tribute while the names of the dead were solemnly read out that he forgot that dark yawning abyss which had opened before him. And when that victim rolled onto the stage in his wheelchair, his legs amputated after a tank crushed them during the massacre, and thanked them all tearfully for twenty-three years of support . . . Only then did he forget. What was that like, he thought as the man laid a wreath for the dead, to feel a forty-ton tank rolling over your legs? Yes, for a time he was there, back in 1989, watching that night unfold on television for all the world to see – the shouting, the flames, the helmeted troops, the unmistakable sharp bark of small arms fire . . . He heard again that student leader's voice rising unsteadily as the troops approached; heard the students singing defiance; saw ordinary people making barricades, setting buses and lorries ablaze; saw limp bleeding bodies being carried away; heard again those desperate voices shouting, '*Tell the world! Tell the world!*'

The speakers went on and on, but the singing, the fist-pumping, the defiant exhortations – that made him uneasy; they always reminded him of the Red Guards he used to see, holding up their little red books and mindlessly chanting their Maoist mantras, just as sure of themselves then as these people were now.

But that was different, he reproved himself a moment later. These people here now and those students then, they were right, while the Red Guards were wrong, mad and wrong.

Right? Completely, utterly and absolutely right? Down to the last detail? Really? Weren't there splits in the leadership then, personal jealousies? Weren't there today? Weren't some of those students in Tiananmen more concerned about the state of their dormitories than the state of China? Weren't others more intoxicated by their own rhetoric, giddy with the glamour of it, than really thinking things through –how to get a real democracy going and not end up in chaos? Really? Not a single one of them? Not that that justified the massacre. How could it? That was why he'd been coming here all these years, the massacre. But what would have happened if those students had prevailed? A Chinese Spring like the Arab Spring? Look what happened there. Blighted summer and a long, harsh winter of anarchy or bloody civil war.

Yes, but then again, how could you reform a repressive regime without protesting? And how could you protest without unleashing anarchy or being crushed? That was the question, the unanswered question. Besides, hadn't that regime lifted the country out of poverty now, however ruthless or corrupt its officials might be? Or had they just stepped aside and let people get on with it, so long as they didn't interfere with their own profits and power?

But then he heard Chan's smooth voice again, politely telling him, while delicately avoiding the word itself, that he would soon be dead, and all those questions drifted away like shredding mist while the speakers' urgent exhortations on the stage faded to a remote and uncompelling murmur.

He was standing on the brink again, peering into the void.

Sitting silent beside him, Mila was remembering too. Remembering, not Tiananmen, but that day in Shanghai twenty years before, that day the baying Red Guards came for her. Those glaring eyes, those strident accusations, those stabbing fingers; all twisted and forced, all marshalled by a few mad zealots. And then that rush to hurl her from the stage, the sickening crunch of her fall, the wild taunting jeers still sounding in her ears as her mind dissolved in pain . . . *'Imperialist's whore!'* How did they know, she often wondered; who told them Dimitri was her lover? And years later, that man Lo shamefacedly apologising – *'I had to do it.'* She heard his sheepish voice. *'We all had to, otherwise . . . It was the madness of the time.'* He wouldn't meet her eyes as he spoke, but neither would she meet his. One of the strongest dancers, he was then, he could lift her so easily. Yes, the madness of the time, when friends denounced friends and children their parents. But hovering over all those straying memories was the dark shadow, the shadow that diminished everything else, the shadow cast by Dimitri's words: *metastasised . . . Not much time . . .*

*

Some time later she touched his arm. 'Let's go.'

He nodded and blew into his glowing white cone. The candle flame guttered and died. Yes, time to go now, time to go. Time to leave this field of candles glowing in the dark. The moon was higher in the sky, he noticed. Smaller, paler now. Cold and remote.

San-san stood up with a fluid, uncoiling motion, smoothed down her white silk shirt and stretched out her hand to help him, but he shook his head. At least he could still get to his feet without help. Help humiliated him; he hated it. So did pity, and pity was bound to come soon too. Ungracious perhaps, but there it was.

And then he saw that girl again, the one from the tram. She was sitting upright and cross-legged as if in a yoga pose, just a few rows in front of them, glancing round as they began to edge away. She gave him another faint smile, a smile of recognition, then looked back down at the candle's flame burning steadily in her sheltering hands. Yes, it still mattered to her.

'It looked as though there were quite a few people from the mainland here tonight,' San-san said absently. She frowned. 'I wonder what happens to them when they go back home.'

'Someone's probably watching them,' Mila answered. But it was Dimitri she was watching, quietly probing. 'They'll end up on some list.'

'The girl who gave me my candle was a mainlander,' San-san said mildly. 'She didn't seem worried.'

'Must be the one who spoke to us,' Mila said.

'Perhaps she was there to watch the others,' Dimitri suggested bleakly.

San-san shrugged. 'She said she's a postgraduate student here. In music.'

'Good cover, perhaps?' How strange, he thought, his voice sounded almost normal, as if all this still mattered to him.

Neither San-san nor Mila answered and they walked silently on, past row after row of people. Mainly young people, too young even to have been alive when the massacre happened, but also parents with their children and older people who might have been refugees from China thirty years ago. Perhaps they'd swum like Mila across Deep Bay, desperately hoping they wouldn't get shot or die between some prowling shark's savage jaws. Some of them glanced up and smiled at them as that young girl had. There was a camaraderie there, as if they were all worshippers at the same church. Well, they were, weren't they?

'So how did it go in Shanghai?' he forced himself to ask San-san at the gate, where street vendors had set up their stalls. One was selling the old colonial flag, he noticed, the Union Jack on a deep blue background. Another was offering T-shirts with *Democracy Now* in Chinese characters printed across the front.

'The concert was fine.' San-san's tone insinuated something else wasn't.

'But?' Yes, how strange, he could act as though nothing had changed. And even sound quite convincing. Only he wasn't really there in his words, it was as though he was hearing San-san and himself, both, from some other dimension, a dimension where he now belonged.

Mila was holding her hand out for a taxi. 'We'll drop you off first, San-san. Did you see the Yus in Shanghai? Did they come to the concert?'

'Lai-king did.' Again that faint insinuation.

'What about Guodong? I thought he loved chamber music?'

'He's been . . .' – San-san hesitated – 'arrested.'

'Guodong?'

'A month ago. He's in detention somewhere.'

A taxi pulled in beside them. 'I'll go in front,' San-san said. 'As I'm getting out first. It's a wonderful hall,' she added almost wistfully. 'I mean the acoustics . . .'

'What happened?' Mila slid onto her seat with a little stifled grimace as her back complained. 'What's Guodong done? Why did they . . . ?'

'Lai-king said he was helping some people from his home village. They were protesting about their land being grabbed by local officials and sold off to developers. You know, the usual thing. He put some petition online.'

In the air-conditioned cocoon of the taxi the driver stiffened faintly and glanced sideways at San-san.

'Online?' Mila repeated slowly as she turned to buckle her seat-belt. 'What did it say?'

'It was taken down almost at once,' San-san shrugged. 'Apparently quite a lot of people saw it, though. The trouble was, he said something about democracy as well. Lai-king said that made it worse.'

'It would,' Dimitri heard himself saying. 'Especially in the run-up to the Tiananmen anniversary. The authorities are always touchy then.' There he was again, talking as though nothing had happened. San-san would never guess.

'Best thing would be to stop the mainlanders all coming over here,' the driver muttered in a low growl of Cantonese as if he was talking to himself. He nodded sourly at the people on the crowded pavement, as though they were all mainlanders.

After a second or two's surprised pause, 'You don't like them?' San-san asked uncertainly, switching to Cantonese herself.

He shook his head. 'Locusts!' He seemed quite young, but hunched over the wheel he had a surly discontented look about him. 'They send their wives over here to have their babies, and we have to pay for them. Then they fill up the schools with their kids. The rich ones come over with suitcases full of cash and buy up all the apartments. I know, I've had them in my cab. And where did they get all that money from, I'd like to know? We can't even get baby milk powder now, they buy it by the ton and take it back over the border because their own stuff's poisoned. Stop them coming, I say. Keep them out.'

He drove on in a sullen, bristling silence now, and seemed to have silenced them as well, each solitary in their own thoughts. Yu Guodong, Dimitri reflected, gazing up inattentively at the neon signs hanging out like illuminated flags over the pavement. Twenty-five years his colleague at the university. Guodong's face hung there like a borderless photo in his mind. Always cheerful and honest, even when honesty wasn't the best policy. His parents had given him the English name Faustus in Shanghai when they sent him to a Catholic school, either not knowing or not caring what the fathers would think of it. And, being Jesuits, the fathers had taken it in their stride. That must have been just before the communists took over. Now he was in purgatory, in Shanghai again, sixty years later. 'Well,' he murmured drily, 'it never rains but it pours.'

'Why, has something else happened?' San-san glanced round at him.

He looked at Mila before he answered, a warning look. 'No. Nothing, really.'

Mila took his hand, gripped it almost. 'He saw Chan this afternoon,' she said firmly. 'To get the results of his check-up.'

Dimitri frowned at her, withdrawing his hand. San-san's eyes widened, turning to Mila now.

He looked away out of the window. At the shuffling crowds on the pavement. At a big-character banner proclaiming Falun Gong an evil cult and, nearby, a rag-tag group of demonstrators filing along the street with placards denouncing the recent election of Hong Kong's leader as a farce. Which it was, he thought detachedly as he watched the straggling and, it seemed, dejected procession – a few hand-picked electors choosing between a few hand-picked candidates while the voteless millions looked helplessly on. Now there was a busker, playing a saxophone, and an old woman begging by the traffic lights, grey-haired and worn-faced. But what had any of that to do with him now? And all the time that faint churning in his stomach. He felt San-san's concerned gaze like a gentle yet unwelcome hand upon his cheek.

'It wasn't good news,' Mila added deliberately.

Dimitri pressed his lips together, closed his eyes and leant back. If he spoke, he knew, his voice would crumble.

'Apparently the cancer's come back.'

3

San-san felt the jolt of the world stopping for an instant. Then it went on, but it was a different world now, spinning on a different axis. 'Come back?' she repeated stupidly. 'I thought it was cured?' Then, recovering, 'What did Chan say? I mean, what does he recommend?'

'More chemo–' Mila began.

'Do we have to discuss this here and now?' Dimitri asked acidly.

San-san flinched. 'Sorry, I–'

'In a taxi of all places?' He was speaking to both of them, but it was San-san who turned back like a scolded child, while Mila merely reached for Dimitri's hand again. He left it still and passive in hers, unresponsive to the pressure of her fingers, and gazed stubbornly at the back of San-san's head, her dark hair pulled up taut into a topknot, a strand falling gracefully loose beside her ear.

The taxi-driver was glancing at Dimitri in his mirror, San-san noticed. He might understand more English than they thought. 'I'm sorry,' she murmured contritely again. 'I didn't think–'

'It's all right.'

She gazed at the road ahead, starting its long climb up towards the Peak, and searched for something to say that wasn't clumsy or forced. But there wasn't anything to say. How bad was it, she wondered. She'd known him most of her life, her father's closest friend. She'd just found out he was very ill, perhaps dying, and there she was, sitting dumb in a taxi as if nothing at all had happened. She started absently counting the street lamps with their haloes of light in the hot humid air. One, two, three, they filed past. Four, five, six . . . She lost count and glanced furtively at Dimitri. He was gazing rigidly out of his window now with tightened lips. Perhaps he was counting the street lamps too? Or just staring into endless, empty night? She thought of her father's death, her younger brother's, then her mother's, and felt the chill that death always brought her, the death of someone close. As though a great bird of prey had just swooped past her and she'd felt the rush of air, heard the throbbing beat of its wings. She imagined Dimitri clutched limp and helpless in the great bird's talons as it soared away.

'We can talk about it tomorrow,' Mila's voice sounded behind her, quiet and firm as ever.

She nodded. Did Mila ever show emotion? Did she have any?

'About Guodong, perhaps,' Dimitri was saying in the same dry, bitter tone. 'Not about me.'

When Mila didn't answer: 'Lai-king hoped we could help somehow,' San-san murmured.

'How?' Mila asked. 'What could we do?'

Dimitri smiled wryly. Mila's tone implied there was nothing anyone could do once you were in the authorities' power. And after all, wasn't that how it had been with her?

'I think she meant get it known in the press here and so on,' San-san said almost meekly. She hated disagreements, even mild ones.

'It'll probably get picked up by the press anyway,' Dimitri said. 'Not that a paragraph in the paper here will do much good.' For some reason – perhaps it was those schoolchildren he'd seen going to the vigil – he thought of those two Catholic priests mentioned in the press, who just disappeared in the Chinese Gulag twelve or so years ago. 'Human Rights Watch, Amnesty, Avaaz, Change org.?

Maybe better than nothing, but not much better. They just get blocked in China.'

'Or it might make things worse,' Mila said. 'Best to phone Lai-king first, find out what exactly's going on. I mean, does he have a lawyer?'

'Not that that does much good either, usually,' Dimitri added. Yes, he could speak as though nothing had happened and he was no nearer death than anyone else. But all the time the thought of it was dragging him down like a great boulder while everything else receded, dwindling into an infinite distance.

The road wound up towards the Peak, growing emptier the further they went. Soon they were alone, on the narrow road that looped round the hill and led to the house San-san's father had left her, the last vestige of his vanished wealth. The dark emptiness outside accentuated the heavy silence in the car, making it more and more unbearable. Even the driver seemed uneasy.

'I'll get out here,' San-san murmured suddenly. Then: '*Needoh lok che*,' more loudly to the driver. *Stop here.*

'We can take you all the way,' Mila protested without conviction as the car slowed.

'No, it's all right. It's easier to turn round here. You know how narrow it gets further on.'

She wanted to say something encouraging or at least comforting as she got out, but nothing came. Dimitri raised his hand and let it fall while Mila smiled a faint goodbye. 'I'll phone tomorrow,' San-san called out, and watched the taxi turn and drive away. Neither Mila nor Dimitri looked back at her.

She had two or three hundred yards still to walk, but that was what she wanted; she'd been rudely shaken out of life and needed time before she stepped back in. Walking past the tall trees that had been there all her life – trees where barking deer used to roam, Dimitri had told her once when she was a child – she wondered if Alex knew already.

The wrought-iron gates were open, one hanging slightly on its hinge as if it was lame. *Must have it mended*, she thought in one small part of her mind while the rest stayed blank. Alex's Toyota was parked in the drive. Lights shone from the windows, she could hear the children's voices. As she let herself in, Jason came to greet her, claws clicking on the parquet floor. She laid her hand absently on the Labrador's warm skull and fondled his smooth, floppy ear.

'Hi, Mum,' Michael called from the living-room. 'How was it?'

'OK.' She took a breath and stepped back into life again. 'Where's your father?'

'In the study, helping Cathy with her maths.'

'Have you finished your homework?'

'Of course.' He returned to his iPad, sitting on the floor and leaning back against the sofa, his light brown hair – it certainly wasn't black – falling over his face.

How strange, she thought as she walked down the hall, lined with prints of old Hong Kong, how strange – it was Lai-king's harassed expression after the concert in Shanghai she was remembering now, not Dimitri's in the taxi she'd just left.

'You're back early,' Alex said, glancing up from the blackwood desk that used to be her father's. 'Not over already, is it?'

So he doesn't know yet, San-san thought.

Catherine looked up from her textbook and tossed her glossy black ponytail back over her shoulder. Yes, she could be taken for pure Chinese with those eyes, those cheekbones, although she was only half – no, something a bit less than half, San-san calculated as she ran through her own complicated ancestry – her mother Chinese, her father half-Chinese . . . And Alex English. So yes, Catherine and Michael must be a bit less than half. But why was that even going through her head now, at a time like this?

'How's the maths tutorial going?'

'Nearly finished.' Alex glanced at her. 'Why?'

'Oh . . .' She shook her head and shrugged. 'Want some tea?'

'OK.' He watched her walk towards the kitchen and, with a faint puzzled frown, stayed watching the space she left for some seconds until: 'I can't do this one,' Catherine complained sulkily.

'Ma'am?' Lena asked, looking up from the sink.

'No, it's all right,' San-san said. 'I just want to make some tea. You finish clearing away.'

She stood there gazing at the kettle, while Lena noisily loaded the dishwasher. Lena. She'd worked for them for nine years now and San-san knew little more about her than that she'd come from Cebu in the Philippines to support an indolent husband and two children she saw once a year.

'How's the family, Lena?' she asked as the kettle began to hiss.

'All right, ma'am.' Lena glanced at the photo that, after shyly asking San-san's permission, she'd placed on top of the refrigerator. A boy and a girl, almost the same age as San-san's own children, all brushed and washed and neatly dressed. There was no picture of her husband.

San-san glanced at Lena now. She looked tired tonight, the faint lines in her face a little deeper. Well, after all it was late. She wanted her son to become a priest, San-san remembered, but he wasn't very good at school. She skyped her children for a few minutes nearly every night and was often sad afterwards. But usually she was cheerful all day long. What else did San-san know about her? Much less for sure than Lena knew about all of them.

The kettle began to boil.

*

'Maybe it's not so bad,' Alex said, gazing into his teacup. 'Maybe he just needs some more chemo.'

She was sitting opposite him on the edge of the deep armchair. 'It didn't sound like that.'

He nodded, glanced at his watch. 'Perhaps I should phone them?'

'Not now, Alex.'

'It's not too late. They don't go to bed till midnight.'

'I think they just want to be left alone at the moment.'

'How can you know that?' he bridled. 'They didn't say so, did they?'

'Not in so many words, no. But Mila said let's talk about it tomorrow. And when I said I'd phone tomorrow, they sort of agreed.'

He leant back and sighed. 'Well, I suppose tomorrow will do. It may not be as bad as you think, anyway.' But his eyes, which were just like his father's, were far away and unfocussed. And there was a little more grey in his hair, she noticed. Yes, they were in their middle years.

He sipped his tea, put the cup down, and looked away at the night pressing its blank face against the window.

'Why don't you phone Chan?' she asked. 'He could tell you.'

'Assuming he'd be willing to talk and not say it's confidential.' He glanced at his watch again. 'Tomorrow, though. Ten-thirty at night's a bit late, isn't it? For a medical consultation? Anyway, I should talk to Mila first.' Mila, he thought, not Dimitri. His father's inmost feelings were a closed book, a book that no one except Mila ever opened and read.

They watched the tea cooling in their cups.

'I wonder if Elena knows?' Alex asked at last.

'I shouldn't think so, if you didn't.'

'I could call her now.'

'You could try,' San-san said sceptically. She knew Alex's sister perhaps better than he did. While he phoned, she gazed round at the walls of the room, still hung with many of her father's paintings and scrolls. How many times had she seen Dimitri there, poring over the books or unrolling the scrolls her father never hung? How many more times would she?

Of course all Alex heard was a voice asking him to leave a message after the tone. He ended the call at once.

'Well, how was Shanghai, anyway?' he asked, imagining Elena's unanswered phone like a lost spacecraft floating somewhere far away beyond Earth's orbit.

San-san told him about Guodong's arrest. 'Lai-king was really desperate,' she ended.

'I should think so,' he nodded. But it was his father he was thinking of.

Jason's claws clicked across the floor. He placed a paw on Alex's knee and looked up with mute appeal in his glistening brown eyes. 'Better take him out, I suppose,' he sighed again.

San-san's phone rang as she was carrying the tray back into the kitchen. Lai-king's voice sounded harsh, urgent and distorted in her ear. 'Lai-king, I can't hear you well,' San-san said slowly and distinctly. 'I – can't – understand!' But Lai-king's voice rushed on and on until after a few seconds the line went abruptly dead.

'Who was that?' Alex asked as he came back.

'Lai-king.'

'Lai-king?! What did she say?'

'Nothing. At first I couldn't understand her and then she got cut off.'

'Well, they're probably monitoring her phone.' His eyes drifted away from San-san as he thought of his father with Guodong – or Faustus, as they always called him – at some function in the university, a lifetime ago it seemed now. Graduation Day, probably.

Then, inexplicably, he remembered his mother saying goodnight to him. Only it wasn't really goodnight; it was goodbye, the night she killed herself. And she never actually got to say goodnight, because he pretended to be asleep, watching her covertly through his scarcely parted lashes. Watched her at the door, waiting till she came closer and he could scare her with suddenly wide-awake eyes. But she didn't come closer. She stood there a long time without saying a word, then turned and quietly closed the door. He heard her saying goodnight to Elena and then he fell asleep. Would she have changed her mind if he'd opened his eyes and said something? It was almost the only memory he had left of her. No, there was another, of her playing the piano, intent and absorbed. Would Faustus and his father fade from his memory, too, in time? But he knew they would. Everything faded with time. Yes, his mother playing the piano. He wished he knew the name of that piece. He could play a recording of it. He imagined listening to it, remembering more vividly, although he didn't know much about music. Perhaps San-san would recognise it. Perhaps it would draw other memories out from the haze of time that veiled the past. But then, perhaps they would be unhappy memories? Now he recalled his mother sitting limp at the piano, her head sunk forward, shoulders sagging.

'Let's go to bed,' he said at last, while Jason circled

round and round in his basket and finally curled up, head on paws, to sleep. 'Not much else we can do tonight, is there?'

San-san was gazing out of the kitchen window, out over the garden, out over the moonlit sea and the dark humped islands beyond. Then she stirred. 'I'll just try Lai-king first.'

But Lai-king's number was always busy.

'Send her an SMS,' Alex suggested.

how r u? San-san texted. *any news?*

'You didn't say how the concert went?' Alex asked as they climbed the stairs.

'Oh, pretty well. They actually said they'd like us to come back and do some master classes.' For a moment she saw herself climbing those stairs as a young girl, climbing them fearfully up into the haunted dark, where nightmares awaited and every shadow was a lurking monster. And then she was remembering that day her father was arrested. She was practising in her room when, glancing out of the window – some sudden premonition turned her head – she saw the police car driving away, her father seated between two detectives, one British, one Chinese. Her stomach still stirred at the memory.

'Did they? When?'

'What?'

'The master classes.'

'Oh.' The memory faded. 'October, November. It was a bit vague.'

'And will you?'

'Don't know,' she shrugged. 'It depends on the rest of the quartet. Teaching, family and stuff.'

'As usual.'

How easy it is, she thought as she undressed, *how easy to step back into life again. Too easy.*

'What's this?' Alex called from her dressing-table.

'What?'

He was holding up a scrap of paper with Chinese characters scrawled on it.

'What are you snooping in my handbag for?' she smiled. 'Looking for love letters?'

'It wasn't in your handbag, it was here, by the mirror.'

'It's my lover's phone number, of course.'

He was frowning over the characters, never very good at them. 'Jianping. Who's he?'

'*She*.'

'What? I thought it was a boy's name. So you've got a lesbian lover?'

'She's a mainland girl at the vigil. She was handing out the candles at Victoria Park.' *Yes, how easy, how comforting.*

'A mainlander? Wow, what are things coming to?'

'There were quite a few there, she told me.'

'Well, you can usually tell, can't you? Just by looking.'

'Or listening. She said she'd come to our next concert.'

He watched her wriggling into her nightdress, running her fingers through her hair. 'You haven't changed, San-san, you know. Since . . .'

'Since when?' She smiled ruefully as she shook her head. 'Yesterday?'

Yes, how easy. And yet, while Alex's head lay comfortingly heavy on her shoulder, she lay awake gazing out at the distant moon. Like an old face, she thought, pitted and scarred by time. She remembered Dimitri's set expression in the taxi, remembered Lai-king's urgent voice on the phone.

Alex stirred.

She glanced down at him. 'I thought you were asleep?'

'No, I was thinking.'

'About Dimitri?'

'Mm.' He sighed and rolled onto his back. 'Strange, to think he might be going soon. It makes you realise . . . how short it all is, in the end.'

San-san nodded. But it had happened to her already – father, mother, brother. She was the last one left – except for her two older brothers, she recalled almost guiltily – John, retired now from the law and playing golf in California, and Peter, settled in Australia after Tiananmen. But then those two, several years older than her, had always been distant, almost like another branch of the family.

And then Lai-king's anguished face slipped back into her mind again.

Alex was remembering a day on the beach – South Bay, wasn't it? – some summer when his mother was still there and his father was teaching him to swim. It seemed like yesterday, and yet it also seemed remote, embalmed in another dimension, unreachable. But he didn't want to tell San-san he'd been remembering that, feeling obscurely that the memory would tarnish in the light of another's gaze, even San-san's. So he turned his head to look at her. 'What were *you* thinking about?'

'Just then I was thinking about Lai-king. When she came to the concert, I mean.' Lai-king's strained, anxious face, her eyes wide and fearful. How she kept looking round as though she thought she was being followed – as she might well have been. 'She looked so . . . distraught.'

Alex nodded, gazing up at the dim, blank ceiling. 'Not much anyone can do about that, though, is there?'

'I suppose not,' she admitted reluctantly. But wasn't there always something you could do, however small?

Now Alex was picturing his father and Mila lying awake too, staring up at an even blanker ceiling. 'Ah well,' he sighed, 'it may not be so bad after all.'

'Guodong and Lai-king?'

'Dimitri.'

4

'I can't understand you!' Lai-king heard the words blurred and faint as if shouted through a long dark tunnel. Then the tunnel closed. She waited some minutes for San-san to call back, then laid the phone slowly down on the table and stared through it with dulled eyes, stared at that officer's ungiving face at the police station yesterday. '*Your husband's case is still under investigation. We will notify you when it's possible to see him.*' Four weeks, four and a half, and still no word. And when she went to the edge of the window and looked down at the street, there was the police car parked as usual, with two men sitting inside and two, a woman and a man in plain clothes, standing by the entrance to the building. It was eleven at night, and the streets were slowly emptying. The massive new shopping mall almost opposite had closed and she watched the cleaners going in, the security guards standing by the doors while the shop assistants left in ones or twos and hurried to the bus stops where people waited wearily for buses that would take them to their distant suburbs. Just like Hong Kong, she reflected, except that here they didn't queue. No, they bunched, ready to shove their way in when the buses arrived. That was one of the first things they'd both noticed when they came to Shanghai. 'The people are so rude here,' she'd complained to Guodong. 'So pushy.' But he'd only laughed. 'That's what the Singaporeans used to say about Hongkongers. It's all relative.'

There were a few late shoppers leaving, too, elegantly dressed, carrying their purchases in fancy bags. No buses for them – their own shiny cars or at least a taxi ordered on their smartphones. Would they care if they knew about Guodong? No, they'd been bought off with Gucci, Armani, Louis Vuitton. Besides, there was the Olympics for them to goggle at when they got home, or the trial of Gu Kailai if they wanted a bit of scandal, the woman who was supposed to have murdered that Englishman. Then Gu Kailai's husband would be tried next. 'There are always bread and circuses,' Guodong used to say, although she'd never quite known what he meant – something about how the Roman emperors used to keep their citizens docile. That TV shot of Gu Kailai's face flitted across her mind, and then one of her once-powerful husband. As usual, they were sandwiched between two police officers who were a head taller than them. 'To make them look small and weak compared to the might of the law,' Guodong had said only a few weeks ago. 'You know, *how are the mighty fallen* kind of thing.' And then the show-trial would come. Bread and circuses.

The policewoman was looking casually up at her window now, speaking on her phone. Lai-king wished they'd bought curtains; she could have shut that woman out. But Guodong had never wanted them. Just a blind in the bedroom to keep out the light. Not in Hong Kong either. '*What d'you want curtains for?*' he would ask. '*We're on the tenth floor, who's going to be looking in?*' And anyway, the police would probably have told her she mustn't draw them, so they could keep an eye on her. She moved away and sat down on the bamboo armchair they'd brought with them from Hong Kong. She remembered the shop where they bought it years ago, that old place in Wanchai. Long gone now, she supposed.

It had seemed so interesting, Shanghai, when they first arrived. And of course it helped that they'd been able to buy this fairly large apartment with their Hong Kong dollars before prices rose here. And not far from the Bund, too, the river bank with all its old colonial buildings. *Bund* came from some Persian word for 'embankment', Guodong had told her once. But that was long years ago now; it seemed another age. She was gazing at the scroll hanging on the wall, she realised, and yet not seeing it at all. A wonderful piece of calligraphy, Guodong said when he bought it all those years ago in Hong Kong, but calligraphy never moved her very much. Yes, he'd found it on Cat Street of all places, he said, but not, of course, where the tourists shopped. How she wished now they'd never left Hong Kong, not even for Guodong's father's sake. None of this would have happened then. He could be going to Cat Street now, where the dealers would invite him into the back to show him something unusual.

What was happening to him now, though? Why wouldn't they tell her? And why didn't San-san phone back? But perhaps she was asking Dimitri Johnston now, asking him to help? It was the only hope she had, to get some publicity for Guodong, so they were careful how they treated him. Strange, she used to think of Hong Kong as a stuffy, undemocratic, colonial place, but now it seemed like a beacon of freedom and hope compared with here; her only hope now.

On Guodong's desk lay the novel he was reading when they came for him. She couldn't bring herself to close it and put it away; it would be like giving up on him, like treachery almost. She imagined him seeing it there when he came back, picking it up and reading on where he'd been interrupted, as if he'd only been away an hour or two, not four long weeks. It was one of those novels by a Western author that the critics so admired, but she couldn't see anything in it. Couldn't they write about something more important than well-heeled intellectuals and their lusts and loves? Didn't they care – did they even know –about the world out there beyond their self-limited horizons? The world where their petty concerns shrunk to the glossy triviality of a fashion show? 'Navel-gazing novelists,' Guodong used to call them. 'Or groin-gazing, more likely,' Dimitri had once drily added. Yet they read them all the same. But that was in the distant carefree past.

She should go to bed, she was tired, but she knew she wouldn't be able to sleep. Oh why, oh *why* had Guodong put that petition online? What good could it have done? If only he'd asked her before he did it. Why didn't he *think*? He'd done it impulsively, as if he was still in Hong Kong. When the Tiananmen anniversary was coming up, too, and the authorities here were so jumpy! Perhaps that's what it was – after ten years he still hadn't really realised mainland China was different from Hong Kong. And he always was so impulsive, never thinking of the consequences.

*

When the phone beeped, she started out of a shallow doze and looked round anxiously, forgetting where she'd left it. Of course! There on the table. A new message. From San-san, she saw. She scrolled down. It was illegible, just a row of x after x after x. Had they blocked her phone then? But naturally, they must have done.

Before she went to bed, she peered guardedly out of the window again. The two officers at the entrance were gone – at least, she couldn't see them. But the car was still there, or another just like it.

*

It was just after ten the next morning when the doorbell rang. She'd been trying to call San-san, but never getting through. When she opened the door the few inches its tethering chain allowed, she knew at once the man and woman standing there were plain-clothes officers, although she hadn't seen them before. Her stomach crimped.

'Yu Lai-king?' the man said. As if they didn't know.

She nodded, holding the door still on its chain while she looked from one to the other. Old Mrs Li from across the hall was just coming out of the lift, a bulging white plastic bag dangling from her hand. So she'd been to the market, Lai-king thought detachedly, and wished she herself was coming back from the market, with nothing more on her mind than what she'd bought and whether she'd paid too much. Usually Mrs Li would greet her and exchange a few words, but now she glanced away as soon as their eyes met, as if she was embarrassed or even afraid to acknowledge her.

The woman officer, quite young and pleasant-looking, was peering past Lai-king, as though she thought someone else might be there in the room. Lai-king's stomach curled again in sudden panic – had Guodong escaped? Were they looking for him?

'Open up, please,' the man said. 'It won't take long.'

So it wasn't that, then. They weren't looking for him. They wouldn't talk like that if they were. Besides, she thought as she unhooked the chain and opened the door, who ever heard of people escaping from prison in China? Prison or detention centre, whatever they called it. There were faint smudges on the door, she noticed, smudges left by people's hands. She ought to wipe them off, but she no longer had the heart for that.

They walked in, scrupulously wiping their shoes on the mat, and looked round appreciatively, as if she was selling the place and they'd come to view it. Then they turned to her and stood courteously, waiting till she gestured them to sit down.

'Can you show us your papers, please, Mrs Yu?' the woman asked.

'Again?' she said, almost sullenly.

The woman smiled and waited.

Lai-king went to get the papers. When she came back, the woman was talking in a low voice to the man. She paused as Lai-king approached, then took the papers politely with both hands and nodded her thanks. The man looked round the room again as though considering whether to buy the furniture as well as the apartment. 'Worth quite a lot, a place like this,' he said approvingly, turning back to Lai-king. 'Ever thought of selling it?'

Lai-king's stomach crimped yet again as she shook her head. What did that mean, *thought of selling it?* She watched the woman take out a pair of glasses with brown tortoise-shell frames from a grey case, which she then closed and placed carefully on the table. *I thought they had to have perfect eyesight*, registered faintly on the surface of Lai-king's mind while deeper down there was only this dark stirring of uncertainty and alarm. The woman bent her head over the papers, scrutinising them word by word. She had a mole on her cheek. Didn't they use to call that a beauty spot in Europe? She was frowning slightly too, frowning down at Guodong's detention notification, which two uniformed policemen had brought her the day after he was taken away. *Why did I put that there?* Lai-king wondered. The woman, smiling faintly, laid it carefully aside. Meanwhile the man was gazing up at the ceiling, leaning back comfortably – too comfortably – as though the place was already his and herself, Lai-king, the visitor.

The woman handed the permit back, again courteously with both hands, and nodded to the man as he glanced at her with one lifted eyebrow. While he spoke she folded her glasses and placed them carefully back in their case. Lai-king was aware of her precise movements all the time she was listening to the man.

'Well, Mrs Yu, your husband should be coming home soon.' He seemed quite pleased to be bringing her good news. He raised his hand, however, when Lai-king opened her mouth to ask when. 'But there are certain conditions,' he went on. 'He must stay here in Shanghai, not go back to that village again. He must not put anything online that is subversive or threatens stability. No blogs, no emails. Remind him of that when he comes back, would you?' He paused and tilted his head. 'And the same for you, Mrs Yu. Nothing about that village. And then there's that Hong Kong musician you spoke to at the concert on Saturday . . .' He smiled as he saw her start. 'Be careful what you say to her. Don't get her involved in this. There are foreigners trying to stir up trouble in Hong Kong, you know. Trying to foist Western ideas on us. You don't want to get mixed up with that. It's for your own good, both of you, you understand?'

Yes, she understood. She nodded, anxiety not yet soothed by tremulous relief. 'When–'

'If he does break those conditions, he could end up in a labour camp or prison. Remember that. And so could you.'

Again she nodded, dumbly, obediently. Despising herself.

The man glanced at the woman now, again raising one eyebrow. The woman leant forward towards Lai-king. 'Don't you have a daughter in America, Mrs Yu? In California?'

Lai-king nodded once more, her stomach suddenly churning with a new apprehension. What now? What now? She hadn't been able to contact Fung-ying since they took Guodong away. And in any case, she was afraid she'd rush over here once she found out, and who knew what might happen to her then?

'And three grandchildren? You must miss them all, I expect? Especially the children growing up?'

'We visit them quite often.' Her voice blank as a closed door. 'And they visit us here.'

'So far,' the woman agreed amiably. 'About once a year. But sometimes it's difficult to get a visa, isn't it?'

'Difficult?' For a second Lai-king was puzzled, then she understood. 'For them or for us?' Her voice really sullen now. She heard it was. And felt the brief flare of resentment in her eyes.

The woman smiled pleasantly again. 'There could be difficulties getting in and difficulties getting out,' she said blandly. 'Couldn't there?'

Lai-king looked away at the scrolls hanging on the wall. But she wasn't seeing them; she was seeing closed faces, heads shaking, papers being pushed back across the counter.

The two officers watched and waited.

'When will he come back?' she asked at last. 'My husband?'

'Quite soon, I expect,' the man said with a sigh as he got to his feet. 'If he behaves himself.' He paused. 'And you do too.'

She closed the door after them and slid the chain back in its slot. She felt no relief now, only new tremors of anxiety. Anxiety and guilt, as though, however innocently, she'd betrayed Guodong by talking to San-san. San-san, how could she get a message to her not to do anything? They might be writing to the press or Amnesty or whoever right now, and that would only make things worse for Guodong. If only she hadn't told San-san. She'd waited four weeks, why hadn't she just waited a bit longer? She must get a message to them somehow! To San-san or Dimitri.

She walked back into the room and slumped down on Guodong's chair. There lay that novel, still open on his desk, gathering dust. What were they doing in Hong Kong? She imagined them all at their computers, composing letters to the press, formulating petitions just as Guodong had done, and now that could only make things worse.

But perhaps they weren't doing anything at all? Perhaps they'd forgotten them already?

Petition Gets Hong Kong Academic
Arrested On Mainland

Retired university teacher Yu Guodong has been detained in Shanghai for putting a petition online protesting against the local authorities for what he called a "land grab" in his ancestral village.

A former colleague, Dimitri Johnston, said last night that Yu had never been very interested in politics, but was "not afraid to speak his mind".

Reporters were unable to contact Yu's wife, who was born and educated in Hong Kong. A mainland police spokesman, who would not give his name, said he could not comment on the case.

The Yus' daughter, who lives in California, posted a picture of herself with her parents on her Facebook Page with a message that she was "shocked and very worried".

5

Mila sat upright in Dr Chan's waiting-room, absently gazing at the wall above the rack of fashion magazines. An elegantly dressed Chinese woman was sitting opposite her, leafing languidly through the latest *Vogue*. Mila heard the pages rustling while she tried to think what to ask Chan. But there was only one question really: would this new treatment do Dimitri any good? No, there was another: how long does he have, with and without the treatment? Every time she rehearsed those questions in her mind, she felt something cold and hard clutching her – cold, hard and familiar. She'd felt it when her father died, she'd felt it when the Red Guards came for her, that feeling she'd suppressed for years, yet which was always there like a shark lurking in the depths of a calm, bright sea. Was it fear of death, she wondered. No, not exactly. More the sense of how fragile everything was, how transitory – no, not even that. It was the sense that everything else had been play and illusion, but now the games were over and there was nothing left but bleak brutal reality. That, and the thought that you never realised it until it was too late.

'Mrs Johnston?' the nurse's impersonal voice sounded at her shoulder. 'Doctor Chan will see you now.'

How strange, Mila thought as she followed the nurse. *She's Chinese, I'm Chinese and yet we speak English to each other. Is it because I'm down on her list as Mrs Johnston?*

'Hello, Mila.' Chan turned from an X-ray on the screen behind him, the grey-white bones of someone's chest. Could it be Dimitri's, she wondered.

'Hello. Thanks for fitting me in.'

He shook his head. '*Hou ma?*' *How are you?*

'*I'm* all right. It's Dimitri I've come about.'

'Ah yes, of course.' He nodded with a little start and gestured to the chair. 'How can I help?'

So they were speaking Cantonese, Mila thought as she sat down. Of course they were. Why then hadn't the nurse, she wondered detachedly as she went on: 'He doesn't want to take this course of chemotherapy you're recommending.'

'No,' Chan smiled faintly as he smoothed his greying hair down – he always was a little vain, she remembered. 'He told me so.'

'He says it isn't worth it, with the side-effects and everything.'

Chan smiled again, shaking his head. 'He's being too negative. It's the best treatment available.' Now he clasped his hands on the desk. 'Naturally it isn't pleasant, but I really think he ought to.'

'But how long . . . how long will it give him? And what about the side-effects?'

'Mila' – he looked directly into her eyes now – 'if he doesn't take the chemo, he'll probably be . . . probably be gone in six months. If he does take it, he might have a year, two years, even longer. We can't tell exactly, it hasn't been around that long. Some patients respond better than others. But it's certainly better than six months. And don't forget, new treatments are being developed all the time. Who knows? In two years we may have something better still.'

She nodded slowly. 'And the side-effects?'

'They're manageable.' He shrugged. 'He'll lose his hair.'

'Again.'

'But it will come back.' He hesitated. 'Probably.'

If he lives long enough, she thought. But aloud: 'So he really might have two years?' she asked slowly.

The intercom beeped. Chan turned to answer it. 'Yes?' He stretched his arm out to glance at his watch. Gold cufflinks, Mila noticed. 'In five minutes, yes.' He turned back. 'Sorry?'

'I said he might have two years?'

'Statistically speaking, between one and two. And as I said, some people have survived longer than that.' He shrugged again. 'If it was me, I'd take it. But it's his call in the end. I wouldn't leave it too long, though, if I were him.'

'I see.'

He smiled, tilted his head and waited.

Wasn't there something else she had to ask? Was there really nothing else? Could it all be said, a matter of life and death, in a couple of minutes? Chan certainly wasn't offering more, anyway. She stood up. 'Well . . .'

He rose to open the door for her. 'How are the children? Grown up and married, I suppose?'

She stopped in the doorway. 'There's no chance of a cure, then?'

'Remission,' he said, smiling regretfully like a waiter announcing her favourite dessert wasn't available today. 'For a year or two. Who knows? Maybe longer. But a cure?' He shook his head. 'Only if something else turns up. That's what the statistics tell us. Of course, sometimes people do buck the trend.'

'I see,' she said again.

'But that's something we can't predict. And who knows what treatment they'll come up with a year or two from now?'

'Yes, of course. Well, thanks. Thanks very much. The children are fine.'

'Grown-up and married by now, I expect?'

'Yes. Well, Elena's divorced.'

'Ah. She was the ballet dancer, wasn't she?' As though divorce was only to be expected from a ballerina.

'Yes.' *But I was a ballet dancer too once,* she thought.

'Grandchildren now, I expect?'

Grandchildren? Why should they be talking about that now? 'Yes, grandchildren,' she answered absently.

The middle-aged woman glanced up from her *Vogue* as Mila passed, then let her lids droop again. Walking to the receptionist's counter, Mila heard the nurse speaking to her in Mandarin. Was she one of those rich mainlanders then, the ones who came with suitcases full of dollars? She glanced down at the goldfish in the bubbling tank beside the high counter. How long did goldfish live, she wondered. How lucky they were they couldn't foresee their end.

'No charge,' the receptionist smiled.

The lift lobby was empty and so was the lift, except for a messenger with a large brown envelope who got out at the next floor. As the lift smoothly descended, she gazed at her reflection in the mirrored wall. Her eyes were empty, too, as though the life behind them had drained away. Then, where her image had been she saw Dimitri's face, ravaged with pain; saw him lying in a hospital bed, tubes snaking out of his body; saw his eyes glazing, a nurse laying his gaunt hand down on the sheet, shaking her head . . . But when she shook her own head, she saw him alive and well beside her in the lift a year from now. Or two years, who knew?

The atrium was crowded as usual with people swiftly going about the business of life. Quick-stepping, eager, absorbed in a thousand projects and plans. Chattering to each other, chattering on their phones. She felt she was a shadow passing among them, as though they could walk through her without noticing.

She found a coffee shop on the ground floor, an empty

table in the corner. She watched herself sit down, watched herself deliberately open her handbag, deliberately take out her phone. She watched her fingers touching the keys. She held the phone to her ear and listened to its insistent, purring ring. Ring after ring after ring in empty silence.

A waitress sauntered over. '*Caffé*,' Mila said.

'*Yi caffé?*' *Hot coffee?*

'*Haihya*,' she said, nodding. Then, into her phone: 'Elena? Listen . . . No, listen! I've just seen Chan. We've got to persuade Dimitri to take this treatment . . . What? It's his only chance, Elena, it's really good . . . Yes, I know . . . Thursday, yes. Alex and San-san have invited us all.'

When the coffee arrived, she sat motionless for a long time, watching it slowly cool. It was as if she was looking into a pond, a deep, dark pond where vague shapes she could not make out moved shadowy below the surface.

After some time her gaze was drawn away from the glimmering pond by the sound of a young girl laughing. At a table by the window a Chinese woman was sitting opposite a girl of twelve or so, about the same age as San-san's Catherine. The woman, her mother surely, was showing her daughter a necklace she must have just bought – the wrapping paper lay crumpled beside her plate. It was a small stone, Mila couldn't see what, suspended on a fine gold chain. At first she thought the necklace was for the mother, but no, the girl leant forward, raising her long, dark hair for her mother to fasten it round her neck. Then she leant back, her hair falling down loose over her shoulders, while she held the pendant in her hand to examine it more closely. She was smiling with delight. Perhaps it was a birthday present?

Mila looked away as the woman glanced across. Her lips tightened faintly. She gazed down into the dark pool of her coffee again, blank and impervious now, while in her head she heard another doctor telling her thirty years ago she couldn't have a child. *The damage from that fall in Shanghai* – yes, she'd told him it was a fall, not that she'd been hurled from the stage – *had made it impossible. If she'd had it treated right away* . . . He'd shrugged. *But now* . . . Seeing his regretful face in the calm, black mirror of her coffee, she stirred it with her spoon to drive the memory away. Then, taking a few sips, she raised her hand for the bill.

'Something wrong with the coffee?' the waitress asked, nodding at the almost full cup.

'No, it was fine, but I have to go.' She gave the girl a tip and left, willing herself not to look back at that woman and her daughter.

*

Dimitri was watching the sunset from the balcony when she came home. He glanced at her over his shoulder then looked back at the western sky. The sun was fading into the haze of pollution from the mainland. You used to be able to see the distant hills, every one of them – Lantau Peak, Sunset Peak, Sunrise Peak – sharp and clear against a crystal sky, but now they were all smothered in that grey industrial smog.

'How are you feeling?' she asked.

Dimitri turned, his lips puckering into a wry smile. 'It doesn't happen that quickly, Mila.'

'What have you been doing?'

'Nothing, really. Contemplating eternity. And thinking of Guodong . . .'

'Yes?' Mila was kicking off her shoes.

'I've been trying to phone Lai-king too, but . . .' He shrugged. 'So I'll probably never see them again.'

She shook her head faintly, not dissenting exactly, more brushing the thought away.

'What about you?' he asked.

'What have I been doing? Oh, a bit of shopping in town.'

She hesitated. 'I saw a woman in a coffee shop with her daughter. They looked so happy.'

Dimitri considered her standing there alone, barefoot and suddenly forlorn in the shadow of dusk. 'It would have made it easier now, wouldn't it?' he said slowly. 'If we had . . . ?'

'Perhaps.' She closed her eyes a moment, remembering that girl raising her hair to place the gold chain round her neck, eyes luminous with delight.

'So why wouldn't you–?' Dimitri began.

'I saw Chan too,' she interrupted firmly. 'Listen.'

6

'Of course you must try it,' Elena declared, as though that settled the matter. 'You can't just give up!' Her cheeks were flushed and there were tears in her voice, though not in her wide blue eyes, which were almost glaring at him. They matched the blue earrings – what stones were they? – quivering from her ears.

He glanced round at them all. The grandchildren had gone to their iPads next door and now the rest of his family sat there considering him, each one through their own personal prism, almost as though they were interviewing him for a job. He looked from one to the other while he toyed with the stem of his empty wine glass, twisting it constantly this way and that between his finger and thumb. His son, Alex, headmaster at an international school, and Alex's violinist wife, San-san. His daughter, Elena, a choreographer at the ballet. And Mila, who had taught Elena ballet as a child and later became her and Alex's young stepmother. What did they each see? One thing for sure. He saw it himself, as if he was a moment inside their heads: a crusty, sick, old man who'd soon be dead. Must be the wine, he thought. He'd drunk quite a lot for him. Why not? It dulled the pain – well, not the pain; the sense of that deep black hole churning inside him, which accompanied him everywhere now, sometimes fainter, sometimes stronger, but always there, even in his sleep. The pain hadn't really started yet, but it would come, it would come.

'You must!' Elena repeated fiercely. 'You can't just give up!'

Alex glanced at his sister almost reprovingly, as though she was one of his teachers who'd gone too far with a recalcitrant pupil. 'We just don't want to lose you before we have to,' he said quietly. 'That's all.'

Elena nodded vigorously, her face still flushed. San-san glanced from Alex to Elena. Mila simply looked deep inside him. Well, she knew him best of all. That quiet amused smile of hers, the first time he spoke to her, a young girl then, leaning composed and alone on the balcony of that flat – no, not the first time, the second time. The first time was in the concert hall, that night the riots broke out and the Cultural Revolution came to Hong Kong. Yes, he remembered the curfew announcement coming through the loudspeakers, the worried audience making for the exits; his wife, Helen, stopping reluctantly to introduce Mila as Elena's ballet teacher . . . The second time was the real meeting. But whose flat was it? Jan's, that's right, Jan's. His mother's best friend, another white Russian. Long dead now, forty years ago. Before . . . before every bad thing happened and Mila went back to China and he thought he'd never see her again. For a moment he felt once more that deep void he'd felt then as he watched her walk across the border at Lok Ma Chau, into the bloody chaos of Mao's revolutionary China. Forty years ago. No, he calculated, forty-three . . . And now it was he who was leaving. He felt the smart of tears threatening his eyes once more and looked away. The children's voices sifted through the door, laughing and chattering. They were quite clear and yet they seemed far off, detached, as if from another place, another time. *The voices of children are heard on the green . . .*

'You may not want to lose me before you have to,' he said drily at last, looking down at the smooth glass stem still turning this way and that between his finger and thumb. 'But you surely don't want to keep me when it's agony to stay? You know – *They hate him that would upon the rack of this tough world . . .*?' They didn't know of course, none of them except Alex. But it was Alex he was speaking to.

'What?' Elena frowned at him, shaking her head as though he'd spoken in some foreign tongue or even lost his mind.

'*King Lear*,' Alex murmured to his sister. '*They hate him, that would upon the rack of this tough world stretch him out longer.*' She was still shaking her head and frowning while he nodded recognition to Dimitri and gave a twist of a smile. But it was *He* hates him, not *They*, he couldn't help mentally correcting his father, then felt immediately ashamed of being so schoolmasterly pedantic.

Now nobody spoke until the maid came in with her tray.

'Yes, please, Lena,' San-san said. While Lena was clearing the dishes they all remained silent, gazing down at the table, occasionally glancing sideways at each other, listening absently to the chink of crockery, the faint clatter of cutlery on the tray, the children's voices rising and falling next door. Lena smiled briefly at Dimitri as she took his glass, and he wondered if she knew too. Why not? She must have heard them talking.

'Well, I'll think about it,' he sighed at last, when Lena closed the door behind her and there were only the voices of the children to listen to and the quiet whir of the air-conditioner. 'Since you all insist. Can we please talk about something else now?'

But the preoccupied silence hung there, palpable, until at last: 'Have you heard about the Yus?' San-san managed to ask Elena.

'Which Yus?' Elena had curled her fingers to her palm and was staring down at her bright red lacquered nails, indifferent just then to all the Yus in China. Strange, Dimitri thought, she was angry with him for wanting to go now rather than a few months later. As if he owed it to her to cling to life, whatever the cost.

'Guodong's been arrested.'

'Guodong?' Elena asked uninterestedly. She was still staring down at her nails. 'The one that used to be at the university?'

'My best friend in the department, you mean?' Dimitri answered sharply. 'Yes. Do we know any other Yu Guodongs?'

Elena blinked and flushed.

He saw the hurt in her eyes and relented. 'They went back to Shanghai about ten years ago,' he went on more gently. 'Remember? Guodong and Lai-king? Guodong's father still lived there. He was ill, but they wouldn't let him out to come here. So . . . they went there.'

Elena glanced up from her nails at last. 'Why wouldn't they let his father out?'

'The authorities didn't like him much. An economics professor.' Dimitri spoke in jerky, truncated laconicisms, as though recollecting things bit by bit, dragging them out of the jumbled chest of the past. 'Had a bad time in the Cultural Revolution. Then wrote a book the Party didn't like. After he was . . . what's the word?'

'Rehabilitated?' Alex offered.

He nodded. 'So he remained *persona non grata*.'

'Not much of a rehabilitation, then,' San-san interjected.

Dimitri shrugged. 'Seems Guodong's following in his footsteps. He never could keep his mouth shut when he thought something was wrong.' He smiled, remembering a scene at some Faculty Board meeting where Guodong had objected to a decision he thought was unjust and walked out of the meeting. What was it all about? He couldn't remember now.

'Pity he had to go back to the mainland, in that case,' Alex was saying.

'His father was ill,' Mila said quietly, thinking of her own father. 'What choice did he have?'

'Filial duty, yes,' Alex said, then wished he hadn't as they all avoided Dimitri's eyes.

'They liked Shanghai at first,' San-san offered after a moment, a little too brightly.

And so, awkwardly, they began to discuss the Yus. Like people at a wake, Dimitri thought, talking about the weather all the time as if the dead man wasn't lying there behind them in the room. No, not the weather, he reproved himself guiltily, something far more serious. But all the same, they only talked about it to take their minds off that shadowy thing, that presence that would soon be absence, in their midst. And all the time they kept glancing at him, smiling with sympathy, pity or concern.

'. . . spoke to Lai-king on the phone,' San-san was saying, 'the day I came back from Shanghai. But then I got cut off . . .'

But their voices drifted past him. He was thinking of that last course of chemo five years ago, how it weighed him down with fatigue, as though there was lead in his veins. And the nausea. Could he bear to go through all that again? For another year of wasting life? What for?

'. . . now they could send him to a labour camp for four years without any sort of trial,' Alex was saying. 'Or is it three?'

'They're talking about abolishing labour camps, aren't they?' Elena asked.

'The *laojiao*, yes, Not the *laogai*.'

'What exactly is the difference? I never really got it.'

'*Laojiao* means "Re-education Through Labour",' Alex began patiently. '*Laogai* means "Reform Through Labour".'

'Yes, I know that! But what's the *difference*?'

'Oh, Re-education Through Labour camps are supposed to be for smaller offences. But the point is, the police can put you in one of them for three – or is it four? – years without a trial. Reform Through Labour camps need a trial. For what that's worth.'

'Anyway, it's only talk, isn't it?' Elena said. 'If they do abolish them, it'll be the same thing by another name?'

Alex shrugged.

'Or perhaps they might just put him under house arrest?' San-san suggested hopefully. 'I suppose that's better than a labour camp, at least . . .'

Yes, and a labour camp's better than a slow, agonising death, San-san, Dimitri told her in his mind. *At least you could have some hope in a labour camp. Hope you might get out one day.* Now they were moving on – all except silent Mila – speculating what the exact difference was between one kind of labour camp and another, how many people there were in them and why they were there, what they were really like. Wasn't that what San-san's aunt had wanted to write about thirty years ago, when she escaped from Shanghai and ended up in Taiwan? Escaped only with San-san's father's help, which landed him in prison here for people-smuggling . . . No, *Assisting and abetting illegal immigrants,* that was the charge, not people-smuggling. For a moment he saw the headline in the paper. *Prominent Businessman Arrested . . .* Yes, *The Fourth World,* San-san's aunt was going to call her book, the world of the labour camps. Well, if *he* wrote a book now, he'd call it *The Next World.* Except you couldn't write much about nothing.

'What do you think, Mila?' Elena asked suddenly, as though she'd just realised they were all groping in the dark and only Mila knew the way. She never called Mila 'mother.' Well, of course not, she knew Mila first as her ballet teacher, then as her father's girlfriend, two years after her actual mother killed herself. 'Mother' didn't blend with that history. If Elena thought of anyone as mother, it was probably Ah Wong, their old *amah*, who had cared for her through the long, blank months after her real mother's death. Not that Elena didn't get along with Mila. Better, probably, than she would have with her mother. They were good friends, like sisters, but never mother and daughter.

But Mila shook her head, as if even she didn't know what the labour camps were like. She knew all right, though, she knew. She just couldn't chat about it round a dinner table. Hers wasn't that kind of knowledge; it went too deep.

A gust of shrieking laughter from the children next door pulled Dimitri suddenly back into his own childhood. Not that there was much laughter in a Japanese internment camp. Not in that one anyway. Although he did seem to recall people laughing sometimes. Gallows humour, perhaps . . . Yes, he could see himself back in that camp; see his mother's harassed face, his father lying gaunt and pale on his narrow bed. And beyond them, beyond the barbed wire, he could see the wide blue sky and the innocently glittering sea. But why were these scenes from his life reeling past him now? Because he was like a drowning man, of course. Strange, though, to think he'd never see these kids grow up. Yet not strange at all, really. Just the way things were . . . If only he could calm this churning in his stomach, or get used to it. *You're going to die, Dimitri*, he kept telling himself. *You're going to die. Get used to it*. But it didn't help. Whatever reason said, emotion stubbornly resisted. If only they'd all stop sending those reassuring glances across the table, though, those encouraging smiles. It was all false, they knew he was done for and so did he. Why not admit it?

7

When they left, San-san called the children to say goodbye. Dimitri thought they were eyeing him with a new, awed interest. Michael with dark brown hair like his father's and Catherine with her mother's sleek black hair – yes, she could be taken for a pure Chinese. And Elena's daughter, Tara; half-American, a quarter Russian and a quarter English, but really just Elena, her high-spirited self, reborn and already at thirteen reliving her mother's insouciant teenage youth. Did they know too? Did everyone in the whole damned city? Elena hugged him and said she'd call tomorrow, San-san was talking quietly to Mila. Alex clasped him briefly and smiled some sort of quiet encouragement. As a headmaster would, he thought, and then rebuked himself for this thought. Then San-san held him a moment, quiet and still.

He glanced in the rear-view mirror as he drove away and saw them all standing there, silently watching, even the children, despite the almost irresistible tug of their iPads. When the car was out of sight they'd start talking about him, discussing what to do.

'I suppose they think I'm too ill to drive,' he muttered.

Mila smiled, not at him but at the road winding down the hill, the grey tree trunks lit by the sweep of the probing headlights. 'Or too drunk?'

'Well, I suppose I will be soon.'

'Too drunk?' she repeated. She was still smiling, he saw when he glanced at her, but it was a sad sort of smile.

'Perhaps you think *you* should be driving?' He knew that

wasn't what she meant, but he felt sour as a squeezed lemon, bitter because he was dying and an object of pity.

She didn't answer, glancing away out of the window.

'Sorry.' He laid his hand on her knee. 'But I can't stand all this concern, this anxiety about me. They're smothering me with it.'

She rested her small hand on his, but absently, it seemed, still gazing out of the window at the tangled trees gliding past in the hot, still summer night.

'What are you thinking?'

She shrugged faintly. 'What it would be like to wake up in the morning,' she said quietly, deliberately. 'And you weren't there. Ever.'

He saw her eyes reflected in the glass. The night made them seem dark and haunted. Were they also moist with tears? Was that why she'd turned her face away?

They were approaching the lower reaches of the hill. The city's lights glittered beneath them. And beyond the lights, the ships in the harbour. And beyond the ships, the tiered lights of Kowloon. And beyond those lights, the dark swellings of the distant hills. And beyond them all, the mighty Chinese dragon. It was a clear night for a change. There'd been some sun in the afternoon, some bright blue sky. To think it used to be like that every day in summer, unless there was a typhoon. 'It's funny,' he said when he slowed at the roundabout, 'I don't feel all that unwell. I'm looking at the world just as I always did. Except that . . .'

She was still gazing out of the window, as though intent on some scene in the street now. 'Except that you feel you're leaving it?' she completed the sentence for him. Then she turned to look at him and he saw her eyes were clear. Of course they were, she'd cried all her tears out as a young woman in China. She had no more to give. That was what gave her that detached calm; she'd already seen the worst. 'No need to rush it, though, is there?' she asked mildly with a pleading smile, then looked away.

A taxi hooted twice behind them. Not impatiently, but quietly. Just a reminder that the road was clear. He drove on – on down towards Central, the long way home.

'Where are you going?' She glanced back at him in surprise.

He shook his head, driving on, on through the city towards Sheung Wan. She gazed questioningly at him a moment, then back at the road.

'Remember this?' he asked at last, lifting his hand from the wheel to point at the old buildings, decrepit tenements that would soon be torn down for a new mall, or towering blocks of flats – he'd forgotten which.

She nodded.

Of course she remembered. How could either of them forget that place where their lives had changed, in a day, an hour, a few minutes? Yes, that was all it took, a few minutes. He heard the noise again, the confused shouting, the mindless, rhythmic chanting, the police loud-hailers, the stones and tear gas, the rubber bullets. And that muffled, calmly vengeful voice in the police van. '*Put the boot in!*'

Yes, more than forty years ago now, the . . . what did they call it in a Greek tragedy? The peripeteia, yes, peripeteia. The reversal of their fortunes, Mila's and his.

'Why now?' Mila asked. But really, he thought, she knew perfectly well why.

'I'm visiting my past before I leave it. *Our* past.'

She nodded again, gazing not at the buildings, but at the tram stop in the middle of the road, the very spot where it all happened.

There was a gap in the traffic. He swung the car round in front of a waiting tram. 'All right,' he said grudgingly.

'I'll give that damned treatment a try, since you're all so keen on it.'

Mila smiled; a smile of relief, he saw. And then he himself felt tautened muscles slowly loosening all over his body, as though he'd only chosen what he really wanted all along. Even that uneasy churning in his stomach seemed to fade a little. He imagined it now as a prowling beast slinking away as dawn's pale light filtered through the dark of night. 'I don't suppose it'll do much good, but . . .'

A few yards further on, the flashing blue lights of a police motor-bike appeared in the side mirror.

'Crossing double white lines won't do much good either,' Mila smiled as the policeman drew alongside and gestured to him to stop. 'Didn't you see?'

'Hell, there was nothing coming! Why does he have to pick on me?'

'Pretend you don't know any Cantonese,' she murmured as he lowered the window. 'He might let you off.'

But the policeman didn't. Impersonal and efficient, he even called on his radio to check if the car was stolen or had a whole library of traffic fines against it. 'Lucky he didn't do a breath test,' Mila said as they drove on. She frowned down at the ticket, holding it slantwise to catch the passing street lamps' uncertain light. 'Four hundred and fifty dollars.'

Forty years ago people often left a ten-dollar bill in their licence and that would have been the end of it. Forty years ago. 'Take it off my funeral expenses,' he said, and realised he was smiling – for the first time, he thought, since he'd been in Chan's consulting room. The first time, at least, that it wasn't artificial. 'Cheaper wreaths or something.' And now he was almost laughing.

She reached across to place her hand on the back of his neck. It felt warm and comforting, and he stirred, leaning into it like a cat being stroked. 'Don't stop. Do it when I'm going,' he said. 'I want to feel that at the end.' And then he remembered Helen's funeral all those years ago. And that poisonous anonymous note some swine had sent her, that illiterate vicious note that made her kill herself.

WHAT DANCE DOES YOUR POLICE-HATING HUSBAND PERFORM WITH YOUR DAUGHTERS COMMUNIST-LOVING BALLET TEACHER WHEN YOU ARE NOT LOOKING?

All because of that place, that hour, those few minutes.

'Don't stop,' he repeated. 'Just keep on doing it.' As though her warm, small hand could smooth away the scars those words had burned into his brain.

*

She left her hand there till they reached their apartment, not far from the university house where they used to live. That was one thing they'd done right – or Mila had anyway, he was too impractical – buy an apartment with a view over the sea before the prices rose out of their reach. They even had bamboo growing outside and the hill sloping up behind them was as green as ever. The developers hadn't got there yet. And wouldn't, in his lifetime at least.

He swallowed his tablets and sat on the bed, watching Mila stroke the brush through her long black hair. She'd cut it short once, thinking she was too old to wear it long; then, when he reproached her, she'd let it grow again, although she never wore it loose any more.

She glanced at him in the mirror. 'When will you start the treatment?'

'I'll phone Chan tomorrow.' He shrugged. 'He said I don't have to start by yesterday, but I shouldn't leave it too long. Why?'

She shook her head. 'Just making sure.'

'What was San-san saying to you when we were leaving? Something about me?'

She smiled slyly, the brush momentarily stilled in her hair. 'We don't only talk about you.'

'What was it, then?'

She was regarding her own face now in the mirror as if it was herself she was talking to.

'It was about Guodong.'

'Oh?'

She started brushing her hair again, sweeping the bristles through it in long slow strokes. It sounded like the sea, he thought, the distant sea. 'He's got some heart condition, apparently, and Lai-king's worried he might not be getting his medicines.'

'Ah. Who knows?' He lay down and closed his eyes, feeling suddenly very tired. Was that what it would be like at the end? Just terribly tired, dragged down by the great leaden weight of it?

He remembered Guodong talking to him at one of the university graduation ceremonies – when was it? Long years ago – talking about his anthology of world poetry. His life's work, he'd said cheerfully. His life's work. Always cheerful. And now . . . He opened his eyes and gazed up at the ceiling. 'So one of us probably gets a medicine that won't help,' he muttered, 'and the other possibly doesn't get a medicine that would.'

'Perhaps it will help you, Dimitri. Why don't you admit that? Why always look for the dark side of the moon? You know you don't really mean it, anyway.'

'Not the dark side, the whole round bloody thing. The side-effects. The probabilities, the minuscule probabilities of surviving for long.'

'Two years isn't short, is it? It might be longer. They might even have a cure by then.'

She switched the light off and he gazed up into the sudden, endless dark until his eyelids slid wearily down again like shutters closing on a desolate room. 'All right,' he said, almost contritely. 'Maybe two years, if I'm lucky. But don't you go hoping for a miracle.' The sheet rustled as she lay down beside him. She took his hand and held it still, stroking it thoughtfully, it seemed, with her forefinger. Up and down, up and down, soft as a bulbul's feather. He remembered how it felt forty years ago, when their hands were smooth and supple and they imagined they'd live forever . . . When their hands were smooth and supple . . . When their hands were smooth . . . When their hands . . .

'After all, if it was me,' Mila was saying slowly, quietly, 'wouldn't you want to have me for as long as you could? Wouldn't you hope for a miracle?'

But he was asleep.

8

Dimitri gazed up at the thick plastic bag dripping healing poison into his vein. It was hanging on its metal arm like a body swinging from a gallows, he thought, which led him to visualise his obituary. But all he could see up there on the off-white ceiling was his date of birth and words that trailed off and made no sense. Was he dopey from the chemo? Or was that, after all, the story of his life?

He looked out of the window at the hill outside the hospital. A man and woman were laboriously climbing the concrete steps leading straight up the steep slope, the man leading, the woman following. Every few steps, the man stopped and held out his hand to the woman, who seemed to disregard it, hauling herself up without his help. On either side of them the tangled green undergrowth and trees grew as they always had. No, amid all the frenzy of new building, that scene hadn't changed since he was a boy. They were quite old those two, plodding up step by step until they reached the level conduit path that wound round the hill from the reservoir to the filter beds. Going to practise tai chi probably, at one of the spaces where there was good fung shui and you could look out over the sea. As they vanished at last behind the trees that lined the path, he imagined how easily the bushes could grow back and cover that flight of steps and the path they led to. Then perhaps archaeologists from some far future generation would stumble across the remnants and speculate about the ancient inhabitants of that desolate place, as distant from them as the stone age was from him, perhaps imagining human sacrifices to the sky god – if there were archaeologists, or even a generation, that far in the future.

The nurse came in, glanced at the slowly emptying bag, glanced at the needle in his arm, glanced at him and, smiling briefly, asked, '*Hou ma?*' *How are you?*

'*Gei hou*,' he lied. *Quite well.* The nausea was starting already.

'Soon be finished.' She adjusted the tap on the bag and left him with another slip of a smile.

His eyelids were heavy. He let them drift down, picturing the chemo now as a toxic tide flowing sluggishly into the estuary of his vein, then slowly trickling down through all the branching rivulets and streams that still nourished his ageing island body. Then Guodong's face appeared in his head, and then Lai-king's. Where was it they'd had that farewell dinner before Guodong left for Shanghai, the four of them and several former students? That Shanghainese restaurant on Queen's Road, probably. He couldn't be sure now, it was years ago after all. Ten years at least . . . or was it more? Mila always got on well with Guodong, he remembered that, because of their common Shanghai connection. Their fathers had known each other vaguely. And there was that student whose name he'd forgotten – he was there too. Forgotten his face as well, it must have been twenty years at least since they'd last met. A teacher then somewhere, but in his student days he'd been a member of the students' union . . . He'd said how proud the students had all been when he gave evidence at that trial, he and Mila both. Proud! That trial, which led to that vile anonymous note. Which led to Helen's body moving sluggishly to and fro like a waterlogged sack in the waves gently lapping the beach. Which led to – he heard the door-latch click and opened his eyes.

Mila sat down on the chair beside him.

'I was just thinking about you,' he said slowly. The words felt furry somehow and too big for his mouth.

'How do you feel?' she answered.

'Like someone being executed by lethal injection. Better than a bullet in the back of the head, I suppose.' But actually, he knew, he felt faint stirrings of hope whenever the chemo trickled into his veins, as though the drug that weighed his body down was really hope itself. And, he had to admit, since he'd started the treatment, he'd begun to feel better. That ceaseless churning inside him, that had diminished too. Sometimes he even noticed it wasn't there at all. Except when he started awake at night. Then it was there all right. He felt he knew then what it was like for a prisoner in the condemned cell. He would lie awake thinking starkly that that was just what he was – a condemned man waiting for his execution. He was on death row just as much as any murderer. And Nature was an implacable executioner. Often cruel, too. Almost as cruel as man, which was saying a lot. He would lie there for an hour or more nearly every night, staring with still eyes into the abyss. But then the thought of the drugs slowly dripping into his body would give him the sense that there might after all be a stay of execution – who knew, perhaps for years. You couldn't really tell, they'd told him before he started. Some patients went into remission for quite some time. He didn't ask how long 'quite some time' was. Then the churning inside him would slow and weaken, and he would slide gratefully back down into deep sleep once more.

'What were you thinking about me?' Mila was asking.

'Oh, things.' About Helen's suicide, but he didn't want to revive that all over again. 'I was thinking about Guodong as well.'

She inclined her head slightly and waited.

'Do you think there's anything we could do to help?'

'Not until we know more. Otherwise we might just make things worse.'

'As you keep saying. Well, you should know, I suppose.'

'Besides . . .' Her voice dragged.

'Besides, I'm at death's door?' The lassitude was dragging him down again. His eyelids drooped.

'That door may not be open yet, Dimitri. Not for . . . for who knows how long.'

'But it's ajar all the same. I can feel the draught,' he muttered. 'I can feel the draught.'

'Draughts can come under a closed door too.'

He had to smile; he had no answer to that.

'San-san said she'd come round this evening. Alex has a parent–teacher meeting.'

'Elena yesterday, San-san today – all making their goodbye calls?' But he was smiling more broadly now, smiling at his absurdly resolute pessimism. She was right; it might not be goodbye yet, not for . . . well, for quite some time at least. Quite some time. *Carpe diem.*

She took his hand and held it. He let his eyes close. Did she just say something, or was someone else in the room? That nurse perhaps? Or a doctor? What were they saying? He ought to listen, he ought to open his eyes and look . . .

But the deep, slow tide carried him irresistibly away.

*

He woke slowly, as though floating up to the surface through heavy water. Those were Cantonese voices he heard, surely, women speaking Cantonese? Where was he then? And then his eyes opened and he saw Ah Wong sitting with Elena at his bedside. Elena was murmuring something to Ah Wong, who, perched uncomfortably on the edge of her chair as though she had no right to sit there, was watching him with her head on one side as she used to watch Elena, he remembered, when she was sick. '*Kamyat houdee*,' he heard Elena say, *Better today*, then Ah Wong laid her bony, vein-ridged hand on Elena's and leant forward, peering concernedly at him with faintly hooded short-sighted eyes. '*Hou ma, sitau?*' she asked. *How are you, master?*

'Ah Wong! What are you doing here'?

'Elena brought me.' She glanced approvingly at Elena a moment as though she was her daughter. As well she might, he thought hazily. She'd been more mother than *amah* to her, ever since Helen's death. And perhaps before. 'All the way from Fanling in her car.'

'And the traffic in the tunnel was terrible,' Elena added. 'Sorry we're late.'

'Are you?' He smiled faintly. 'Late, I mean.'

'I thought we'd be here an hour ago.'

He let his eyes close again as an image floated across them. Ah Wong early one May morning, carrying three- or four-year-old Elena piggy-back down the hill to the market, Elena's arms clasped round Ah Wong's neck, her fair hair against Ah Wong's jet black queue, yelling something excitedly in her ear as Ah Wong turned her head to listen . . . Yes, some things remained. He hoped that memory would stay till the very end, whenever it came. He would like to take it with him. He opened his eyes. 'Where's Mila?'

'Gone shopping,' Elena said. But they both knew that Ah Wong, their *amah* long before Mila appeared, regarded the second wife as inferior to the first, however much she fought with the first over what she considered her interferences in the kitchen. And Mila knew it too – how could she not? – and kept her distance.

'How are you, Ah Wong?'

'*Hou, hou*.' *Well, well.*

But she was shrivelling year by year. It was fifteen years now since, still a robust woman, she'd left them with obstinate determination, convinced it was time to prepare for death. Nothing he said could make her change her mind, and in the end: '*She wants to go, Dimitri,*' Mila had told him. '*Can't you see? She wants to go.*' And so away she went, solitary to her little room in a faraway government housing block, and gradually, year by year, her body had shrunk and shrivelled, as if to prove she'd been right and it had indeed been time. But then how much had he shrivelled too? And now he was nearer death than she was.

'How are *you*, master?' she asked again, eyeing him shrewdly.

'Oh, getting better now.'

She didn't look convinced. 'You got Chinese medicine here?' she frowned, looking round the room.

While he hesitated, '*Chidee*,' Elena answered soothingly. *Later*. 'He's going to have that afterwards.'

'And how's Suk-yee?' he asked as Ah Wong looked doubtfully back at him.

And so they talked about Ah Wong's pretty niece until Mila returned. About her pretty niece, who years ago had slipped across the border from China, and about her distant relatives still there, whom Ah Wong hadn't seen in years and probably would never see again. What had become of Suk-yee, Dimitri wondered absently, remembering how embarrassed Ah Wong was one day years ago when he came in to find the girl sitting on a chair in the kitchen calmly varnishing her toenails, her thin pyjamas taut over her shapely, upraised leg.

Ah Wong stood up as Mila entered: '*Tai tai*,' *Madam*, she greeted her with her usual cool politeness. 'I'll go now, master,' she said decidedly. Reaching into a large plastic bag that had lain at her feet, she pulled out a blue quilted high-collared jacket – Mao jackets, they used to call them

– and laid it on the bed. 'Too cold in here,' she declared, nodding at the air-conditioner. 'Better wear this, master.'

'*Dohjeh*, Ah Wong.' *Thank you*. A jacket like that must have cost her quite a lot. But he would repay her somehow. Or if he wasn't able to, Elena would.

'*M'sai hak hei.*' *Don't mention it*. She reached out and touched the bed. 'Take care, master. Go and see a Chinese doctor.'

He nodded. 'Yes, all right.'

Elena stood up too. 'I'll come with you.'

'No, Elena, no need. You stay with master.' But of course there was a need. Ah Wong couldn't read or write. She needed guidance in this part of Hong Kong, where she was as much a stranger as any newly landed *gwei lo* (*foreign devil*).

'I'll put you on the bus,' Elena was saying determinedly. 'I can't take you all the way, I've got a rehearsal this evening.'

Mila stood smiling faintly till the door swung shut, listening to Ah Wong expostulating and Elena insisting. 'I've got some food for tonight, when San-san comes.' she said composedly as their voices faded. Then, looking up at the bottle swinging on its gallows: 'It's finished.' She reached behind the bed and pressed the bell. 'We can go home now. What are you going to do with this jacket? Give it to Oxfam?' She accepted Ah Wong's exclusion of her as the second wife, but it still pricked her sometimes. She remembered the steely glint in Ah Wong's eyes the first time they met, as though she knew full well why the first wife killed herself.

'Wear it in the winter, I suppose. If I'm still alive.'

'And next winter too,' she smiled.

'And the winter after?'

The nurse came in, eyebrows questioningly raised.

9

They sat on the balcony after dinner. In the evenings it was cool enough now, there was a faint breeze. The scented smoke from the dark green mosquito coil Mila had placed on the tiled floor drifted lazily past them. Dimitri leant further back in his bamboo chair till his head rested against the wood. His eyes took in the tall rubber tree in the corner with its waxy leaves and the delicate fern fronds clustered round it, while San-san spoke – took them in as things he knew would still be there when he was not.

'I still can't get through to Lai-king,' she was saying.

'No, nor can we,' Mila said. 'And without that it's hard to know what we should do.'

'When I saw her in Shanghai, she said you'd helped some people here once? It was also something to do with the police? You and Mila?'

'That was different,' Mila said after a moment's silence. 'Not like Guodong's case at all.'

'Very different,' Dimitri agreed.

'My father told me about it once, I remember. But I never really . . .' She paused, waited, invited.

Dimitri hesitated. He'd never talked about it properly to anyone, least of all his own children. Not the whole story. And yet he'd always felt he ought to sometime, he ought to tell it all once before he died, full and complete. Was this the time? Was San-san the person he should tell it to? 'It was during the Cultural Revolution . . .' he began at last, uncertain how far he would go. 'It didn't end very well.'

'That depends where you think the end was,' Mila said.

'I mean that particular episode. Of course there was a, a . . .'

Mila rose from her chair, walked with that dancer's level glide of hers back into the living-room and turned towards the kitchen. She still preferred not to talk about it, even to hear about it, after all those years. She had locked it deep inside her and thrown away the key.

'. . . There was a kind of epilogue,' he resumed. '*That* ended better. But the beginning didn't end well. That didn't end well at all.' He glanced down at the mosquito coil glowing by his foot. A long grey segment of ash dropped into the old cracked saucer it was standing on. The heavy incense-laden smoke curled up and glided slowly past them like a ghostly snake, away into the night. 'Anyway,' he went on, 'I was giving Mila a lift to the ferry. I'd seen her at the bus stop as I was leaving the library and . . .' He hesitated again, gazing now at the rippling silver blade the moon had laid across the sea. It was pointing at him, he realised. Directly at him. Accusingly, perhaps. Because that was a lie, the lie he'd told Helen. He hadn't been in the library, Mila wasn't at the bus stop – they'd been in each other's arms all afternoon. 'I was married to Alex's mother at the time,' he went on slowly. 'It wasn't a very happy marriage . . . She was very depressed, suicidally depressed in fact. She'd wanted to be a concert pianist, you see, but she had to give that up when she married me and came to Hong Kong. So, well, she wasn't happy here.' He looked away now from the moon's cold blade. 'She had an offer to play at the Edinburgh Festival. Only as a substitute, but it would have been her big chance, I suppose. At least she thought it would. But it came too late, after we'd left for Hong Kong. That was in the days when you travelled by boat and people sent telegrams. Remember them?'

San-san smiled, nodded, waited.

'The telegram caught up with us eight weeks later, when we arrived. ' He shrugged. 'That really hit her hard.'

When he glanced round, he saw San-san was nodding – of course, Helen's depression was something she must know about already. Her father would have told her, and so would Alex and Elena, for that matter. But why exactly she killed herself none of them knew. He'd never told them. The children had just accepted it as part of their childhood – their mother died and Mila came gradually into their life, or back into their life as far as Elena was concerned, two years or so later. That was all. At least, he hoped it was.

'Anyway,' he resumed, 'it was during the worst time of the Cultural Revolution on the mainland and the local Maoists were trying to overthrow the government here. It was pretty ugly sometimes – bombs, assassinations and whatnot. It even looked as if they might invade – they fired at a police post from across the border at Sha Tau Kok one day and killed several policemen. The British had to send troops up to rescue the rest. So you can imagine it was rather tense for a time.'

San-san nodded yet again.

'Well, I was driving Mila down through Sheung Wan on the way to the ferry when we ran into a fairly violent demonstration near Rumsey Street. We were held up while the police tried to contain it. They had snatch squads that went after the ringleaders and we saw one man being taken – hustled, I mean – into a police van next to us. Then we heard them beating him up . . .' *Put the boot in!* he heard in his head once more, and then the muffled screams of pain that soon faded into silence. 'Then a day or two later it turned out the man died in custody, so I – we – felt we had to give evidence at the inquest. You know, tell them we'd heard the police beating him up and so on. And then there was a trial after that and we gave evidence there too. It caused quite a stir at the time, but in the end no one really got punished–'

'Why not?'

'Oh,' he waved his hand. 'They were found guilty at first, but then there was an appeal and the verdict was quashed – insufficient evidence, they said.' His raised eyebrows placed ironic quotation marks round *insufficient evidence*. Closing his eyes, he recited in a deliberate judicial voice, '*The prosecution failed to prove beyond reasonable doubt that the injuries the man died from were inflicted on him in the police van.*' He shrugged. 'Maybe they were right . . .' But his tone said he didn't believe it. 'So we didn't really achieve much, giving our evidence. And that was that.'

He paused again. He'd come to the brink. Should he step over, or pull back – there was still time – back into the safe, dark cave of secrecy in which he'd hidden all those years? Somehow the words came almost of their own accord and suddenly it was too late to stop them, he'd already stepped into the void. Perhaps, he thought fleetingly, perhaps it was the chemo that was loosening his tongue?

'Well, actually not quite that,' he said slowly. 'You see, Mila and I – we were seeing each other at the time. I mean, we'd been seeing each other for a few months.' He glanced at San-san to make sure she understood. 'And, well, I suppose one or two people must have known it. Or suspected, at least . . .' Yes, he knew one who did. Peter Frankam, high up in the colonial bureaucracy. Frankam's familiar dapper face flitted across his mind. He gazed steadfastly out into the night, unwilling to meet San-san's eyes again. Would she understand the joy Mila gave him, the relief from that enduring despair of his failed marriage? 'Anyway, someone – an outraged copper, I suppose, or . . . someone – wanted to get his own back because we'd given evidence against the colonial police. So they sent an anonymous letter about us to Helen – my wife.' He closed his eyes and read it yet again in his head – how many times had he read it already?

WHAT DANCE DOES YOUR POLICE-HATING HUSBAND PERFORM WITH YOUR DAUGHTERS COMMUNIST-LOVING BALLET TEACHER WHEN YOU ARE NOT LOOKING?

Opening his eyes, he still saw only those clumsily printed words on that innocent sheet of A4 paper. Sometimes he'd wondered if that vain man Frankam could after all have been the one who sent it. But no, it couldn't have been him, that would have been too low. Besides, he was well-educated, he wouldn't have omitted the apostrophe – unless deliberately, he suddenly thought, to divert suspicion?

'She didn't tell me about it,' he went on slowly. 'It must have arrived in the morning while I was at the university. She didn't confront me or anything when I got home. She just re-addressed it to me and put it back in the post. To make sure I wouldn't see it till the next day, I suppose. And . . . well, she took some pills while we were at a beach party we went to that night. I found her much later on the shore, when . . . when it was too late.' Behind his eyes he saw her body once again, wallowing in the placid waves of the incoming tide. And then the wailing ambulance with its flashing lights and the police, the crunch of the policemen's boots on the sand, the slither of the paramedics' shoes as they carried Helen's body away on the stretcher.

He waited till the ambulance's siren had faded in his head. 'Then I got the letter the next morning,' he said slowly. 'After she'd died.'

'Oh God,' San-san breathed quietly.

There was the faint chink of crockery from the kitchen.

'The funny thing was' – he smiled wryly at his use of the word *funny* – 'I was just plucking up the courage to tell her about Mila. But whoever it was got there first.'

'You never found out who it was?'

'I didn't want to. I never told the police because then it would all have come out about Mila and me. So . . .' He paused, hesitated. 'Well, I did wonder sometimes about someone in the bureaucracy who must have known about Mila and me. I didn't really like him much, he was always so full of himself, but I knew him at Cambridge and he invited me to a lunch with some eminences – I don't remember who now – to celebrate his promotion. He got a bit tipsy, I think, and he made some sly remark to me about my acquaintance with *a certain Chinese dancer*.'

'In the bureaucracy? Who?'

Peter Frankam, he nearly said, then shook his head. Wasn't Alex quite friendly with Frankam, something to do with the school's governors? 'It doesn't matter now. I'm pretty sure it wasn't him, anyway.'

He felt San-san, quiet as a nun, beside him. Now he'd told it. And, yes, somehow it was a relief. A relief, too, to know it was San-san he'd told it to. 'And then,' he stirred, 'a few months later, after the inquest, Mila went back to China and I thought I'd never see her again.'

San-san glanced round towards the kitchen, as though it was China, and Mila might not come back from there.

'Of course, some people said we shouldn't have given evidence against the police at a time like that,' Dimitri went on, gazing back now at the mosquito coil's glowing tip, 'while others said we should. Obviously the cops didn't like it; they'd been having a pretty rough time of it. Well,' he shrugged, 'if you'd seen one of your pals have his throat ripped out by a cargo hook, you probably wouldn't handle the next bunch of demonstrators with kid gloves either.

Anyway, you can see it didn't end very well for anyone. Nobody got punished for the man's death, my wife killed herself and Mila went back to China. But then two years later she escaped from the mainland and phoned me out of the blue. That was the epilogue, the happy ending.'

'I never thought we should give evidence,' Mila said flatly, coming back with coffee on a tray. 'I never thought it would do any good.'

'But you gave it all the same,' San-san said. Had Mila really been waiting in the kitchen till Dimitri had finished?

Mila shrugged, as if to say, *Yes, I'm crazy.*

'Why did you go back to China, though,' San-san asked hesitantly, 'when it was so awful there then?'

'After what happened I didn't think I could stay with Dimitri and his children. After all, their mother killed herself because of me. There was too much . . . well, guilt, I suppose. Besides, I wanted to dance, San-san.' Mila gazed out over the balcony into the dark and the past. 'I wanted to dance. There wasn't a ballet company here then and' – she shrugged – 'I didn't think I'd get a visa to go to England after' – she smiled ruefully as her voice strayed – 'after that controversial trial. In fact I got a phone call telling me I wouldn't–'

'From the government?'

'Oh no,' Mila smiled. 'It was anonymous, of course. Like that letter to Dimitri. Perhaps it was just an empty threat, but . . .' She shrugged again. 'So, China seemed the only place left. I was born there, after all.' She shrugged again and glanced down at the cups trembling faintly on the tray between her hands.

'But weren't you scared?'

'Oh yes, I was scared all right. But they told me – I mean people connected to the Party here . . .' Mila placed the tray carefully down on the table, speaking now calmly and detachedly, as though about someone else, someone she scarcely knew. 'They told me it would be all right because I'd given evidence against the colonial police. Although it wasn't all right as it turned out.'

No, it wasn't all right at all, Dimitri thought. *The Red Guards nearly broke your back.*

They watched Mila pouring the coffee, handing round the cups. They were the blue and white rice-patterned teacups, but they used them for coffee anyway. They'd had them for years. They might be there for centuries. Why did things last longer than people? But then people did more harm than things.

'So you see, sometimes you try to help someone and it doesn't help them at all,' Mila said. 'It just makes things worse.'

San-san nodded, if a little doubtfully, and sipped her coffee. Gazing out over the balcony at the islands and the sea, she remembered Alex telling her – years ago, it must have been, soon after they were married, anyway – about Mila's entry into his life. Some kids at school sneered about his father's 'slitty-eyed girlfriend', he'd told her. But she was so different from his tempestuously moody mother, so calm and easy to get along with, *'like an older sister, really,'* that he'd just shut his ears to all that. And of course Elena had been fond of her as her ballet teacher from before: '*She said her next teacher wasn't half as good, she was glad to have Mila back.*' When they got home from school, Alex said, it was always calm, not sullen or stormy. But didn't he find Mila *too* calm, San-san had asked him once. Cold, almost? *'Well, where would you rather learn to swim?'* he'd answered. *'In a cool calm pool or a hot stormy sea?'*

'By the way,' Dimitri interrupted her reverie, 'this is all confessional, so to speak, about Mila and me.' Would she understand *confessional*? Of course she would, she'd been to a Catholic school. 'You won't tell Alex, will you? Or Elena. I've never told them, never told anyone. Except Mila.'

'Okay.' San-san nodded slowly, imagining Dimitri's first wife dying on the beach. Which beach, she wondered. Perhaps she herself had been there as a child or with Alex, lain on the same sand. She glanced across at Mila, who was gazing out into the night as though preoccupied with her own thoughts, no longer listening.

'I shouldn't really have told you,' Dimitri was saying now. 'And as I never even told the police about that anonymous letter, I suppose I could be accused of withholding evidence or something. I shouldn't have told Mila, I never meant to, but somehow it just slipped out.' And as he spoke, an image slid into his head, behind his eyes. He saw Mila sitting in that café in Alexandra House, brows knitted as she read that anonymous venomous note he'd impulsively handed her. 'As far as the inquest went – that was the second inquest in one year. I guess I'll never go to another – the verdict was simply that Helen killed herself because she was depressed. Which was certainly true, if not the whole truth.' He stopped abruptly, remembering that other bit of the truth he'd never told – the words Helen had written on the note in her round, childlike hand beneath those bare, malicious lines:

If you can be happy with her, it gives me one more reason to go away, doesn't it?

He stirred. San-san was sitting there, watching him, waiting. 'I just didn't see any reason,' he went on, 'why the children should know any more than that their mother was depressed. They'd been through enough already, I mean.' Or was he really afraid they'd blame him for Helen's death – him and Mila? Yes, of course. That too. He looked away at the cold bright face of the moon. Hurt, uncomprehending eyes staring up at him? At Mila? How could he have borne that? How could they? No, some truths could not be told. Let them believe Mila and he became close only after she came back from China. So why had he told San-san now? Yes, it must have been the chemo. Or was it really the weight of it all, a burden of guilt he could no longer bear?

'Please' – he glanced back at her, then away as if afraid to meet her eyes – 'don't ever tell them. They never knew that Mila and I were . . . what's the word? Involved, yes, involved.' He thought of the meaning of the word and imagined Mila and himself rolled, folded, into each other. '. . . That we were already involved before their mother killed herself. Helen certainly never suspected anything before that poison-pen letter. She'd have said so if she had. She was away in England with the kids when the trial took place. She didn't come back till just before the appeal.' Now he did look at her, pleadingly, almost. 'We have to keep it that way.'

She nodded once more, slowly and deliberately, like a nun, he thought again, a nun hearing confession. Except that nuns couldn't hear confession. Better, by far, if they could. He smiled his thanks, his trust. Was that how sinners felt, he wondered, after they'd confessed? And suppose that anonymous letter had never been written? Suppose he'd intercepted it? Helen might not have killed herself. Not then anyway, not like that. And what would all their lives have been like then?

When no one else spoke: 'You're looking well on this treatment,' San-san said quietly at last. 'Isn't he, Mila?'

'I feel dopey most of the time. Perhaps that makes me look well.' Yes, dopey. That's why he'd told San-san about Mila and himself, not because he couldn't bear the burden. Burden? What burden? Was it a burden to keep something secret that his children should never know? *Yes, it was,* a voice inside him whispered, a voice he'd tried to still for forty years. *A burden of guilt. Their mother killed herself because of your affair with Mila. And you never told them. That was your guilt. Didn't Mila just say so herself? Wasn't that the real reason she went back to China? She felt guilty. And so did you.*

Mila replaced her cup quietly on its saucer. 'Why don't we try phoning Lai-king again?' she asked.

They both looked at her in surprise. Was it Dimitri's health she wanted to avoid discussing, San-san wondered, or just the past?

'Now?' Dimitri frowned.

'Why not?'

'I don't think you'd get through,' San-san said uncertainly. 'They still seem to be blocking her calls. I tried again this morning, but . . .'

After a moment's perplexed hesitation, Dimitri shrugged. 'No harm in trying, I suppose. We've got to find out how things are somehow.' He took up his phone from where it lay inert on the table and scrolled to Lai-king's number.

Abstractedly watching him, San-san imagined Alex asking her what they'd talked about tonight. *About your mother's suicide,* she heard herself saying. No, not that. *Oh, nothing much,* then. No, that wouldn't do either. About Guodong? Yes it would have to be that. *About Guodong,* she'd say. But she'd never lied to Alex before, never withheld the truth. It made her feel as though some invisible barrier would – no, already had – come down between them. Would he sense that too? She wasn't a good liar. Now she imagined herself telling him the truth one far off day when Dimitri and Mila were both gone. Would that be breaking her promise to Dimitri? Would it raise that invisible barrier or lock it more firmly down, Alex hurt and angry that she hadn't told him before? Why did Dimitri have to tell her anyway, if he didn't want Alex or Elena to know? To confess? To ask for her understanding? Or even, after he was dead, for theirs? Well, perhaps–

'Lai-king?' Dimitri said suddenly into his phone. 'Is that Yu Lai-king?'

10

Lai-king was inattentively watching the television, something about the President of China in Hong Kong for the inauguration of the new leader there. She never used to watch television much, especially in China, where everything was censored and sanitised. But now that she was alone, she found she turned it on more often, almost as if she might see something about Guodong on the news, although she knew that was absurd. Now there were the usual congratulatory speeches and stiff patriotic pronouncements and she was sitting there, half-watching, half-listening to it all, when the doorbell rang.

She rose from the couch with that familiar anxious stirring in her stomach – nobody called on her any more except the police – and went to the door. Leaving it on its chain, she opened it a few inches – and saw Guodong standing there! At first she could only stare at him, his head bowed as if he was weary or ashamed. Then he looked up and smiled, a crooked, almost embarrassed, sort of smile. 'Aren't you going to let me in?'

She was still staring at him. 'You're back, then?' she said weakly.

'Aren't you going to let me in?' he repeated. He glanced round, almost alarmed, as steps sounded from the stairs below. Only one of the cleaners, but he watched her all the same until she passed.

Lai-king fumbled with the chain and for a moment couldn't loosen it, then the door was open and he was inside. He was home. She locked the door again and slid the chain back in its slot before she turned to embrace him.

He stood there still, his arms hanging by his side, then slowly, tentatively, put them round her.

'Are you all right?' she asked against his chest. His shirt smelt of sweat and something else – what was it? Prison?

She felt him nod. 'Bit tired, that's all.'

After a while he eased himself loose. 'I'd better have a shower.'

'Have you eaten?'

'What?' He was looking round the room as though he hadn't seen it for years. 'Oh, let's have some tea first. Oolong, is there any? I've been dying for some Oolong tea.'

'Guodong, did they hurt you?'

He shook his head. 'I'm all right.' His gaze wandered away as though he didn't want to look her in the eyes. Away to the TV screen. Still Hong Kong, she saw. Still a lot of rigid, robotic figures making rigid, robotic speeches. Guodong switched it off as he passed towards the bathroom.

She made the tea and put out the cups. Guodong was still in the bathroom. He used to sing in the shower, snatches of opera. He had a light tenor voice, although it was getting lower with age. But now he was so silent, she waited anxiously at the door until she heard the water turned off.

He came out in the blue and white striped dressing gown that had been hanging there on the door since the day they took him away, gulped down a cup, then leant back and closed his eyes.

'Hungry?' she asked.

'Don't know. Maybe.'

'I'll make something. What would you like?'

'In a minute.' He raised his hand. 'Tell me what they've been telling you first.'

'Who?'

'The police. What have they been telling you about me?'

When she told him, he nodded as though that was what he'd expected. 'They kept on at me to say who put me up to it in Hong Kong,' he said. 'Seemed to think I must have collaborators there.' He thought of that bare room where they questioned him. 'As if people wouldn't complain unless someone put them up to it, when officials grab their land. I was there–'

'I know.'

'I saw it. The whole village was up in arms. Wasn't that enough? Anyway,' he shrugged, 'that's why they kept me so long, they said. Trying to get me to give them some names.'

He was silent for some time, gazing across the room, but, Lai-king guessed, not really seeing it.

'San-san was here,' she said tentatively.

'Who?'

'San-san. You know, Dimitri Johnston's daughter-in-law.'

'Oh, San-san! She was here?' He looked round the room with detached incredulity.

'No, in Shanghai. For a concert.'

'Ah. When?'

'Three weeks ago. I managed to see her. She said she'd contact Dimitri and try to help.'

'Dimitri? What could he have done?'

'Well, nothing happened anyway. When I tried to call her in Hong Kong, I could never get through. It must have been the same for her. Anyway, from what the police said, it's probably just as well.'

He nodded. 'So it seems we're living in a cage. And we can't do anything about it. While those damned officials in the village are probably having a banquet right now to celebrate.' His words were angry, yet his voice seemed only fatigued, defeated.

Lai-king went to the window and looked down. 'The

police are still there,' she said. It sounded like a warning. 'What would you like to eat?'

'Actually, I think I'll just have a rest first.' He stood up, looked down at the novel lying open where he'd left it on his desk, then closed it with a flap of his hand as though it could no longer interest him. 'Just a few minutes. Catch up on some sleep.'

It was only just gone five o'clock. Lai-king drew the blind down in the bedroom as he slumped onto the bed. 'I was afraid they might send you away to a labour camp,' she said into the blind.

'So was I,' he muttered. 'Looked as though they might at one point, too. Probably only to scare me, but all the same . . . They just wouldn't believe no one in Hong Kong had put me up to writing that petition.'

'You sure they didn't hurt you?' She turned to him.

He shook his head. His eyes were closed.

'What about your medicines?' she asked from the door. 'Did they let you have them?'

But he was asleep already, his mouth sagging open. She stood there, gazing down at his face. It seemed unchanged, unlined even, considering his age. Yes, he was just the same, except tired and a bit thin, of course. And yet she felt as though there was a stranger lying on their bed. He hadn't said a word about being glad to be home, either – perhaps he just didn't feel he was yet.

If only they hadn't left Hong Kong, she thought yet again as she quietly closed the door. None of this would have happened. Instead of coming home morose and leaden from prison, or detention centre, or whatever it was, Guodong might have spent an evening with Dimitri and come back light-hearted and slightly tipsy. Dimitri was almost the only person he enjoyed a drink with. She took his medicines out of the cabinet in the bathroom and laid them on his desk. He should see the doctor tomorrow; make sure he was all right. She ought to be glad he was back, she thought guiltily. But it was true, it just didn't seem as though he was back yet, not completely. They hadn't been separated for so long since they were married in Hong Kong. Was that the reason? She wondered uneasily what tomorrow would be like, and the days after tomorrow.

*

When her phone rang, she started. She no longer expected anyone to call.

'Lai-king? Is that Yu Lai-king?' a strange voice asked.

'Yes?' she answered guardedly.

'Dimitri here.'

'Dimitri!' Now she recognised his voice. But how had he got through to her when San-san couldn't? Had they unblocked her phone?

'We've been trying and trying to reach you, but–'

'Where are you?' she asked, still more guardedly. Of course they must be listening – she pictured people in some dark office with headphones and recorders. She'd seen a film like that once in Hong Kong. She and Guodong, before–

'I'm in Hong Kong. How are you? How's Guodong?'

'Oh, he's fine.'

'Fine? I thought–'

'No, he's fine. He's come back, he's asleep now. Everything's fine,' she said, thinking of all those headphones. Then, after a pause: 'How are you?'

'I'm fine too.' Dimitri's voice had a more wary tone now. 'So everything's really all right?'

'Yes, yes. He's just a bit tired and . . . How's Mila?' she asked quickly, before he could ask more about Guodong.

'Oh, we're all fine here.' Now his voice dragged, as though he was giving something up.

She couldn't think what more to say, letting the uneasy silence lengthen and lengthen. 'I'll tell Guodong you called,' she said at last.

'Yes. Yes. It was in the papers here . . .'

'Was it?' A tremor in her stomach. 'Did you tell them?'

'What? Oh no, no. They must have got hold of it somehow. Well, they did call me and ask a few questions–'

'Did they?' Again that tremor. 'What did you say?'

'Oh nothing, nothing, Just Guodong was a nice chap, sort of thing . . .'

'Ah.' She breathed a relieved sigh.

'We did want to help, of course, but–'

'Oh no, please! Really! That's not necessary, not necessary at all. Everything's fine. Really fine.'

Neither spoke for several more uneasy seconds, until: 'Well,' Dimitri said, 'glad you're both okay.'

'Yes.'

'Tell Guodong to call some time, won't you?'

'Yes, of course.'

'When he has time. Goodbye, then.' He hesitated, then added in a tone shaded with unsaid meaning, 'I'll wait for him to call.'

'Yes. Goodbye. Thanks for calling.'

As she laid the phone down, she imagined those people with headphones again, glancing at each other, nodding, stopping their recorders. And then she remembered what that film was. *The Life of Others,* that was its name. About life in communist East Germany. That's right, they saw it on one of their trips to Hong Kong; they'd never have been allowed to see it on the mainland.

She went to the bedroom door. Opening it very quietly,

she peered inside. Guodong was wide awake now, hands clasped behind his head, staring up at the ceiling.

'I thought you were asleep?'

His eyes didn't move. 'Who was that?' he asked. 'It woke me up.'

11

'It was astonishing,' Elena said. 'There we were sitting in this taxi on Hennessy Road and we simply couldn't move. It was completely blocked with demonstrators – quite a few mainlanders as well as locals. Placards about everything from this new 'national' curriculum they want to teach in the schools here – well, that was the main thing, of course – to land grabs on the mainland, democracy, corruption . . . You name it, it was all there. There were lots of school-kids as well, and even a few people waving the old colonial flag, would you believe it?' She sat down on the bed. 'How's it going, the treatment?'

'Going?' Dimitri glanced up at the thick, clear bag, almost empty now, hanging from its stand. He thought of it more as a lamp-stand than a gibbet, now that he recognised he was feeling better. 'It's nearly gone.'

'But how do you feel?'

He shrugged. 'It knocks you out for a time. What the long-term effect will be we just don't know. Chan is of course suavely optimistic, so I keep my fingers crossed.' But really, he knew, he was as hopeful as Chan said *he* was. Only it would be tempting fate to say so.

'Well, you're looking good on it, honestly. Much better.'

'You prefer me bald?'

'So it saves on barber's bills.' She patted his shoulder as if he was a querulous child. 'It'll all grow back, anyway. Besides, you've still got your wig from before, haven't you? You looked great in that. But your face is fuller, really. Better than a few weeks ago. Honest.'

'You sound almost convincing.'

Now she gave his hand a little slap. 'Have you seen this new "national education curriculum", though, that they're trying to foist on the schools here?' Her eyebrows rose and she tossed her head when she said 'national'.

He nodded, but she didn't notice.

'They say there's hardly a word about the Cultural Revolution, the Great Leap Forward, the Mao-made famine, God knows how many millions wiped out.'

'Something like the entire population of England,' Dimitri said. 'Forty million or so. As far as we can tell. Just the famine, I mean.'

'My God, I didn't know it was that many.'

'No, they don't want you to. The Cultural Revolution was comparatively minor. Only about a million, I think.'

'No wonder Mila escaped to Hong Kong.'

'And Suk-yee. Thousands did.'

'Yes, that's right, so she did.' Elena remembered now, remembered Ah Wong talking about it with her niece Suk-yee in the kitchen one evening. It was after dinner, the time when Ah Wong used to tell her one of her 'ghosty stories', and she was impatient to hear a ghost story, not Suk-yee's real one. She smiled at the memory.

'Of course no one really knows how many they killed when they took over the country,' Dimitri was saying. 'As in every civil war. Another million at least. They set quotas for how many "counter-revolutionaries" they were supposed to liquidate in each province.' An image floated into his mind. A column of open trucks being driven to a public execution ground somewhere in China, the condemned with bowed heads sitting guarded in the back, with placards detailing their 'crimes' hanging at their chests, the cowed people watching from the pavement.

'And then Tiananmen, of course,' Elena was saying.

'Where a few thousand, at most, were killed – we just don't know. But it so happened the world's cameras were on them. The media barely noticed the millions slaughtered before that because they didn't die in the limelight. No dramatic photos, nothing to hang a story on. So no story. And so much for the world's press.'

Elena hesitated. She'd never seen him quite so sardonic. 'Well, anyway,' she went on. 'Not a word about any of all that in this so-called national curriculum. Nothing but praise for the great Chinese Communist Party and its selfless devotion to the welfare of the people. It's sickening. No wonder Hong Kong parents are protesting. I would, too, if Tara went to a Government school. But then I don't suppose many of the local big-wigs' kids do, either. No patriotic national curriculum for them, it's off to the most expensive private schools they can find and then on to Harvard or Oxford. Like on the mainland. All they want from the other kids is blind faith in the Party.'

'Sounds a bit like some of the right wing in America,' Dimitri said, glancing up at the chemo bag again. 'Only the myth is creationism there, not communism.'

'You're outrageous,' Elena smiled. 'Don't forget I was married to an American.'

'How is he, by the way?'

'Tom?' She shrugged. 'Pays up on time. Mostly. He's not a creationist, anyway.'

'A procreationist, perhaps?'

Now she laughed delightedly. 'With other women, yes. You're really quite witty, you know, considering.'

Considering what, he wondered. That he was still lingering at death's door, he supposed. Although he felt – yes, he felt now – it might not swing open just yet. Not for some time, anyway.

A nurse came in, smiled minimally, glanced at the bag,

fiddled with the control, smiled minimally again and left. Was she the same nurse as before? He couldn't remember.

'How many more weeks?' Elena asked after a moment.

'Four more, I think.' He let his eyes close. 'Then comes the verdict.' He imagined a prisoner at his trial, waiting for the jury to come back. And yet that young shoot of hope was still sprouting in his chest, each day a little stronger, the hope that his verdict would be *Not Guilty*. Or rather, since we were all guilty in Life's Supreme Court, that the sentence would be some indefinite stay of execution. Which, after all, was the most that any of us were granted.

'You should come to our next performance,' Elena was saying brightly. '*The Rite of Spring*. It should be good.'

'Yes.' She was afraid of silence, he realised. She felt she had to keep his spirits up. 'When is it?' Rite of autumn might be more appropriate for him, he thought. Or winter.

'Next month. I'll get some tickets for you and Mila.'

'Better ask her first. I'm not sure . . . not sure what'll be going on then.' Actually, he wouldn't feel like it, he thought. Not only because he would have just have finished the treatment – more because he'd never cared much for ballet. Classical ballet, anyway. Too much narcissistic posturing, too many artificial smiles. Oh it was graceful all right, elegant, great if you still liked fairy tales. But in the end it was . . . well, just too damned *airy-fairy*. Compared with Indian dance, for instance. Some of it, anyway. That belonged to the solid earth. But *The Rite of Spring* might be all right, he supposed, better than *Coppélia* or *The Nutcracker* or . . . But then there was Giselle, of course. Or Manon. They were pretty good too . . . He began to feel the weariness creeping into him. If only he could sleep till it was all over.

'Have you heard any more from the Yus?' Elena's voice seemed to come from a misty distance now.

'What?' His eyes opened. Yes, her face was misty, too. 'No. Just that one phone call. They never called back. And I sensed Lai-king didn't want us to call them again.'

'I wonder what's going on.'

'Nothing, probably. Guodong just has to watch his step. I suppose that's why they aren't phoning. The security people might still be keeping an eye on him, after all. But San-san's probably going to Shanghai again in the autumn . . .' His eyelids drooped again. He couldn't hold them open. 'For another concert and . . . she might find something out then.' He wondered how he would be in the autumn – or *if.* But of course he would, it was next autumn that he might be gone. He felt that familiar void opening inside him when he remembered that. But then he remembered Chan's words, remembered his smooth face when he started the treatment. Yes, he felt sure now, he'd have two years, maybe more. And then, who knew? And Guodong, what would have happened to him by then? Perhaps, after this treatment, he could go and see him in Shanghai? He knew why Mila had suggested they phone Lai-king that evening with San-san. She thought it would give him something to live for, another reason to keep on with the treatment – well, of course she cared about the Yus as well, but that was the main reason. However, the only thing that had really persuaded him to take the treatment in the first place was the thought of Mila lying alone in their bed night after night, coming back to an empty apartment day after day. Yes, that was why he was letting them pour this stuff into his veins, to spare her that a little longer. Or was it really? Wasn't he in the end as much afraid of death as the next man? Wouldn't he cling to life until death prised his weakening fingers away one by one? Yes, it's in our genes, he thought drowsily, we can't avoid it. The fear of death, it's in our genes . . .

'What?' Elena said, somewhere far away.

'Hi,' a voice said.

He dragged his eyes open. Alex was just entering the room, the door swishing shut behind him. 'How are things?'

'You were talking in your sleep,' Elena said. 'Something about jeans. Funny, I've never seen you in jeans. Not very suitable for a concert, anyway.'

Concert? Of course, they were going to San-san's concert tonight! That was why Alex was here. He'd completely forgotten. He glanced up at the plastic bag, empty at last. What was that stuff doing to his mind, turning it into a blurry fog? Mila would be waiting for them at home, they were going somewhere for a late dinner afterwards. He hoped he wouldn't be too tired and just flake out.

'How are things?' Alex asked again.

'Okay.' He stirred. 'At least they will be when they take this damned needle out. If only it didn't make me so dopey.'

'Well, it must be doing you good,' Alex said. 'You look much better.'

'Yes, didn't I say so?' Elena chimed in. Was there anxious foreboding lurking beneath the cheerful tone of both their voices? Of course there was. There had to be.

12

Yes, he was dopey during the concert, but it was only as if everything else had been dulled, allowing him to hear the music and only the music, undisturbed. The coughs and rustles, the mere fidgety presence of other people, which usually distracted and irritated him, were somehow muted in his mind and the music reached him through a soft, languorous haze. Perhaps he wasn't listening as attentively as a critic would, yet he felt completely absorbed by it, without another thought or feeling in his head, not even that ever-recurring sense of death remorselessly approaching.

Before the last chord had quite faded: 'Viola fluffed that last entry,' a woman murmured behind him, proud, he imagined, of her acuity. Did she only come to listen for mistakes? Then the applause started.

They were called back three times but, thank God, didn't play an encore. The spell was broken; you couldn't revive it just like that. He sat there still while seats flapped back all round him and people stood, turned and gossiped, walked slowly back towards the exits. Yes, perhaps he should just have music plugged into his ears when he was dying, and his eyes covered so there was nothing but night and magical sound. Didn't they say hearing was the last sense to fail? That last piece they played, for instance, the slow movement. That would be good to go out on, whenever he did. *Music hath charms* . . . But *his* breast wouldn't be savage then. Ravaged would be better. Yes, *music hath charms to soothe the ravaged breast.*

'Are you okay for dinner?' Alex was asking solicitously.

Mila glanced at Dimitri, eyebrows half-raised.

Not really, but he nodded and hauled himself upright.

*

They went backstage. People he didn't know were talking to the musicians as they packed their instruments away. A schoolgirl was asking them all to autograph her programme, Mila was talking to the cellist, Brian, who was some years older than the others. Derek, the first violinist, was laughing with the violist whose name Dimitri could never remember, as they loosened their bows. Why wasn't San-san the first violinist, he wondered. Because she was too pliant, he suspected, too retiring, never seeking a place in the sun. He thought her playing was just as sensitive as Derek's – but what did he know of a chamber quartet's dynamics and politics? He found a chair and sat down to wait. At last the people began to leave, with quick hugs, pecks on cheeks, air-kisses or handshakes.

'Tired?' San-san asked at his shoulder.

He nodded, then shook his head. 'I liked it,' he said simply. It didn't sound like much to say, but she smiled as if she understood the weight that lay behind it. Or was she thinking of his 'confession', the secret they shared? They hadn't met since that evening on the balcony.

'This is Jianping.' She turned to a girl standing a pace behind her. 'From the mainland.'

He stood up with an effort – God, yes, he was tired – and shook the girl's hand. '*Nie hao?*'

'How do you do?' the girl answered in English, then they both laughed at the absurdity of each speaking the other's language. She wasn't pretty, he noticed, but nor was she plain.

'Jianping's a graduate student here,' San-san went on.

‘I saw you in Victoria Park on June the fourth,’ Jianping said. She glanced at San-san: ‘With San-san.’

‘Ah,’ he remembered. ‘You’re the one who was handing out candles?’

‘Yes.’

‘Unusual for a mainlander.’ He looked at her again. There was something very definite about her, frank and . . . what was it? Firm, he supposed. Firm. ‘Isn’t that a bit risky?’ he asked.

She smiled and shrugged, as if it was nothing really.

‘Where are you studying here?’

‘Look, why don’t you join us for dinner, Jianping?’ San-san interjected.

‘Oh no, I don’t want to intrude.’ Jianping shook her head.

Intrude, Dimitri noticed. She really was at home in English.

‘I mean, you’re all family and–’

‘No, really.’ San-san appealed to Dimitri.

‘Yes, why don’t you?’ he said. ‘We’d be delighted.’ *Or would we,* he wondered.

She bowed faintly. ‘Well, thank you.’

‘Why do all mainlanders speak such perfect English?’ he asked. ‘The ones who come here, anyway?’

She laughed, shaking her head. ‘I make many mistakes.’

‘You should hear my Mandarin.’

He saw Mila smiling at him across the room. Smiling perhaps because he was. ‘You must meet my wife,’ he said. ‘She’s from the mainland too, a long time ago.’

Jianping’s eyebrows rose fractionally as she glanced at Mila.

*

At the restaurant he assumed his usual role, watching and listening while the others talked. There was a large table nearby, noisy with mainland and local businessmen. He half-listened to their conversation, half-listened to the talk at his own table. Always the detached witness at social gatherings, now he was even more so, as though he'd taken another step back before quietly turning to leave the room. San-san, relaxed and slightly flushed after half a glass of red wine, that loosened strand of dark hair straying down over her cheek . . . Would she keep his secret forever? Well, till after Mila and he were gone anyway? Yes, he knew she would, he'd known her since she was a child.

He watched them all, one by one: Alex small-talking with the violist and Brian, all three perhaps finding it a little trying; that mainland girl, Jianping, a bit out of it, smiling politely but vaguely at references she didn't understand; Mila nodding at something Derek was saying while her glance hovered over him, watching him watching them . . .

'Why did you go the June the fourth vigil here?' he asked Jianping abruptly across the wide, round table.

The other conversations stopped like cars pulling up at an unexpected traffic light, stopped and waited. Jianping hesitated, glancing round the table before she answered. 'Because I couldn't go to one on the mainland,' she said simply. 'I only found out about it three years ago, when I came to Hong Kong. In China – on the mainland, I mean – we aren't told anything about it. Except that it was just some foreign-inspired disturbance. It was a big . . . surprise? No, shock. Shock for me when I heard people talking about it.' She smiled and shrugged. 'So I decided to find out more. You can discover a lot on the internet quite easily here, which you can't on the mainland. And so . . . I went to the vigil last year. And then again this year.'

Dimitri's glance strayed to the boisterous table nearby. They were drinking a noisy toast now. 'Do you know about house arrest?' he asked, returning to Jianping. 'Black jails? Labour camps?'

'Of course.' She looked down. 'A little.'

'Better watch your step, then, when you go back to the mainland,' he said. 'A little knowledge can be a dangerous thing.'

Jianping looked up, held his glance. 'We aren't all sheep there,' she said, a keen edge glinting in her voice.

The uneasy silence lengthened at their table while at the others' the merriment continued and expanded; they were getting drunker, getting louder.

'You know that last piece we played tonight?' San-san said with an effort. 'The *Dissonance Quartet*? They were a bit worried about us playing it in Shanghai. They thought the authorities might find the word "Dissonance" subversive. Apparently, there was quite a debate before they let us play it, and even then they didn't print "Dissonance" in the programme, just the opus number.'

'Well, it is only the subtitle, so to speak,' Derek drawled negligently.

'That's not the only thing that happened in Shanghai,' Dimitri reminded San-san quietly.

'No. I told Jianping about that.'

'Did you?' He glanced at Jianping with raised eyebrows. 'I'm surprised.'

Jianping returned his gaze without speaking, but with a smile straying round her lips, as though she was holding back another retort.

'They've confirmed us for those master classes in November, by the way,' Derek said. 'I got an email this afternoon.'

And so the halted traffic began sluggishly to move again.

*

'Why did you interrogate that girl like that?' Mila murmured as they were leaving. Murmured, but there was reproach in her tone.

'Interrogate? I don't know, it just came over me.' He shook his head. 'I was listening to that table near us, did you hear them? There they all were, celebrating some business deal – what do they care about Tiananmen or black jails or labour camps, so long as they're raking in the money? I wondered why she was different. If she really is.'

'What do you mean, if she really is?

'Well, how do we know she doesn't work for the government?'

'Dimitri, she was handing out candles at the vigil.'

'Exactly. A good front. That's why I was surprised San-san told her about Guodong. You don't tell that kind of thing to complete strangers in China.'

'Then why did you bring it up? Besides, she's hardly a complete stranger, is she?'

'Isn't she?'

'Well, San-san knows her, doesn't she? She's met her a few times, she told me.'

'A few times? Is that enough?'

Mila shook her head slowly. 'Really, you're being paranoid.'

'Put it down to the chemo,' he answered curtly.

'Which everyone can see is making you better,' she smiled, unperturbed. 'If that's the price, I suppose we can pay it.'

Alex was waiting for them at the door. 'San-san's giving

the others a lift to Braemar Hill. We can grab a taxi and drop Elena off on the way. It was nice, wasn't it, the dinner?'

'And the concert,' Dimitri added drily.

'Well, of course.' Alex was practically tone-deaf and could never hold a tune.

*

In the taxi, a remorseful weariness stole over Dimitri, a creeping fog that shrouded his mind and seeped thick and heavy through his body. 'Sorry,' he murmured to Mila, leaning back against the headrest.

'What about?' Elena asked, always alert.

He closed his eyes, pretending he hadn't heard.

'It tires him out, this chemo,' Mila said quietly. She gazed away at the still of the harbour, at the glistening lights on the long, lonely span of the bridge that led through the humid haze of night to the distant airport and the far, far rest of the world.

'Anyway, I wonder how Guodong is now?' Dimitri muttered.

13

They nearly always went out together now, as though, Lai-king thought, that was somehow safer. At least she wouldn't come home to find him gone. But now that he'd been back several weeks and the police were no longer there downstairs, she began to feel that wouldn't happen. The more certain they were they weren't being watched, the more they felt able to go out. Not just briefly to shop, but also to stroll about the streets in the evenings when the heat had faded, although it still lay heavy over the city, a sullen polluted haze. Usually they only walked along the Bund, where the air was cooler and a little cleaner, and they could look out over the river at the new glittering city of Pudong. But sometimes they would walk all the way down to People's Square as far as Da Shi Jie, which Guodong's father often used to talk about. *The Great World*, where in the old days you could get everything you wanted, from sex and drugs to food, acrobatics, opera and plays. Most of it had been closed for years now, a lifeless relic, and there were only a few fashionable shops left, selling tea and whatnot on the ground floor.

Sometimes they thought they were being followed, sometimes they weren't sure.

Life was almost normal, and yet they both still felt a hand might be laid on Guodong's shoulder at any moment. Was that why he'd lost interest in reading? He sat about all the time, gazing at nothing, or occasionally going to the window to see if that unmarked police car was there again. Sometimes he did pick up a book, but then he laid it down after a page or two. It was as if he couldn't settle to anything because he was waiting for that sudden knock on the door. Even his nearly finished anthology of world poetry, which he'd been working on forever – even that didn't interest him now. It lay there untouched in his rarely opened computer like a toy he'd outgrown. What had happened to him during those weeks in detention, what had they done to him? He wouldn't tell her, he could only repeat, 'Nothing really. It wasn't too bad.' Was it like that when soldiers came home from war, she wondered, bearing scars they could not show, tales they dared not tell?

But in the deep of the night, while she lay asleep beside him, he would often start awake, a trembling of anxiety in his stomach, as if he was still there in that cell, the light glaring in his eyes, a guard banging on the metal door with his baton. Yes, he heard that harsh clanging in his head. Or as if he was back in that bleak room again, being questioned once more. Sometimes he wondered what it was, why those memories disturbed him so deeply. He hadn't been beaten after all; he wasn't locked up with murderers or drug-runners. The worst was that he didn't always get his heart pills. No, it was nothing physical, it was the helplessness, the knowledge they could do what they liked with you, that abiding anxiety, those leaps of fear whenever they called your name. And in the end he had broken, something in him had snapped. He'd tamely agreed at last, agreed not to go back to the village, not to put another 'subversive' petition online. Yes, that was what had broken him. But he'd thought it was either agree or be sent to a labour camp, and he didn't think he'd survive that. Not at his age. But that had crushed something in him. He was ashamed; humiliated and ashamed.

Once there was something about his village on one of

the internet sites – something about a disturbance there – but then it was deleted. So they were still protesting, he thought, but the thought was dead. He never called Dimitri or San-san back and never answered emails from abroad except from their daughter, Fung-ying. For several weeks now he'd hardly been online at all. Fung-ying was supposed to be coming with the children next year. He thought that would be the test. If she had no trouble, then life could really go on normally again. Except for the people in the village. It wouldn't go on normally for them, they'd lost their land. 'Sometimes I feel like going back there,' he told Lai-king once. 'Just to see what would happen.'

'And be in a labour camp when Fung-ying comes?' she answered sharply. 'Or she wouldn't be allowed to come at all?' But she knew he didn't really mean it.

*

Late one sultry Saturday afternoon they walked all the way along the manicured pedestrian walkway of Nanjing Lu, past the high-fashion shops and the occasional beggar, past a woman skating up and down selling skates like those she was wearing, past elegant cafés and restaurants. At the crossing a legless youth lay inert in a small, shabby cart, a beggar's bowl on his chest, while a grey-haired old man beside him scraped a melancholy tune on an erhu. Waiting for the traffic lights to change, Guodong dropped some coins into the metal bowl. Then across the wide space of People's Park to Renmin Avenue and finally on to the Grand Theatre. 'Let's go in,' he said when they reached the steps. 'I'm dead tired. We can get something at the café.'

Lai-king looked round. There was nowhere else except that drab kiosk in the square. 'All right.' She trudged up the steps, worn out herself.

At the foyer Guodong stopped. 'Look. They're doing *Dream of the Red Chamber* tonight. Maybe we can get tickets?'

An opera based on that classic she hadn't read since she was an undergraduate? She hesitated. But it was the first time he'd shown real interest in anything since he came back. So: 'Yes,' she said. 'Why not?'

She ordered some coffee in the café while he stood in line for tickets.

'I couldn't get the best seats,' he said when he joined her. 'But they should be all right.'

'How much?'

'Three eighty.'

She smiled. 'We deserve a treat.' Yes, they were free, relaxed, for the first time since he came back. Perhaps they really could put it all behind them now, forget his ancestral village and all its troubles.

The theatre was nearly full, mainly with people as old or older than themselves, people who might have seen a piece like this in their youth, before the strident socialist kitsch of the Cultural Revolution. Was that why they came in their old age? Or was it just to rest in some cool air? Some of them looked as if they'd nodded off already. 'This should be interesting,' Guodong whispered to Lai-king as a young couple sat down in the seats beside them. She nodded and shrugged simultaneously. A young couple, she thought. Unusual, that. Young people didn't usually listen to that kind of music any more.

After the first scene, the girl sitting next to them picked up the programme that had slipped off Lai-king's lap and gave it back to her.

'Oh. Thank you.'

'Did you like it?' the girl smiled.

'Yes,' Lai-king answered cautiously. 'Did you?'

The girl nodded. 'I don't know much about this kind of opera, though.'

'Well, you're too young,' Lai-king acknowledged.

'I know more about Western music,' the girl went on apologetically. Now the young man on her other side leant forward to regard both Guodong and Lai-king, smiling faintly. 'I think you like Western music too?' he asked.

Guodong nudged Lai-king with his elbow and frowned, minimally shaking his head.

'It's all right,' the girl said. 'I know a friend of yours in Hong Kong. San-san Johnston.'

The music started again. They looked back at the stage. The actors returned.

Throughout the rest of the performance, Lai-king kept glancing uneasily at the girl, who for her part seemed absorbed by the opera. San-san? She knew San-san? Why had she sat in that seat next to them, why had she spoken to them? Guodong sat there beside her, stiff and faintly frowning. She couldn't tell if he took much notice of what was happening on the stage now, but she knew what he must be thinking in the theatre of his mind. When it was over, neither he nor Lai-king spoke to the young pair, who followed them silently yet watchfully in the shuffling, murmuring throng towards the exit.

'San-san wanted me to say hello,' the girl said abruptly, yet quietly, behind Guodong. 'And so did Dee . . . Demeter . . .'

He turned back. 'Dimitri?'

'Yes, Dimitri,' she smiled. 'I had dinner with them a few weeks ago. After San-san's concert. She's coming here again in November.'

They had stopped by the door. He looked back at the empty auditorium, at the heavy curtain masking the stage, behind which they could hear the stage-hands already dismantling the set. 'How did you find us? Have you been following–?'

She nodded. 'I had your address from San-san, but I thought you might not want us to call on you there, so . . . yes,' she confessed with a smile, 'we followed you.'

'What do you want?' His tone was curt, unfriendly. He still didn't trust them, whoever they were.

'Just to give the message,' the girl answered calmly. 'And to take an answer, if you like. I'll be going back in three weeks. I'm studying there. I mean, I'm from Zhejiang, but I'm doing a postgraduate degree in Hong Kong. This is my friend, Yiming.'

The young man bowed. He wore large, black-framed glasses which gave him an owlish look.

They were outside the theatre now, standing on the busy street. *Ask them home,* a mad voice whispered in Guodong's head. 'Well, tell them we're fine,' he answered the girl coldly, as though to silence that disturbing inner voice. 'Everything's fine.' He took Lai-king's arm and turned away.

'D'you think they were genuine?' she murmured as they walked off towards Xizhang Road. 'Or . . . ?'

He shrugged. 'How do you tell?' Then he frowned. 'I think they were standing behind me in the queue at the box-office. I remember some young people were.'

'Oh, Mr Yu?' the girl's voice called again quietly at his shoulder. 'Here's my phone number. If you want to call me?' Her voice rose questioningly, as though she wasn't at all sure he would.

'Thank you.' This time he did smile briefly and even nodded goodbye.

'They're still pretty angry in your village, I hear,' the girl added as she turned away.

He glanced sharply at her now, but she had already rejoined her friend and was sauntering off with him towards the underpass to People's Square, their heads inclined towards each other. Watching them till they disappeared down the steps into the tunnel, he put the folded slip of paper into his pocket and held it there as he walked slowly on with Lai-king until they found a taxi.

She glanced at him in surprise when he told the driver to take them to the Bund instead of their apartment. Perhaps he thought they might be being followed? They got out at the end of Fuzhou Lu. Standing by a lamp-post, he carefully unfolded the slip of paper. *Jianping*, he made out under the pale light. And then a mobile number. He passed the paper to Lai-king. She frowned down at it, shook her head and gave it back to him.

'Will you call her?' she asked as they walked on.

He didn't answer for some steps. She watched their shadows lengthening as they left one lamp-post and then shortening as they approached the next. 'I don't know,' he said at last.

'Didn't she say San-san's coming again in November?'

He nodded, glancing across the darkened river at the great Jin Mao Tower and the tapering pinnacle of the World Financial Center soaring still higher, glistening in the pollution haze he could taste in his throat. *We are so modern now*, he thought. *Except* . . .

'I remember she said something about coming back for some master classes when she was here,' Lai-king said slowly.

He stopped to watch a late-night ferry crossing the river. She glanced at him, then stood and watched it too. They didn't move until it had docked at the pier on the other side. Then they walked silently on.

'It's funny,' Lai-king said as they turned at last towards home, 'Mrs Li started talking to me again this morning. I met her in the lift.'

'Did she?'

'Of course, she didn't say anything about you . . .'

'Maybe I *should* phone her,' Guodong said.

'Mrs Li?'

'That girl, Jianping!' he said impatiently as he took out his keys and shook them. 'If Dimitri knows her, she should be all right.'

14

This time Mila insisted and he surrendered. Perhaps, he thought, he wanted her there after all. Perhaps he didn't want to sit alone in that featureless office and hear the sentence pronounced without her calm, comforting presence beside him. But what would the sentence be? A stay of execution? Yes, he'd settle for that, he wouldn't appeal . . . They sat still and taut while Chan read the scan report on his computer. *He's frowning*, Dimitri thought. *It's all over*. It was as if he'd fallen out of a plane. His stomach lurched. He saw himself plunging down towards the earth.

'Well,' Chan said, looking up from his screen at last, 'it looks pretty good. At the moment you're all clear. In remission. The tests are all negative.'

'All negative,' Dimitri repeated slowly, as if he didn't understand, hadn't yet taken it in.

'That's very good news,' he heard Mila say.

Chan nodded. 'The best we could hope for. Let's hope it stays that way.' He leant back in his chair and smiled. 'So you can go about your normal life.'

Dimitri hesitated. 'How long for? I mean what's the prognosis now?'

Chan shrugged, glancing past them out of the window. 'We can't say how long exactly . . .' He hesitated. 'Not forever, of course – but then any one of us might walk under a bus tomorrow.'

'Only, I was thinking of going to Shanghai.'

Mila's quick glance was surprised. Of course it was, he

hadn't said a word to her, thinking secretly about it for weeks now, only waiting to see if he'd be well enough to go.

'No problem.' Chan looked at his screen again. 'As long as you don't miss your check-ups. How long are you going for?'

'Oh just a few days, to see . . .' He paused. Did Chan know Guodong? 'To see an old friend. You remember Faustus Yu?'

'Yu Guodong? Yes, of course.' He was distracted, reading something on the screen. 'No problem. Just make sure you don't miss any check-ups. And take your pills.' He looked back at Dimitri now with a smile and nod that clearly signalled dismissal.

'Well, thanks.'

'Not at all. Enjoy Shanghai.' He half-rose to shake their hands. 'How is Guodong? Haven't seen him for years.'

'Oh, you know . . .' Dimitri shrugged. 'No one gets any younger.'

Chan nodded. 'Used to be full of life in the university, I recall.'

'A bit less full now, I'm afraid,' Dimitri said as he opened the door for Mila. And suddenly he felt the force of the image, seeing them all like wine bottles standing in a row – full, half-empty, a few dregs, drained. How full was Chan's bottle? How empty his own?

'He asked after the children when I saw him back in June,' Mila said quietly as they walked down the carpeted corridor. 'And you could tell he wasn't in the least bit interested really. He just says it without thinking. It's like "Have a nice day".'

'I didn't know you saw him in June?'

'Of course you did, I told you. That's when I started getting at you about the treatment. But,' she smiled slyly, 'there *are* quite a lot of things you don't know about me, all the same. Aren't you pleased, though? Isn't it wonderful?'

'Well, it's certainly better than the alternative . . .'

'And just think, you didn't want to have the treatment!'

'. . . even if it is only a stay of execution.'

'One step at a time,' Mila said. 'Who knows? You might–'

'I wonder how Chan's children are?' he interrupted. He didn't want her to go down the false hopes road. That could only lead to a sudden precipice. 'There were three of them, weren't there?'

'Four,' she said, looking away.

'I suppose we should have asked. But he seems too impersonal to care about anyone's kids, even his own.'

'The question is whether he's a good doctor,' Mila declared, 'not whether . . .' She paused as people in the waiting-room glanced up at them from their listless magazine-surfing. 'Whether he's a caring, touchy-feely sort of person,' she concluded in a lower voice.

This time there was something to pay at the receptionist's desk. And suddenly, as he signed his ordinary name on the ordinary credit card slip, it came to him fully at last, in a rush, an abrupt loosening of all his tensed muscles. Yes, it was true! He was free, for a time. He could live a normal life. And Mila was right, who knew what would happen later? For a few seconds he felt weak and giddy with the relief of it.

'What is this about Shanghai?' Mila asked as he slid the credit card back into his wallet. The worn leather was torn, he noticed. 'You never said anything about that to me.'

'There are a lot of things *I* don't say to *you*,' he smiled. 'I need a new wallet by the way.' *Or do I?* he thought a moment later.

She was looking at him – no, into him – with those steady eyes of hers. 'You really mean to go and see the Yus?'

'If I can,' he nodded. 'Before I drop off the perch.'

'You look good enough for years now,' Mila said lightly as they left the deadening blandness of Chan's office. 'Almost perky.'

'Perky?' He pushed the polished brass lift button. 'You don't say that word very often.'

She smiled. 'I don't need to around you.'

The lift was empty. As soon as they'd stepped inside, he put his arms round her and held her tight. She pressed her body softly against his. Oh God, what relief! It was like being born again, he thought gratefully. Gratefully? But who to? He said nothing, just felt her; felt her, rested his cheek on her head, closed his eyes. And saw her again on that evening all those years ago, the evening he first really spoke to her as she leant against the rail of that high balcony. He could hear the hubbub of voices behind them, see the city's lights glistening below, see her turning with a smile to answer his question, whatever it was . . . Wasn't that one of those nights when the whole city was put under a curfew as the Cultural Revolution spread into Hong Kong?

At last he raised his head. 'This lift's taking a long time, isn't it? Perhaps it's stuck?'

'Perhaps we should press one of the buttons?' she murmured.

He pressed twenty-nine, the top floor, and held her all the way up, then all the way down. His eyes were closed, but Mila's were open now, gravely contemplating her face in the mirrored wall opposite. *How long*, she thought floor after floor, *how long*, *how long*?

'If the concierge has been watching the TV screen, he must've had an eyeful,' Dimitri said at last as the doors slid open.

But the man scarcely glanced at them as they left.

Out on the street, the heat was still solid and heavy,

although it was mid-September already. It was like walking into another element, an added gravity that weighed you down, humid and dense. But the pavement seethed regardless, the buses growled past, the tram bells clanged. Within a few seconds he'd heard Mandarin, Cantonese and English as quick-stepping people hurried past, talking to each other, talking to their phones, talking to themselves, for all he knew. How grateful he was to be part of all that vibrant bustle a little longer, before the great stillness settled over him.

'Let's have some coffee,' Mila said. 'To celebrate.'

He nodded and guided her back towards Alexandra House, where there were several cafés. Now it was Mila who was dialling on her phone. Was he the only one who wasn't? 'Who are *you* calling?' he asked as they walked into the air-conditioned lobby.

'Elena. She's been holding tickets for us until we knew . . .'

'You'll be lucky if she answers,' he warned her. But then he heard Elena's tense voice and Mila's as she smilingly answered. She must have been waiting for Mila's call. Ah yes, *The Rite of Spring*, he thought. *The Rite of Spring*, he felt like going to it now, after all, as though new blood was flowing like fresh sap through his veins. And suddenly there were tears pricking his eyes. He blinked them away as Mila handed him the phone.

'I knew it, I knew it!' Elena was laughing. 'Didn't I tell you? And I've got tickets for all of you! Best seats in the house!'

*

And yes, the savage energy of the pagan dances, the barbaric dissonance of the music really did feel like spring suddenly bursting through the winter of his life. For the first time in months he felt relaxed, carefree, as though a weight that had been dragging him down had suddenly been removed. For a moment he imagined it as a great iron ball chained to his feet, rolling away now, out of sight at last.

*

'Not exactly Mariinsky,' Elena said afterwards, 'But not bad, was it?'

'It was great,' he said, although he knew his opinion scarcely counted. The others all congratulated her too. But of course they were only amateurs, it was the reviews she'd be waiting for. She was exhilarated, as she always was after a performance, but there was some other joy, he thought, and not just for him. She must have a new lover, that's what it must be. But as the chatter went on he forgot all that. He began to think of that sacrificial girl dancing herself to death at the end of the ballet. Wasn't that the best way to go, instead of just limping on bent and worn? Well, anyway, tonight he would forget about death. He'd just let himself sink into this feeling of relief, relax in it like a soft warm bath, knowing it would be all right for a time, it would be all right.

'Isn't it wonderful the government has backed down over that national curriculum for schools?' a vaguely familiar Chinese woman was saying in an American accent.

'What? Oh yes, yes.' He remembered now – he'd met her somewhere before with Elena.

'If only people in Beijing could demonstrate like we did here. I'm not having *my* kids taught Mao was wonderful and the Party's wonderful and all that crap. After all the people they managed to kill between them.'

He nodded, wondering if she ever thought of all the people the Americans managed to kill in Vietnam and Iraq. Did that get a mention in American schools' curricula?

Naive arrogance could be as lethal as revolutionary fanaticism.

'I was here when Tiananmen happened,' the woman announced, as though showing a campaign medal.

'Were you? So was I.'

'I saw the writing on the wall. So off I went to America.'

And what about the protesting students that were shot on American campuses in the seventies, he wondered now. That was no Tiananmen, true, nothing like it. At least not in numbers. And there was an inquiry afterwards, a full accounting. Still, the fact remained, American soldiers shot unarmed students in cold blood.

'My eldest son joined the hunger strike against the national curriculum last week,' the woman was adding proudly. 'Fifteen years old.'

'Did he?' Dimitri nodded approval. 'Perhaps things will get better on the mainland soon, though?' he suggested, since she seemed to expect something more. 'Under the next President?'

'Xi Jinping?' she said scornfully. 'Wouldn't bet on it.'

'Well, wait and Xi,' he couldn't resist saying.

She turned away with a faint raised-eyebrow gesture of amused disappointment and started on San-san now, who listened politely and kept nodding her head, although her warm eyes – yes, they were always warm and open – soon began to stray. The woman was like thousands of others who left Hong Kong after Tiananmen, he supposed. Once she'd got her green card and things had settled down on the mainland, back she'd come to make her life and money here, secure in the knowledge she could get out if things went wrong again. And who could blame her? Well, she'd have no trouble fitting in back there. But she was right of course, the government had wanted to brainwash schoolchildren here as they did on the mainland, and they'd found they couldn't do it so easily after all. Good for all the people who took to the streets to protest. Thousands of them, tens of thousands. School-kids, teachers, parents . . . So it wasn't going to be so easy to push Hong Kong people around. No wonder if mainland officials were getting concerned.

Well, that was *their* problem. Just now all he wanted was to be alone with Mila and that deep sense of fatigued relief. He wanted to go to sleep beside her tonight and wake up beside her tomorrow, that warm, calm tide of release still flooding through his body.

At last they could leave. Elena and San-san embraced him as they always did and Alex gave him an encouraging hug. 'Great news,' he said.

'Not bad,' he conceded almost grudgingly. 'See how it goes.'

They laughed at his scepticism as though they knew as well as he did that it wasn't genuine. And then Mila and he were out into the muggy night air.

'Tired?' Mila asked.

'Wonderfully. Deeply.' He felt for her hand.

But outside the hall there was that mainland girl again, Jianping. Had she been waiting for them?

'Did you enjoy the performance?' she asked.

'Yes. Were you there too?'

She nodded. 'I thought it was very good. You must be very proud of your daughter.'

He inclined his head.

Jianping glanced at Mila, as though for corroboration.

'I'm sure he is,' Mila said.

Now Jianping turned back to Dimitri.

'I saw Mr Yu last month in Shanghai,' she smiled.

'Yu Guodong? Really?'

'He said he was sorry he hasn't been in touch.'

'How is he?'

'Well. They're both well . . .' She seemed to be waiting. Waiting for what?

'Well? Good.'

But still the girl just stood there waiting. Waiting and smiling.

'Ask him to phone me sometime, when you see him next. I haven't phoned because . . .'

She inclined her head, as if to show she understood.

They started walking towards the car park. 'Can we give you a lift anywhere?' he asked reluctantly.

Thank God, the girl shook her head. 'Oh, no thanks. I'm meeting someone.'

'We're thinking of going to Shanghai soon,' Mila said to Jianping, in Mandarin now. 'Perhaps we could meet the Yus then?'

'I'm sure they'd like that,' Jianping replied at once, as if that was just what she'd been waiting for. She raised her hand to say goodbye.

'What did you make of that?' Dimitri asked as they approached the parking lot cashier.

'We'll find out in Shanghai, I suppose.'

'I noticed you said *we* to her?' He paid the fee. '*We* were thinking? I didn't know you were?'

'You don't imagine I'd let you go by yourself, do you?' she smiled, reaching up to straighten his wig.

He stayed her hand. 'I look pretty stupid with his thing on my head, don't I?'

'You won't need it much longer.'

'If I'm lucky.'

'But you already are.'

He nodded. Yes, it was true, he was. They were on the top floor of the car park. He leant wearily, gratefully, on the grey roof of their seven-year-old Honda, gazing out over the harbour. He could make out the lights of Kowloon, but the distant hills were hazy with the pollution of China's industrial revolution. He thought of Macao when he first took Mila there, the placid islands of Taipa and Coloane, Black Sand Beach, the jewelled beauty of the waterfront at night – all gone now, with a ghastly oriental version of Las Vegas in its place. 'They're destroying everything,' he muttered. 'And they call it progress.'

'Would you prefer they let them all stay half-starved peasants,' she asked slyly, 'and kept the exotic, pretty view for rich foreign tourists to enjoy?'

He raised his eyebrows in rueful acknowledgement. 'All the same, there ought to be a better way.' He handed her the keys. 'Here, you drive. I just want to lie back and–'

'Enjoy the view?'

He snorted. 'Slitty-eyed, commie Chink bitch.'

'Pink-skinned, neocolonial foreign devil,' she laughed.

He got into the car and held her hand until she gently withdrew it and turned on the ignition.

'It's slipped again,' she said. 'Your wig.'

'I don't care.' He closed his eyes, sloped his seat back and let himself feel the slow, steep descent down the ramp, the brief halt at the barrier, the turn and glide into the pulsing ribbon of traffic, the long, steady climb up the hill.

15

They were always extremely polite, Lai-king thought. Too polite. That girl Jianping, for instance. She reminded her of the policewoman that day they came to tell her Guodong was going to be released. She was polite too. Why, they even looked quite similar, they could be sisters. But though Guodong hardly knew these two here today, he was warming to them both; she could see that. He'd only met them two or three times and now he'd invited them home. And all because they kept talking about his ancestral village, which they themselves admitted they'd never heard of before Guodong put that petition online.

They smiled and made way for her as she brought the tray in from the kitchen and slid it onto the grotesquely ornate Ching table that Guodong had insisted on keeping because it had been his father's. 'Oolong tea,' Guodong said. 'That's what I missed most in that detention centre.'

'Really?' The young man – what was his name? Yizhi, wasn't it? – leant forward with his puzzled owlish look. 'You missed that most? That was the worst thing about it?'

My God, Lai-king thought. *How naive can you be*?

'Well, of course that wasn't really the worst,' Guodong admitted with a smile. He let Lai-king pass the teacups to everyone before he went on. 'That was nothing, really. It was mainly the uncertainty, not knowing what was going to happen next. The helplessness, I suppose, that was the worst. I mean, I was only being detained – it wasn't prison, after all – but still I felt I might never get out. They told me if I made trouble, I'd be sent to a labour camp.'

'What did they mean, make trouble?' Jianping asked.

'Anything,' he shrugged. 'Step out of line, complain . . . Anything.' He smiled wryly. 'I didn't ask. I didn't always get my medicines either. But yes, it was that feeling of helplessness that was worst. And yet – you can ask Lai-king – when I came back, the only thing I wanted was some Oolong tea. Right, Lai-king?'

'You wanted a shower first,' she said tartly. It sounded almost like an accusation, that he hadn't been telling the truth. 'And after the tea you went to sleep.'

'Sleep? Ah yes, I missed that all right, too. No, you're right, the first thing I did was have a shower, wash the smell of that place off. That was . . . cleansing.'

The young couple nodded uncertainly. Yiming – that was his name, she remembered now – sipped his tea and said, 'Oolong, good.' Only it wasn't sipping really, it was sucking it up with a horrible slurping noise. Lai-king's eyelids drooped involuntarily with faint disdain. Sometimes she was ashamed she could never forget the good manners she'd learnt in Hong Kong, but the fact was, she couldn't. Spitting in the street, slurping up your food and drink – it shouldn't really matter so much to her, it was merely the way they'd been brought up here, after all. And yet she couldn't help feeling it was a symptom of selfishness, of unconcern for others, like that constant elbowing your way into trains and buses. Me first, me first, that was the trouble in China. But then she felt a bit guilty, thinking how polite this young couple were otherwise. Besides, the girl didn't slurp her tea at all – she might have gone to the same Girls College as she herself had, for all you could tell.

But she didn't trust them, that was it. There was something too friendly about them, too polite, too eager to please. Guodong had dropped his suspicions now and taken to them. But that had always been his trouble – he trusted people too easily, even after those ghastly weeks in prison, or detention or whatever they called it. Once he'd decided that girl was all right, he'd opened up completely. But what did he really know about her, about the two of them? She sat there tense, with tightened lips, watching and listening. And that tremor of anxiety that had kept her awake night after night when they arrested Guodong – she could feel it creeping quietly, insistently, back like an ugly little maggot writhing and wriggling in the dark of her mind. She pictured it loathsomely white and fat, deep in some crevice of her convoluted brain.

'Of course, if it's a choice between democracy and stability,' Jianping was saying now, 'we'd all choose stability.'

'We don't want to end up like Libya or Egypt,' Yiming added.

'No,' Guodong was laughing now. 'I should think not. Least of all Syria.'

How had they got on to that? You didn't talk like that with strangers in China! And that's what they were, strangers. Was Guodong mad? How often had they met? Five or six times at most? Did he want to go back to prison?

'The best thing would be if we all minded our own business,' she said sharply. 'And didn't stir up things we don't understand. Learn to live with things as they are, make the best of them.'

That silenced them, all right, all three of them. At least, it did for a moment. But only a moment. She'd barely raised her cup and sipped her tea before Jianping turned to her and fixed her with that unsettlingly steady gaze of hers. 'So you think people shouldn't complain when some official takes their land for next to nothing and sells it at a big profit to a developer?' Her voice was quiet and polite still, but it had a hidden edge to it, hard and sharp.

'Well, of course not,' Lai-king answered, looking away.

'But there are ways they can complain, aren't there? I mean, going to the provincial authorities or . . . or . . .' Or what? Her thoughts floundered. 'You can even take it to Beijing, can't you, and petition the government?'

'And get put in a black jail for a time and then packed off home again?' Yiming suggested ironically. His eyes, too, held hers for a moment, but then looked politely away as though, after all, he had no wish to embarrass her, make her lose face.

'Or sent to a labour camp,' Jianping murmured in that steely voice of hers.

There was another awkward silence, as though everyone felt some mark had been overstepped. Then Guodong cleared his throat and asked Jianping if she'd heard any more about the village. As he spoke, he remembered a summer there years ago – back in the nineties, it must have been. He'd come from Hong Kong to see his father and they'd gone down to the village for the first time since he was a boy. The old house was derelict, but he'd met that young girl Xiuling, who lived nearby. His father knew her father. Whenever they went back they would see her working in the fields or leading cattle along the rough track. He would stop and talk to her; she had such an engaging smile. Then she married someone and moved to the other side of the village . . .

'The village?' Jianping was shaking her head. 'I thought *you* might have heard?'

Was there a hint of reproach in her voice, Lai-king wondered. Guodong seemed to think so. At any rate, when he answered it was in an almost apologetic tone. 'Well, they warned me off. And I felt I couldn't really . . .'

As if he felt he ought to have done more, Lai-king thought. As if he hadn't got into enough trouble as it was, trying to help them!

Jianping nodded, but her eyebrows were raised as though to say she understood, yet didn't entirely agree. Yiming slurped more tea and put his cup down on the saucer with a loud chink. Glancing at Jianping, he tapped his watch.

'Wouldn't you like some more tea?' Lai-king asked stiffly as the silence lengthened. Well, at least he hadn't cracked the saucer, she saw.

'No, thank you.' Glancing at Jianping, Yiming stood up. 'We'd better be going.'

'Thank you very much,' Jianping said. 'Oolong, it was very nice.'

Lai-king nodded. There was a coolness now that seemed to chill them all as Guodong accompanied them to the door.

'Oh, I forgot,' Jianping said as they were leaving. 'Your friend Dimitri said he might be coming to Shanghai soon. With his wife. Actually, it was his wife that said it. Apparently he's been ill.'

'Ill? What was it?'

'Cancer, San-san said.'

'Cancer?'

Jianping nodded. 'He was wearing a wig. Last month, I saw him.'

Guodong slid the chain into its slot after he'd closed the door. He was particular about that now. And he always looked through the spy-hole before drawing the chain and opening. Lai-king followed him to the window, where he stood watching the two of them as they crossed the road below, dodging between a bus and a taxi. They didn't look back, she noticed. The wind stirred Jianping's hair as, without a glance, they passed the gleaming entrance to the mall. They walked down the crowded street and turned the corner, talking as they went. Probably heading for the Bund, Lai-king thought. The sun was setting and you could sense the first chill of autumn creeping into the air. No police car down below, she noted. At least there was that relief.

'Cancer,' Guodong said, turning from the window. 'Who would have thought it?'

'Why not?' she asked irritably. 'Anyone can get it, can't they?'

'Yes, but . . .' He sighed. 'And I never phoned him back.'

'How could you, after what the police said?'

He shook his head slowly in self-reproach. 'What must he think? Anyway, it would be good to see him again. And Mila.' He stood there still, gazing down into the street while she set about clearing the table. 'You were almost rude to them,' he said mildly at last. 'Jianping and Yiming.'

She placed the last cup deliberately on the tray before she answered. 'I don't trust them,' she said flatly.

He turned towards her now, shaking his head. 'They're just young and idealistic.'

'Perhaps. Perhaps not.' She lifted the tray. 'You don't know anything about them, really, do you? And even if they are "young and idealistic"' – she made that sound faintly ridiculous – 'they don't know the difference between Oolong and Pouchong. "Oolong, good," indeed! That was Pouchong I served them. We're out of Oolong.'

He shrugged. 'Pouchong, Oolong, near enough. Seems I don't know the difference either.'

'Of course you do. Pouchong's greener. Anyway, you shouldn't let yourself get mixed up with them. Haven't we had enough trouble already? I mean, things are slowly getting better, anyway, aren't they? Compared with how they used to be? Just give it time.'

He tilted his head a fraction, just like Jianping, as if to say, *Well, yes, but* . . . then followed her into the kitchen and silently helped her with the dishes. Placing the teapot on its shelf, he recalled that day when they came to arrest him. That long, imperious ring of the doorbell, those peremptory knocks on the door. That sudden void in his stomach. Lai-king's anguished face as he was taken away. His own shock and fear. Had it all been a waste, then, pointless and unnecessary? Was there really nothing you could do to help those people in the village? Jianping and Yiming seemed to think there might be, they hadn't given up. It made him feel faintly ashamed. But then they hadn't been arrested and detained, it was easy for them.

'Will you meet them if they come here?' Lai-king asked in a low, dull voice as she placed the cups one by one back in the cupboard. 'Dimitri and Mila?'

'Of course. Why?'

'Because it might make them suspicious again.'

No need to ask who she meant by 'them'. He frowned. 'How could I refuse to meet him when he comes here specially to see me and he's just had cancer? Or still has it, for all we know?'

'Well, what did he do for you when you were in prison?'

'I don't know,' he said, suddenly sharp. 'Presumably he was having treatment for his cancer. What d'you think he should have done?' His voice grew hard now, sarcastic. 'Jump out of bed and . . . and *what* exactly? Besides, it wasn't prison, it was a detention centre.'

He stalked out of the kitchen without waiting for an answer. Not that she had one. Now, she knew, he was really angry, for the first time since he'd come back. And he was thinking of something, she could tell that. Something to do with the village. Those two young activists were trying to put him up to something, she was sure of it. Gazing bleakly out of the window, she dried her hands absently on the red and white chequered cloth while that slimy maggot of anxiety wriggled further into her brain. Then she heard Guodong speaking loudly on his phone. 'Dimitri? Dimitri? It's me, Guodong . . .'

A gust of wind rattled the pane, sending yellow leaves fluttering past the window. Yes, summer was passing, the year turning to its end.

16

'What's going on over there?'

'Where?'

They were driving through the crowded streets of Sai Wan on their way to Central.

Mila pointed. 'China Liaison Office. A protest of some sort. Look at the police.'

'On China's national day as well.' Dimitri slowed down. 'Let's take a look.'

Mila glanced at her watch.

'Just for a moment,' he said.

She shrugged.

He found a space on a side street between a money-changer's, where a pale young man with small rimless glasses surveyed him indifferently through a barred window, and a massage parlour's narrow entrance, brightly illuminated footprints flashing on its gaudy sign. Did people really go for a massage, or whatever, in the middle of the morning?

'It's not a parking space,' Mila warned him.

'It's a public holiday. The police'll be looking for demonstrators, not peaceful parking offenders.'

They started walking back towards the massive building. 'Are you all right to walk this far?' Mila asked.

'I'm supposed to be better, aren't I?'

She smiled, a wince of a smile, and looked away. She thought Dimitri was breathing harder already, and slowed her steps.

A ragged group of some fifty people – old, young, smart, untidy, long-haired, short-haired – were shouting slogans outside the sternly locked and barred entrance to the Beijing Government's headquarters in Hong Kong. Some of them, he noticed, were waving the old colonial flag with the Union Jack on it. TV cameramen, reporters, a small crowd of onlookers and a posse of police officers looked on with what seemed impassive, even bored, faces. 'I am a Hongkonger!' some of the demonstrators were chanting, and 'Give me back Hong Kong!' Dimitri saw a big-character poster held high and crooked for a moment. *We have the right to vote for our future!* Some demonstrators were kneeling by the gates, offering mock funeral gifts for the 'dead' Hong Kong government. The onlookers watched with only casual interest, as though it was a street show they'd lingered a moment for and would soon forget. And there was a self-consciousness about the demonstrators, as though they felt they might look foolish, might even be so. One young man waving the old colonial flag seemed almost embarrassed. And yet all they were asking for was what people elsewhere took for granted – an independent government they'd elected themselves. But why wasn't everyone on the streets? Why did people walk past – he saw them now – as the wealthy walked past beggars, as if they hadn't seen them, yet with a faint uneasy sense of guilt or shame?

It was over in a few minutes, then another group appeared, all wearing black T-shirts. At first Dimitri couldn't make out what it was they were carrying, then: 'It's a coffin,' Mila said and he understood. They placed the coffin carefully down and also offered mock funeral gifts for the 'dead' Hong Kong government. Then someone set a photo with some small placards on the pavement against the entrance to the building. Dimitri made his way forward, followed hesitantly, reluctantly even, by Mila, under the alert and expressionless gaze of two policemen. The photo was of Liu Xiabo. The placards demanded his release from prison in China.

'Let's go,' Mila said in a low, urgent voice. They were being photographed and recorded, he knew she thought – and not just by the TV cameras. He glanced up at the blank windows of the building, the impressively closed doors. She might well be right; how would he know?

'Liu Xiabo,' he said as they walked back towards the car past shops filled with unconcerned holiday shoppers. 'How long's he in for now?'

'Eleven years this time, I think.'

He thought of Liu's face on the photo, an agreeable, unremarkable-looking man with glasses and a friendly smile. Once an uncritical admirer of the West – Dimitri grimaced as he recalled his absurd adulation of America, his naive support of the Iraq war – Liu had later evolved into a more balanced critic of the Chinese government. All he asked for, after all, was a few human rights, like those demonstrators just now. So China locked him up.

He watched his scuffed shoes pacing slowly along the pavement. His stride was shorter now, he realised; an old man's stride, if you could call it a stride at all.

Then Liu was awarded the Nobel Peace Prize, which probably made things still worse for him, although some people said his prison guards actually gave him a dinner to celebrate, believe it if you like. But again, how could you know? It was like looking into a cave. All you ever saw were dim shapes and shadows, insubstantial glimmerings. A few lines of the poem Liu wrote for his wife, under house arrest for no better reason than that she was his wife, came into his head. He remembered a brief smuggled video he'd seen of her. Distraught and anxious, eyes large and haunted, with a guard always at her door. A woman lost and desperate, she seemed, teetering on the edge.

They didn't speak again until they were back in the car. No parking ticket, he saw with mild, mundane relief. 'What are you thinking?' Mila asked as he drove off, followed by the speculative gaze of the pale young man at the money-changer's.

Dimitri glanced at her almost mischievously. 'Remember the first time you asked me that?'

Memory softened her eyes. 'You said you wanted your inner life left undisturbed or something,' she smiled.

'Something pretentious like that, yes, I expect. Actually just now I was thinking of Liu Xiabo. Then I wondered if that's how the Tiananmen demonstration started twenty-three years ago.'

'Like those people back there?' She shook her head. 'It would have been pathetic if it did.'

'Perhaps it was at the start. Besides, isn't that what people would have said about Sun Yat-sen when he started a hundred or so years ago? And here in Hong Kong too? We're not a mile from where he used to live, by the way.'

She shook her head more decidedly. 'Sun Yat-sen was different. That little protest back there was more like what Guodong must have been doing in his village. Very small-scale.'

'Enough to get him arrested.'

Mila shrugged. 'Still small-scale. Hong Kong isn't Beijing, there's no Tiananmen here,' she said firmly, as if that settled it. 'Besides, political demonstrations don't work in China. They get squashed before they can really start.'

'They didn't get squashed before they started in Tiananmen.'

'And look how they got squashed later on,' she said fiercely. 'In the end they all got shot or put in prison. The only real change comes from people with guns, like the communists. Like Sun Yat-sen. And who wants another civil war? In any case' – now her voice was resigned – 'there aren't enough people who care.'

'Demonstrations don't get squashed here,' he persisted stubbornly.

'Yet.' She closed her eyes a moment and shifted in her seat. 'What about ten years from now?' Ten years from now, she thought, suddenly guilty for having mentioned such a distant future time. He wouldn't be here then, unless there was a miracle. He wouldn't be here. But then nor perhaps would she.

He glanced at her. 'Your back hurting?'

'No . . .' Her tone implied *No, not my back.*

But what? he wondered, yet didn't want to ask. He knew there were scars she wouldn't allow to be probed, not even by herself. He glanced at her again, sitting poised and, for all it might have hurt, straight-backed. She was looking away across the harbour at the soaring tower of the International Commerce Centre, Hong Kong's cathedral to trade, its omnipotent windows indifferently splintering the autumn sunlight, then at her reflection in the car window, shadowy and withdrawn. Perhaps she was right; perhaps in ten, twenty, years political demonstrations and protests would all have been squashed or smothered here as they were in the rest of China. Well, he wouldn't be here to see it.

'In that case,' he wondered aloud, 'why keep on going to Victoria Park every June the fourth?'

'Just to let them know we haven't forgotten, I suppose.' Her voice was suddenly subdued, unsure even. 'If we didn't go, Tiananmen would be completely forgotten. And all the rest.' She smiled ruefully, 'I suppose I'm not being very consistent?'

'Conflicted, I think the buzz-word is. You're conflicted. Well, that's what they want.'

'Me conflicted?'

'Tiananmen forgotten. Historical amnesia. The Cultural Revolution, the Great Leap Forward, God knows how many millions dead. Forty, fifty million? They want it all forgotten.'

'And so do most of the people round us now, I should think. If they haven't forgotten already.'

She glanced now at the grey stone classical pillars of the old colonial Supreme Court building as he steered into the lane for Mid-levels and the long climb up Cotton Tree Drive, where she couldn't remember ever seeing any cotton trees.

Law courts, Dimitri thought as he followed her glance, what would happen to them a few years from now? Would they turn into tools of the state in the end, like on the mainland? Would there be the same laws here as there, black jails, labour camps, house arrest? But of course there would. How could Beijing tolerate the rule of law here when they didn't in the rest of China? They would gradually suffocate whatever rights people had here unless the regime changed, and what hope was there of that? He thought of Tiananmen, how twenty years ago Hong Kong people had been running round in shock, desperately hunting for visas to let them settle in some foreign country – he'd helped some of them himself. Would they be running round in another twenty years – they or their children – as Hong Kong's expiry date drew near? Those that could would have got their second passports in good time. And as for the rest, those at the bottom of the pile, they would just have to lump it, as they always had.

And perhaps it would be better to forget, Mila was thinking dispiritedly. *After all, most people have.* Wouldn't she herself rather forget, if only she could? Then she heard Dimitri murmuring the words of that poem Liu Xiaobo wrote for his wife, a poem he must have written in prison. They were level with a crowded 23 bus as, looking up at the faces gazing idly out of the windows, she listened to him reciting the words.

'just let the dust bury you altogether
just let yourself fall asleep in the dust
until I return
and you come awake . . .'

The last line wouldn't come. *'and you come awake . . .'* He frowned, groping for it in the deep pit of memory. *'and you come awake . . . ?'*

'wiping the dust from your skin and your soul,' Mila said quietly beside him.

Now they had drawn free of the growling bus and were climbing towards the Peak, past tall, polished, up-scale, residential towers, each a gated community for the rich. They were silent for some minutes, then: 'And Liu was only telling the students in Tiananmen to leave,' Mila said ruminatively. 'Telling them to leave before the soldiers came. But still they put him in jail.'

'For the first time,' Dimitri added drily. 'It's the fourth time now, isn't it?' He turned onto Peak Road at the top of the hill and suddenly remembered it as it was in his childhood; no more, really, than a pleasant country lane with a few grand houses here and there. Were Chinese allowed to live there then, he wondered. He knew they weren't earlier. What an arrogant racist tribe the British had been then. Well, they didn't have much to be arrogant about now. Not that the Chinese hadn't been arrogant too in their own way, but they were on the receiving end then, whereas now . . .

There was the tree-green slope down to Aberdeen. *Aberdeen*, how the colonials had stamped their names on the land, as though that would make it forever England – or Scotland, he supposed. And there were the fishing junks still, where the crew's children used to be tethered like their dogs on the deck so they couldn't fall overboard. He thought of the two junk gods he had on his bookshelf at home, the paint cracked and flaking now. He couldn't remember how he got them, but he knew they came from one of those boats. Perhaps his mother had bought them for him, bargaining with a family whose children never went to school, hardly ever even left their junk. A faded memory drifted behind his eyes – a junk with patched sails slowly passing some beach where he sat with his mother under a brightly coloured sunshade. Where could it have been? And when? Some summer's day in his infancy . . .

The trees were growing taller along the road now and you could almost believe you were in some piece of rugged English countryside, except that down the green slopes rose the tall white obelisks of residential towers, and at the bottom the drab blocks of Wah Fu low-cost housing estate, one stacked after the other, filing cabinets for people. And beyond them lay the rippling skin of the sleeping sea, the ships, the islands and, thank God, once more today the keen blue sky, in which two buzzards were wheeling on indolent wings. He turned onto Mt Kellett Road, past Matilda Hospital, where he and then his children had been born, and on towards Alex and San-san's house; far beyond their means but for San-san's father's leaving it to her when he died, just about the only thing he could leave her, the only thing he had left.

I shall be sorry to leave all this, he thought almost detachedly. Before, he'd felt a stirring of fear inside him – it returned faintly as he remembered it – whenever he considered his inevitable impending end. And he thought of it every day then. But now, since Chan's ambiguous all-clear a few short weeks ago, death had drifted into the distance, even though his reason gently nudged him, reminding him it couldn't be far off. Death seemed almost as remote now as it was before he learnt he had cancer. As if a dark, menacing figure following close at his heels had considerately dropped back a few paces, so that he was no longer walking in its shadow. 'Didn't Alex say they'd invited someone else tonight?' he asked Mila.

She smiled, glancing sideways at him. 'Your old friend, Peter Frankam.'

'Frankam? Oh God! Some friend!'

'He's not so bad.'

'Bad enough.' For some reason he often thought and spoke of Peter Frankam by his surname only. A relic of his Cambridge days, he supposed, where they'd first met. That was the way in public schools and Cambridge then. Perhaps it still was. 'What makes him so bloody cocksure of himself?'

Now Mila was laughing, the smooth skin crinkling round her eyes. 'What makes you?'

17

'Have you heard any more from that girl, Jianping?' he asked San-san that evening at dinner.

'She phoned the other day. She's going to meet us in Shanghai.' San-san turned to Frankam, 'Jianping's a music student I met in Victoria Park on June the fourth. A mainlander.'

'You don't still go to those vigil things, do you?' Frankam asked with condescending and affected surprise, as if she was a teenager who still sucked her thumb.

'Well, yes,' San-san said uncertainly, tugged between the desire to defend herself and the need to preserve harmony at the dinner table.

'So what do *you* do on June the fourth, then?' Dimitri asked. The children were still at the table and, sensing the challenge in Dimitri's tone, all turned to watch, as though drawn to a playground fight.

White-haired now, but still as sure of himself as when he'd been head of his department in the colonial bureaucracy twenty years before, Frankam settled back into his chair and savoured the last of his wine before answering. He liked an audience, Dimitri saw, even of children, and he liked to keep them in suspense. 'Oh, nothing in particular,' he drawled. 'This year I watched the demagogues in Victoria Park on TV. Thought how irrelevant they've become.'

'Irrelevant?'

'We-e-e-ll, it's nearly thirty years since Tiananmen.'

'Twenty-three and a third, to be exact.'

Frankam's wrinkled eyelids drooped in patient indulgence

of Dimitri's pedantry. 'Twenty-three and a third, then. And things have moved on since then, haven't they? I mean, if you look around at other governments in the region – or elsewhere, for that matter – you have to think the Chinese have made a pretty good fist of it, don't you?'

'Fist is exactly the right word, don't *you* think?'

'Look at the so-called democracies, then. India? A third of their MPs face criminal charges. Need I mention Pakistan? Cambodia? Afghanistan? Basket cases. Now look at China. Efficient and successful. Not that they don't have problems.'

'Corruption, for a start?'

'Name me one country that doesn't.' Frankam raised a languid eyebrow. 'The point is, they've got the structures to deal with the major issues, and they've made a success of it. Perhaps – forgive me, I'm a contrarian – perhaps they've just found the right form of government?'

'You mean the autocracy of the Party, which, by the way, you might as well call the latest dynasty, since it seems to be just as authoritarian as the Ming or Qing were?'

Frankam raised his hand. 'So-called democratic governments get chosen by a semi-literate and ill-informed electorate which knows practically nothing about the issues and votes out of prejudice, tribal loyalty or blind ignorance. D'you think that's better? In China the government is chosen by people actually involved in the running of the country, who can at least be presumed to be better informed than the average voter anywhere, let alone in China. Whereas in democracies it's just a lot of squabbling demagogues out for themselves and telling whopping lies to get themselves elected.'

'Spoken like a true colonial official,' Dimitri said, remembering again that lunch with Frankam in the Hong Kong Club all those years ago. Yes, sometimes he still wondered if Frankam could, after all, have been the one who sent that anonymous note to Helen. But no, he decided, as he always did, that really would have been too low for him, he wasn't vicious. Wasn't he also here in San-san's father's house at that New Year's party years later, though, sounding off about the chances of Hong Kong remaining a British colony? They'd been outside in the garden, he remembered, waiting for the stroke of midnight, when all the ships in the harbour would sound their horns in a blaring yet somehow melancholy chorus to welcome the new year. No, no, it wasn't Frankam, he remembered now. It was someone else, a much less colourful bureaucrat, lower down the hierarchy. And suddenly he was back there, thirty years ago, hearing all the horns bellowing quite distinctly, seeing all the guests self-consciously raising their champagne glasses . . .

'Spoken like a true academic,' Frankam was rejoining complacently, 'still stuck in his ivory tower. But I think you will admit *we* made Hong Kong work too. Better than it works now, if I may say so.'

'How strange,' Dimitri parodied Frankam's supercilious irony now. 'Considering it's almost the same system. You do realise, of course, it's the one advocated in the Republic?'

'Republic?' Frankam smiled patronisingly as though at some callow colonial cadet who'd made an obvious comment at a committee meeting and unwittingly revealed the depths of his naivete. 'The People's Republic? Yes, that *is* what we're talking about, isn't it?'

'*Plato's* Republic.' Dimitri let his eyelids droop in his own version of exaggerated condescension. 'His prescription for an ideal state – I'm sure you remember?'

'Ah, Plato, yes.'

'With its three distinct classes? The Guardians who rule because they're wise and know best, the Auxiliaries who defend the state and keep the people in order, and the rest who do what they're told or else. In China the Guardians are the Party, the Auxiliaries are the military and the police, and the rest do what they're told or else. And China wants it to be the same here.'

'Ah, yes, I must admit I'd forgotten,' Frankam allowed, with a faintly surprised and approving nod, as though the cadet had after all made a marginally useful contribution. 'But surely it's more the Confucian model than the Platonic?'

'Both, perhaps,' Dimitri went on in the same languid, patronising tone. 'But Plato's is more universal. It applies to lots of cases. Take the Catholic Church, for instance. It works on the same principle. The infallible pope and his college of cardinals are Plato's Guardians. The rest of the priesthood are the Auxiliaries, keeping the faithful in order. And then there's the faithful, who do what they're told or else. "Or else" in the Catholic church means hell, incidentally, while in China it means jail or a labour camp, which is pretty much hell anyway. Yes, it seems a pretty old model.'

'Which, may I point out, doesn't mean it's wrong.'

'Oh, and there's the Noble Lie too – that was part of Plato's ideal state, the lie that keeps the lower orders' brains washed. China has that too – you know, the lie about the Great Leap Forward, the lie about the Cultural Revolution, the lie about Tiananmen. And then there's censorship of art; Plato thought of everything, you see. Only sanitised patriotic art allowed, nothing subversive. Doesn't that remind you of China? Come to think of it, the Party might just as well have followed Plato and not bothered with Marx, since they're no more communist now than Ayn Rand was.'

'What's the Noble Lie in the Catholic Church, then?' San-san asked with a slightly uneasy laugh. Like Mila, she had gone to a Catholic school at first, not because her family was religious, but because her father believed, as so many did, the education was better there. Later, however, it was off to secular schools in England and America, for San-san at least.

'The Catholics? Take your pick. Virgin birth, miracles, resurrection. I suppose Heaven and Hell at the back of it all.'

He noticed now that the children's interest was waning as his waxed stronger. They were signalling to each other with raised eyebrows and twitching lips. 'Go on,' he said, nodding to the door. 'Off you go.'

Tara jumped up at once, but Michael and Cathy looked uncertainly at their mother for permission. She nodded and they drew back their chairs. 'Half an hour until it starts,' she called after them. Her eyes followed them until the doors were closed, then turned back slowly and, it seemed, reluctantly to the table.

'Well, Platonic or not,' Frankam was saying, 'it's a system that on the whole seems to work better than the others.'

'Except for *Quis custodiet*?'

'*Quis custodiet*?' San-san repeated uncertainly.

'Latin,' Frankam said with a negligent wave of his hand. 'Your father-in-law can't resist a Latin quotation. It proves he's a member of the elite he affects to despise. I know him, we were both at Cambridge, although not the same year, as I recall.' As he spoke, Dimitri realised for the first time how much Frankam had aged. The dapper self-confidence was still there in every gesture, but the well-shaved cheeks hung from too prominent cheekbones and the skin beneath his eyes was pouched and dark. Well, he was some years older than himself, after all. Perhaps, the thought hovered shadowy on the edge of his mind, perhaps he'd been ill too?

'*Quis custodiet ipsos custodes*,' Alex was explaining. 'Virgil. It means, "Who will guard the guards themselves?"'

'Or in this case who will guard the *Guardians*,' Dimitri continued with both an acknowledging nod and a faintly raised eyebrow. 'Juvenal, actually. Not Virgil.' So Alex couldn't always place a quotation. 'Or in China's case, who stops them from putting people in prison for asking – *asking*, mark you, not even demanding – *asking* for more civil rights?' Guodong's face appeared behind his eyes, then the imprisoned Liu Xiaobo's. 'Like the right to do what we're doing here now – talk freely about whether we have the best form of government. Like the rule of law, a free press, the right to demonstrate? Who stops them from running labour camps, where people get tortured and made to work like slaves on the say-so of some police official or a court that does whatever the Party wants? Who stops them from killing an eight-month-old baby in the womb and then tearing it out of the mother's body because she's not allowed to have a second child?' As he spoke, he remembered that mother's story, pictured her being forced into the local clinic, held down and injected . . . He closed his eyes a moment. 'I assume you recognise what I'm alluding to?'

'There will always be isolated cases of brutality under any system,' Frankam answered airily. 'How many unarmed blacks have white policemen shot in America, pray? How many Muslims were tortured in Guantanamo?'

'Yes, and they were exposed by a free press. When did Xinhua expose the tortures of the Cultural Revolution or the labour camps? Tell me that. Besides, in a democracy there's the rule of law. Governments can be held to account. And then there's always a last resort.'

'I suppose you mean the voters?'

Dimitri nodded.

'But surely you can't think voters in democracies are never corrupt? What's more, they're often blind or stupid. In America, half the voters believe in the existence of Satan, cloven hoofs and all. And half the politicians are bought by billionaires. Is that a recipe for good governance?'

'Of course there's ignorance and stupidity everywhere and of course some democracies are better than others, just as some autocracies are. The fundamental principle is that people have the right to choose.'

'Forgive me, old chap.' Frankam was leaning towards him across the table, one bushy grey eyebrow raised, speaking in a friendly, theatrically lowered – and therefore quite audible – voice. He tapped his forehead lightly with his forefinger: 'I hope you don't mind my mentioning it, but your wig's slipped. It makes you look a bit, well, tipsy almost. Didn't know you wore a wig. Very fetching of course, but . . .'

Dimitri felt himself checked and abruptly emptied, yet at the same time grown heavy. A memory slid, knife-sharp and vivid into his mind. It was soon after the Japanese war had ended, and he was exultantly riding his bike no-handed – it was his first bike, he'd only just learnt to ride – when he'd suddenly fallen off. Jolted, bruised and bleeding, from the heights to the depths in a second. He flushed as he reached for the wig and tried to straighten it.

'Trifle higher,' Frankam said, leaning back to assess the gap, his head on one side, like a society portrait-painter arranging his subject. He pointed upwards. 'Bit more. Just a tad. That's it. Hold it there.'

Dimitri let his hand fall limp into his lap, and gazed down silently at his empty glass. There seemed to be a dead ashen space now in his head, where only a moment before there'd been a hot crackling fire. *What a pathetic figure I must cut,* he thought as he sensed everyone looking at him with pity or embarrassment. *Talking airy nonsense with a cock-eyed wig on my hairless pate.* And what did he really know about it, the facts on the ground? He raised his empty glass as though to drink, then placed it slowly down again. Everyone continued to watch him, he knew, not knowing what to say. Everyone except Frankam, who was silent himself now, gazing down at the table with some pale form of shame creeping, however belatedly, over his face.

'Sorry,' Dimitri muttered at last in a small voice, glancing up at San-san and then quickly down again. 'Sorry, I got carried away.'

'Oh well,' Frankam said in a conciliatory tone now and with another elegant wave of his veiny, age-mottled hand, 'in a few years Hong Kong will have been completely absorbed by China and there won't be any more Tiananmen vigils to argue about, will there? Isn't that how we got into this, er . . .' – again he waved a drooping hand – 'this rather robust discussion?'

Oh hell, Dimitri thought dejectedly, what did it matter? People found a way of dealing with the system somehow, whatever it was, trimming their sails to the wind. And nowadays the winds all blew from China. Besides, he thought still more gloomily, why would a Chinese official looking at the dysfunctional democracies all round him, why would he think democracy was a good idea? Frankam was right, all he'd see – all he 'd notice, anyway – would be squabbling partisan politics, demagoguery and corruption. Why would he think that was the way to go? As the colonial officials used to think before him.

No one spoke until Mila quietly asked, 'Shouldn't we be going to watch the fireworks soon?' and San-san roused herself. 'Yes, yes, I've ordered taxis, we'd never be able to park there today.'

Frankam turned to Dimitri as they rose and walked towards the tall heavy doors. 'Sorry, old man, I shouldn't have mentioned your wig,' he muttered almost awkwardly. 'I didn't mean to embarrass . . .'

'Oh, that's all right,' Dimitri answered casually, almost as if he believed it was, believed he hadn't been humiliated. Self-consciously he touched his wig.

'I mean, I know what it's like.' Frankam hesitated.

'Really, it doesn't matter,' Dimitri insisted. *Know what what's like?* he wondered, but he didn't want to hear now. He smiled at Lena, tray in hand, waiting for them to pass. She smiled back almost complicitly, as if they shared a secret. Of course – the secret, the unspoken secret, was his illness. 'Anyway, Peter,' he turned back to Frankam, addressing him by his first name at last, 'what are you doing with yourself these days?'

'Oh, you know . . .' he began.

But luckily Tara came up to Dimitri, asking if it was true he was interned by the Japanese during the Second World War, and he was able to get away from Frankam with an apologetic smile and shrug.

'Yes,' he told her. 'Why?'

'I'm doing a project on it in school.' She considered him candidly with her blue, inquiring gaze. 'I'm supposed to find out what it was like.' She shook her hair back from her eyes in the way her mother used to when she was a girl, a gesture that foretold a life like hers of carefree enjoyment.

What it was like? No, he thought, she'd never really find that out. It was only the stale dry dust of history for her, as remote as the Battle of Hastings, not the near warm breath of life. Or smell of death.

'I was only a child,' he told her. 'I don't remember anything about it, really. I was less than half your age.' And yet he could remember his father's death, his mother's wasted, worn face. And a food parcel from the Red Cross, he thought he could remember that, too. A cardboard box, sealed with brown tape – or was it just string? – where the Japanese guards must have opened it to check the contents. There were people standing or sitting around in a small dark room, he seemed to remember that.

'Mummy said they killed your father?' As if killing was like swatting a fly. She turned to walk beside him.

'The Japanese?' Elena would have said that in her careless way, assuming that if someone died in a prison camp, they must have been killed. Alex would have been more cautious. But that was how history got distorted. 'No, he just died,' he told Tara. 'Of course there wasn't enough food or medicine, that was why, but . . . well, it was war.' *And may you never know it,* he thought, looking down at her fair wavy hair.

Tara looked disappointed. She'd probably wanted something more dramatic. He thought of the massacre in Stanley Bay at the end of the battle, when the Japanese finally overran Hong Kong – the bayoneting of the wounded in their beds, the raping, then killing of the nurses. Thank God he hadn't seen that – only some faint bloodstains on the floors and walls, slowly fading with the years of internment. But if he had, he wouldn't have told her about it. Nor about the Chinese policeman he saw a Japanese soldier shoot – his first course from the richly varied menu of death. Nor about the beheadings. And so history got distorted again, he reflected. Sometimes it just couldn't be told.

'Let's see the fireworks,' he said and she nodded, the arid past displaced by the dazzling present.

And then, suddenly, there was Elena in her Mini, its headlights decorated to make them look like wide-open happy eyes. She parked outside the gate, blocking the entrance, then hurried towards them, leaving the door hanging open. 'Sorry I couldn't make it earlier,' she said, kissing San-san and embracing Alex at the same time, before hugging Tara. 'I just couldn't get away. Not too late, am I?' Now she was hugging him, then standing back to survey him. 'You look great. Where's Mila?'

The near warm breath of life.

'By the way, I just heard on the radio, two ferries have collided off Lamma Island,' Elena went on breathlessly. 'You ought to be able to see them from here.' So the children ran off to look and the adults slowly followed.

'Well, you were right about Peter Frankam,' Mila murmured to him as they looked down at the coast of Lamma Island.

'"Oh, he's not so bad,"' he quoted her ironically. And yet he meant it. Frankam's crestfallen apology had hinted at a deeper, less assured layer beneath his elegantly smooth and polished surface. 'I should think half the world's on his side, anyway. There aren't that many functioning democracies.'

If the ferries had collided, it must have been on the other side of the island. From where they were watching, there was nothing to see but the usual scattered lights and the power station's tall chimneys on the dark, hilly mass of land. And so they returned disappointed to the road and, climbing into the taxis already waiting there, drove off to the Peak to watch the more exciting spectacle of the brilliant bursting fireworks celebrating China's National Day.

18

The young Chinese woman sitting by the window in the next row was taking pictures with her phone as the plane rumbled unsteadily along towards the terminal. What was there to enjoy in blurry photos of dull airport buildings which all looked alike wherever you were, Dimitri wondered. He touched Mila's hand on the armrest beside him and nodded at the woman. 'Is she going to bore all her relatives and friends with snapshots of airport terminals?' he whispered.

Mila shrugged. 'She had the stewardess snap her, too, a few minutes ago.'

'Lucky she doesn't have a selfie stick, she'd put someone's eye out.'

If Mila heard, she didn't smile. Her eyes focussed absently on the dark asphalt, the grass ribboning past, the ranked planes waiting patiently in their bays like cattle in their stalls; on the low characterless terminal building foretelling wall-faced immigration and bored customs officials, crowded luggage carousels and then, at last, the journey back into the past. Yes, she thought, yes, that's when the journey would really begin. The flight was not the journey, it was just an interlude. She hadn't been back for forty years.

As the plane pulled into its bay and passengers all round them were already unbuckling belts, calling to each other and standing to open the overhead lockers, an announcement sounded through the speakers, insistent and official. 'Did you get that?' Dimitri asked as stewards and stewardesses came through the cabin, hands flapping, motioning people to sit down, closing the open lockers.

'Something about security,' Mila said uneasily.

He glanced at her. Her face had tensed slightly, as if she was afraid. But this couldn't be a bomb scare – they'd be evacuating the plane if it was.

Nevertheless, the same tension seemed to have gripped everyone. They were all back in their seats now, watching, waiting. Then two policemen came down the aisle, preceded by a stewardess. Dmitri saw Mila's hand tighten on the armrest as she watched them approaching. The stewardess stopped at the row in front and pointed to the young woman. After some curt questions and subdued answers, she fumbled in her bag and handed her phone to one of the policemen. He jerked his head, the passengers next to her stood to let her pass, leaning back as though they thought she was contaminated, and she walked tamely, humbly, away down the hushed aisle escorted by the two policemen, one in front, one behind.

For a few seconds the hush remained. Then people began whispering, talking in low voices. Slowly seat-belt buckles were released again, lockers opened, laptops and bags retrieved. But their voices were still low and there was no longer the usual impatient bustle to get down the aisles and away.

'Just for taking those snaps?' Dmitri asked incredulously as he pulled his seat-belt open. 'They took her away for that?'

Mila didn't answer, gazing down the aisle as though she could still see the woman walking, crushed and diminished, between those two policemen.

*

All the way in from the airport Dimitri was remembering his first time in Shanghai. Years and years ago, soon after the Cultural Revolution, when Pudong, on the undeveloped bank of the Huang Pu river, was still largely flat farmland with a few two- or three-storey houses, drab but human. Now it was where the main airport was, and it looked as if Hong Kong's Central district had suddenly loosened its belt and trebled in size – an array of glittering towers, magnificent, but intimidating, dwarfing the creatures who scuttled along the wide tree-lined avenues between them. A more human dimension didn't return until the taxi had gone through the tunnel to the other bank and was driving down the Bund, past all those old colonial buildings that stood there as they had a hundred years before, as imposing in their day as the towers of Pudong were now. Relics of a past that, among all that had been erased, had after all survived. What chance or foresight had preserved them when all the old elsewhere in China was being bulldozed and destroyed? As they passed the old Customs House, the clock chimed in its tall tower. He touched Mila's hand. 'That's where San-san's grandfather used to work.'

Mila nodded. 'Lucky San-san's grandfather,' she said coolly, 'to work on the Bund.' She had been thinking of that woman, remembering how she herself was led away once – no, pushed, shoved, hustled, away. But now she thought of her father, that long narrow alley leading to the shikumen house she was born in, that mixture of Chinese and Western architecture, long since demolished.

'Where did your father work?'

'Out in the suburbs, in the end. In the university before.'

Before the Red Guards came for him, he knew she meant. Or was it one of the Anti-Rightist campaigns? God knew there were enough of them. What was it like to have lived through all those purges, all that violence? There was so much he would never know about her or about China. She had buried it. Perhaps most people who'd been through it did the same – how else could they go on living? Betrayal, humiliation, torture, death. He remembered the rotting corpse that appeared on the beach in Hong Kong in that summer of discontent during the Cultural Revolution, a mainlander with his hands tied with wire behind his back – or was it a woman? Perhaps they were too far-gone to tell. He recalled how deep the wire had eaten into the putrescent flesh. That was Alex and Elena's first taste of death. He saw their shocked yet fascinated eyes again. They were about the same age, he suddenly realised, as he was when he was given his own first taste by that Japanese soldier. And he saw that policeman crumpling as the shot cracked the still air, changed in an instant from a person to a sack of bloodied flesh and bone. No, no one ever talked about such things, neither the victims that survived nor the perpetrators. Small wonder the Party had an easy time denying it. It was what most people wanted anyway – to leave it to rot like that corpse in a salt sea of forgetting.

All the same, buried or not, Mila was tense now; he could hear it in her voice, a certain laconic tightness. Perhaps it was that woman on the plane, he thought, reminding her of her past. Strange, he felt he had to protect her here in her birthplace – she, who had been protecting him throughout these last months. But why not? He could do it; he felt almost fit again, as though he'd been cured, not merely sequestered in some more or less indefinite remission. He hadn't felt so well for . . . well, for quite some time, anyway. But who knew how long it would last? He felt that familiar quiver of anxiety and nudged it aside, gazing out at the imperial buildings lining the street.

Now the taxi was approaching their hotel. He looked up at the green pyramidal roof, then, as the taxi turned, at the side-entrance. He imagined San-san's grandfather, and her father, for that matter, when he was young, going through those same doors seventy or eighty years ago. Only, they must be new doors now – the whole place had been refurbished. All dead now, yet still alive in his and San-san's memory. And Mila's too, presumably.

'When shall we ring them?' he asked as they entered the wide lobby. He could just hear the serene harp-like melody of a guzheng rippling somewhere nearby.

'The Yus? When we've settled in, I suppose. Any time you like.'

'Perhaps we should talk to San-san first. Maybe she knows how he is and so on.'

Mila glanced at him as they waited for the lift. He was unsure, she thought. He didn't know if Guodong really wanted to see them. Or perhaps it was his wig – he was still embarrassed at the thought of them seeing him like that. 'Do you know where she's staying?'

'San-san?' He nodded. 'That hotel next door to the conservatory.'

'Why don't you ring her?'

He nodded again. 'In a minute.' It was only a couple of years since they'd seen the Yus, when they were passing through Hong Kong on their way to America. And yet, everything had changed so much for both of them that he felt he was approaching two strangers now. His resolve to see them was weakening the closer a meeting came. What could he really do for Guodong? Perhaps everything was all right with them now and all they could do was hug each other and reminisce as old men do about the past. The present was too uncertain, and the future both too uncertain and too short.

The lift doors slid apart. The porter gestured deferentially before following them inside, pressing the button and standing silently while the lift glided smoothly up. Dimitri glanced at him standing there beside their cases, eyes studiously unfocussed, self-effacing yet alert. 'Do you have some change for a tip?' he asked Mila quietly. The porter's young face stiffened faintly, his eyes flickering from him to Mila before resuming their statuesque empty gaze.

Mila nodded. 'If you don't want to be understood here,' she murmured in Cantonese, 'you should probably speak Cantonese, not English.'

Now the porter's face remained impassive.

In the room, Dimitri went at once to the window to look out over the river at Pudong. He heard Mila speaking to the porter in Shanghainese, then the door quietly closing. Windows in the towers of Pudong and the surface of the leaden river glowed for a few minutes in the warmth of the setting sun. Then it was gone and the towers darkened a moment before the lights began to flash and glitter and only the river admitted the dusk.

'The phone's over there,' he heard Mila say.

'Okay.' But it was some time before he looked back from the window. Yes, she was tense, and he was too. Why had they come, then? He dialled the hotel and asked for San-san.

She answered at once. He imagined her sitting by the phone, waiting for his call. 'Yes, everything's fine,' she said. 'Guodong wants us to meet for dinner tomorrow. He said he's got something on today. But I could come by the hotel this evening.' Her tone became hesitant, apologetic. 'Do you mind if it's late? We've got a rehearsal till eight-thirty. Is nine too late for you? You're not too tired?'

'San-san!' he chided her. 'Really!'

'Okay, I'm sorry.' And he knew from the way her voice fell that she really was.

He gave her their room number. 'Call us when you get here. We could go to the old Jazz Bar,' he said. 'A bit of nostalgia. It must be more or less how it was in your father's time.'

'Not quite.' He could tell she was smiling to herself. Her father had probably never listened to jazz in his life. 'But as near as you can get now, I guess.'

'I guess? You sound quite American.'

'Well, I did go to an American conservatory for several years.'

'Yes, a perfect example of the people in between.'

'Sorry?'

'Hongkongers. Part Chinese, part Western. In between the two.'

'Oh. Yes, I suppose so.' And now she sounded very English. 'One of the musicians is ninety-three, by the way.'

'What?' For a moment he thought she was speaking of her quartet.

'In the jazz bar.'

'Oh. He could have known your father.'

'I guess he could have,' she said, but in an unbelieving tone.

Now she sounded American again.

When he replaced the receiver, Mila was smiling, for the first time, he realised, since they'd arrived. 'Sometimes I think you're in love with San-san.'

'Jealous?'

'It's in your voice.'

'Well, you should know.'

What had changed? Why were they loose and laughing now, while before they'd been so taut? Then he knew what it was in his case. 'I was afraid in the end Guodong might feel it wasn't safe to meet us,' he said. 'He sounded so, I don't know, strained when he phoned us in Hong Kong.'

'They won't bother him if he doesn't bother them,' Mila said. 'That's the system now, isn't it?' She laid her suitcase on the bed and began to unpack.

'Like with that woman at the airport?'

'Yes, like her.' She glanced at him across her open case. The image of that subdued and humiliated young woman fell like a shadow between them.

'Well,' he sighed and nodded. 'I'll phone Guodong now.'

But there was no answer. He called Guodong's mobile. Still no answer. 'I'll try again later.'

When Mila started to lift his case onto the bed, he held her hand and heaved it up himself. 'Why do you two women always want to turn me into an invalid?' Her small hand was still on the handle, beneath his large one with its loose skin and branching, ridged blue veins. He held it there, feeling all the life they'd lived together move noiselessly beneath her smooth, pale skin, a long winding river flowing down now far from its uplands source, down towards the estuary and the wide dark sea. When he let her hand go, she smiled as at some memory stirring and went calmly on with her unpacking.

His clothes were soon put away. While Mila more carefully unpacked hers, he switched on the TV. How dead it seemed with its censored news and official posing. After a few minutes, he switched it off.

'Let's take a walk along the Bund,' he said as he stowed their empty cases in the rack.

But first they walked down Nanjing Lu, as far as the pedestrian zone, its wide spaces filled with shops and shoppers, a glowing temple where devoted worshippers of Materialism sacrificed and spent. Mila smiled, remembering it in its drab proletarian days.

'That's enough,' Dimitri said after a few minutes. 'Back to the Bund. Or should we try to find where you used to live?'

She shook her head decisively. 'It's miles away. Besides, it's long gone.'

And she doesn't want to revive it, he thought. *It would be like digging up a corpse. Better remember it as it was when it was alive.*

They turned back.

The dark surface of the river glimmered quietly under the Milky Way-like haze of Pudong, in which brilliant still or flashing lights shone like planets and stars. Except the haze was half-pollution, Dimitri thought. At least man hadn't polluted the Milky Way yet. Camera-laden tourists, local and foreign, thronged the promenade, almost as thickly as in Nanjing Lu, snapping Pudong, snapping the old colonial buildings, snapping each other, snapping themselves. Or buying from little kiosks, laughing and shouting in the chill November air. A ferry was slowly crossing the river. 'It's like the harbour in Hong Kong,' Mila said, remembering again the dreary featurelessness of the Bund in her youth.

'And not a soul that stands and stares.' Dimitri leant on the parapet, gazing down at the dark river quietly lapping the bank as it always had, though now a fleet of bobbing plastic bottles floated on its surface, and at the ferry's lights reflected in the wind-ruffled water. Directly across the river was a huge illuminated globe with China coloured blood-red, the rest pale and unmarked. *The Chinese Dream*, he thought.

'Over there,' Mila smiled, pointing to an elderly couple behind them serenely practising tai chi on the wooden viewing platform, moving slowly like mimes through their different poses. 'Is that what you want to see?'

'Maybe.' But he didn't really know what he wanted to see. Perhaps it was just people who didn't live only in the perennially glittering present, as if the past had never been and the future never would be.

'Shall we go as far as the signal station?' Mila asked, checking herself just in time from asking if it would be too much for him.

'Let's see how far we get.'

They walked on. He thought of Frankam. Yes, he was right, the Party had delivered relative prosperity and stability. Why would these people – he glanced round at them all – why would they want democracy? They were doing all right as they were – far better than they could ever have dreamt of thirty years ago. Better than their contemporaries in India, who hadn't had to go through the agonies of Mao's manic revolutionary spasms. Why would they rock the boat in calm water now for the sake of people like Guodong, arrested for protesting against a land-grab in some remote village they'd never heard of? They wanted stability and prosperity, Givenchy and Ferrari. Some of them, he'd read, grown men, rich upstarts, even hired wet-nurses to suck milk from because they didn't trust their own dairies – or was it just for the thrill and vulgar display? And if the price was corruption and the suppression of those who stepped out of line – well, wouldn't they think that better than the alternative? But then perhaps not, he thought again. Now they weren't starving, why wouldn't they want more, why wouldn't they want the rights and freedoms people had elsewhere? That girl Jianping, for instance, if she was genuine. How many more were there like her? And what about the peasants whose land was grabbed, or the millions of labourers from the countryside who survived in the city on the crumbs that dropped from urban prosperity's table, *Gastarbeiter* in their own country? Wouldn't they rebel one day, they or their children? Or would they too in the end find a small place in that urban sun?

He could smell the pollution now, taste it at the back of his throat.

Mila had stopped. He turned back. She was easing her phone out of her wind-cheater pocket. She frowned down at it, shaking her head.

'What is it?' he asked.

She handed him the phone. It was an SMS from San-san. *Can we meet later 2nite, 10.30pm?*

'I thought she was in a rehearsal,' Mila said.

'Perhaps she is. Hence the SMS.' They were near the empty signal station now, its mast bare, its windows dark. Looking back along the Bund, he gazed at the distant green-glowing pyramid of the hotel's roof. It was an expensive hotel, but they'd decided to stay there almost without a word exchanged, as if each separately sensed it was an occasion to be celebrated. Because there wouldn't be another, perhaps? Besides, Mila had got some sort of discount.

'I hope that doesn't mean there's trouble in the quartet,' he said, handing the phone back to Mila. He knew there often was. Family fights, San-san called them. Not that he could imagine her in one. She would always be the quiet peacemaker.

Mila shrugged, glancing down at the screen as she tapped a brief answer. 'Where's your phone, by the way?'

He patted his pockets. 'Must have left it in the room.'

They turned back towards the hotel. The lights glistened and glittered, the people still chattered, laughed, snapped pictures, bought and sold. The elderly couple were still performing their tai chi, staying motionless in each new pose as though embalmed in the amber of time. Dimitri wondered whether someone might have nicked his phone by the time they got back.

But of course not. It lay there on the turned-down bed with San-san's SMS waiting on it. It was that kind of hotel.

*

'Perhaps we should go outside a moment?' San-san said in a low voice when they met in the art deco lobby. It was almost empty, but she glanced over her shoulder as though she thought someone might be listening.

They walked back onto the promenade and leant over the railing, gazing inattentively at the lights of Pudong. They were glistening a little less brightly now, Dimitri noticed, as if the pollution-haze had thickened – or was it just that their mood had darkened?

'Jianping came to the rehearsal,' San-san said in the same low voice. 'I had to talk to her afterwards.' She hesitated. 'Apparently there's going to be another protest at Guodong's village tomorrow and he's going to join it. He's gone there tonight – they might stop him in daylight, she said.'

'Isn't that risky?' Dimitri asked. 'After what happened before?'

San-san shrugged. 'I suppose so.'

'Very risky,' Mila said coolly, pulling at the collar of her wind-cheater. 'I would have thought he'd had enough of demonstrating after all those weeks in a detention centre.'

'I gather something specially upset him and he just decided to go along.' Again San-san hesitated. 'Jianping said – she asked – if we would go there with her tomorrow. To the village.'

'Ah.' *Asked and expected*, Dimitri thought, remembering Jianping's unsettling determined gaze. 'To join the demonstration?' he asked ironically.

San-san smiled as she shook her head. 'Just to see what it's like,' she said.

'Where is she now?'

'Jianping?' San-san shrugged. 'She said she'd meet us at eight tomorrow morning, if we want to go.'

'What about Lai-king?'

'I've called her mobile several times. She doesn't answer. Nor does her landline.' She looked uncertainly at Dimitri. 'You don't have to go tomorrow, you know.'

'No. Nor do you.' He thought of her two children and Alex. 'Maybe you shouldn't.'

'Oh, I don't have anything on. It's our day off.'

'I meant you don't know what you might be getting into.'

'Nor do any of us,' Mila said slowly. She looked away at the other shore, as though Guodong's village was somewhere over there in the sterile urban desert of Pudong.

'Well, if we're only spectators . . .' San-san began slowly. 'Tourists?'

'Let's have something to eat first,' Mila said decidedly. 'And think about it.'

Dimitri realised he was hungry, then that for the first time in months he felt anxiety for someone other than himself. 'But we just have to go, don't we?' he murmured almost to himself, gazing down at the lamps' reflections shimmering on the slow-flowing surface of the river. 'If Guodong's going to be there.'

They turned back to the warm bright lights of the hotel.

19

The car, a black Lifan saloon, was waiting for them on Jiujiang Road, not far from the hotel. Jianping was sitting beside the driver, a young man wearing large black-framed spectacles. 'This is Yiming,' she turned to introduce him in Mandarin as they climbed in.

'Nie hao?' Yiming gave them a fleeting smile and drove off at once. As they passed out of the fashionable centre of the city into the drab suburbs Jianping explained, without turning to them and in a voice as calm as a weather reporter's, how the villagers had formed their own committee and were going to demand the resignation of the village head. 'They are better organised now,' she ended almost proudly, as if that was her doing.

'You haven't told us yet why you wanted us to come with you,' Mila said quietly, but with the hint of a challenge.

'Just to see the protest.' Now Jianping did turn towards them. 'So you can judge for yourselves. And . . .' Uncharacteristically, she hesitated a moment, then smiled almost guiltily. 'And it's better for us with a foreigner in the car.'

Mila's lips tightened. Her eyelids drooped faintly and she gazed away out of the window. San-san and Dimitri glanced at each other. They drove on for some time in dense silence. *Tell them to turn back,* Dimitri thought. *Tell them to turn back*. But he said nothing. After all, they weren't doing anything illegal. It should be perfectly safe. But what did illegal mean in China? He felt that familiar faint sense of unease, like something crawling in his stomach. Yet he would not, could not, tell them to turn back. After all, Guodong was there, he was the one in real danger. They were merely foreign visitors, he imagined himself telling some security officer, innocent visitors to the village. What could they be accused of?

He looked out at a narrow crowded street littered with human debris – broken chairs, collapsed tables, baskets, old cases, flower pots – through which a bulldozer was slowly advancing like a dinosaur trampling bushes and trees. Jianping was regarding him again in the driver's mirror – was she watching him all the time? 'That's where workers from the countryside used to live,' she said. 'They're tearing it down, to make room for a new development. The workers will have to find somewhere else. They are not very happy about it.' She smiled ironically. 'It will cost them money and they don't have much as it is.'

'Still, aren't they better off than in the villages they came from?' San-san asked. 'Otherwise they wouldn't come, would they?'

Jianping considered. 'I would say they are less badly off,' she answered deliberately. 'Yes, they get more money, but they have almost no rights here. They can't get free medical treatment like the locals, their children can't go to state schools, they can be sent back at any time. They are . . .' – she shrugged – 'outsiders.'

Don't lecture us, Dimitri complained silently. *We know about all this. Our news isn't censored.*

'In Beijing they live underground,' Yiming added. 'In cellars and basements. It's all they can afford. People call them the rat tribe. Sometimes there is trouble between them and the locals.'

'I know,' San-san said. 'In Guangzhou–'

'Fights. Riots. That kind of thing. They don't like each other.'

San-san leant back, glancing away out of the window, eyebrows faintly raised.

'I thought the government was planning to change all that?' Dimitri said.

Yiming shrugged. 'Yes and no,' he said enigmatically.

'By the way,' – Jianping turned to look at them all, this time a little slyly – 'it's a Hong Kong developer that's going to build in Guodong's village.'

'We apologise,' Dimitri said drily.

'Oh, I didn't mean that. It's not their fault if the officials cheated the villagers.'

'I don't suppose they'd have cared whether they did or not.'

'That's right.' Yiming chuckled. 'None of their business, so long as the price was right. Capitalism with Chinese characteristics.'

'No,' Dimitri said. 'Just capitalism.'

*

They drove on and on. Dimitri watched the level countryside slide past the window beneath the unremitting leaden sky. When at last they neared the village, Yiming turned off the road onto a rutted dirt track that wandered like a muddy river through open farmland. 'In case they block the main road,' he explained. The track was lined with stunted trees like dwarfs waving stiff awkward arms. They jolted along it for twenty minutes until the village appeared, a jumble of nondescript houses in a flat plain where water buffalo grazed, incuriously raising their heads to watch them pass. The track led past a small pond of dark-green water into the straggling outskirts of the village, became a narrow empty street, then suddenly debouched into a shabby square. There, perhaps two hundred silent peasants in quilted jackets holding placards were facing a double line of police in front of a larger building with the red flag flying over it. Where was Guodong's ancestral house, Dimitri wondered as he looked round at the drab nondescript buildings, some decrepit and bare, all speaking silently of poverty and unremitting labour. Surely not one of those? One, he saw, was stained with mildew seeping up from the ground. An old man in a wheelchair sat watching by its open door, his legs wrapped in a brown blanket.

'We're late,' Yiming said. They got out of the car. Jianping and Yiming started taking pictures with their phones.

A few people glanced round at them, but the rest – women as well as men – stood stolid and grim, facing the police, who were in riot gear with shields and helmets, their own faces sternly rigid and closed. The crowd began chanting slogans, raising their placards. Loud-hailers responded from the police.

'What are they saying?' Dimitri asked Jianping.

'The police? Telling them to disperse.'

Like Hong Kong during the Cultural Revolution, Dimitri thought. Only now he was seeing it from the other side. He glanced uneasily at Mila and San-san. What happened if things got nasty? He noticed a tall woman at the back of the crowd who seemed almost uninvolved in the confrontation, calmly reaching up to raise her long dark hair and drape it back over her shoulders.

'There's Guodong,' Mila said in a low tense voice.

Yes, there he was, a portly, round-shouldered, elderly scholar among all those peasants, standing in front of the crowd, arguing with an officer beside a police car. He leant forward towards the officer, raising his forefinger to make a point, as he might in some polite academic debate. The officer was shouting at him now, while Guodong continued to speak quietly, his hands open, palms up, as though to say, *But how can you answer that? Be reasonable!* Behind the police lines were scattered groups of young men, slouching, leaning against the walls and watching the crowd with a kind of indifferent contempt.

'Those men look like triads,' Dimitri said.

'They probably are,' Mila replied.

Again the loud-hailers warned the crowd and still they shouted back, hoisting their placards. The police started tramping forwards with a cumbrous shuffling step, shoving Guodong along with them, beating their shields with their batons. The crowd shouted defiance. Some of them began hurling stones – Dimitri heard them clashing on the police shields like pebbles on tortoise shells. He saw Guodong stumbling, raising his arm to protect his head. Then, as the two lines met like armies on an ancient battlefield, Guodong was lost in a welter of stones and police batons. The police clubbed a young man to the ground, kicking and beating him. '*Put the boot in!*' Dimitri remembered with stark clarity before some villagers dragged the man away, thrusting at the police with the poles that their tattered placards still clung to. A policeman staggered back, clutching his face. The crowd surged forward, yelling, then back again and forward in a clumsy, barbaric kind of dance; surging, retreating, then surging again. At last the police line began to waver and gradually give way. Now the crowd was rushing forward. They reached the police car Guodong had stood beside and swarmed round it like angry bees, smashing the windows, straining at the wheels, trying to overturn it. Up it rose at last and toppled onto its side. Men were still battering it with their poles, kicking it, even, in their fury.

But the retreating police had regrouped in front of the building with the red flag still limply hanging from its roof. They were aiming guns at the crowd now. Suddenly the peasants' shouting began to fade, their voices dragged uncertainly. For a few seconds there was an uneasy silence, like the silence of birds before a thunderstorm.

Then an order was shouted and the guns fired.

'Oh no!' Dimitri heard San-san gasp.

Canisters landed with dull thuds, blooming into a thick grey-white cloud that swiftly billowed over them. The crowd suddenly disintegrated into coughing, screaming individuals covering their faces, wiping their eyes as they ran desperately to escape the rolling clouds of gas. One of the canisters soared further and with a loud clatter bounced off the car. 'Quick! Get in!' Dimitri shouted. 'It's tear gas. Close the windows!'

They clambered in and slammed the doors. For a few seconds Jianping and Yiming kept taking pictures with their phones until suddenly the car was surrounded by the young men they'd seen before. The men were yelling at them, battering the windows with their fists, yanking and kicking the locked doors. Yiming and Jianping were shouting back at them, but suddenly the windscreen was starred and cracked and Yiming was backing the car away, turning it round, while the young men still shouted and battered its sides and roof. He drove swiftly back down the empty street, peering round the radiating cracks and ice-like greyness in the windscreen. The car lurched and shuddered over the uneven surface, leaving the young men shouting still behind them, their voices slowly dwindling until only the car's engine could be heard – and the distant wailing of a police siren.

As they reached the corner, Dimitri looked back. The square was empty except for those young men, gesticulating threateningly now at a man and a woman sitting on the ground, their heads bowed as if in mute submission, or in prayer. There was no sign of Guodong. But the old man in the wheelchair was still there, slumping, his head lolling as if he was asleep – or was he unconscious? – while the thinning tear gas slowly cleared like autumn mist.

'Lucky the wind was blowing away from us,' Yiming muttered.

'My eyes are smarting,' Mila said.

All their eyes were, blinking and red-rimmed.

San-san was pale, her hand trembled as she wiped her eyes. 'It's all right,' Jianping said as she glanced back. 'They aren't following us.' She gave Dimitri a half-empty packet of tissues.

'What were they shouting?' he asked as he dabbed his eyes.

'Those thugs?' Jianping shook her head. 'Just "Get out!" and swear words and things. But they weren't very clever, they didn't try to grab our phones.' She sounded almost exhilarated.

'Who were they? Not plain-clothes police, were they?'

'Oh no,' Yiming muttered unsteadily. 'Just louts the officials hire to . . . to . . .'

'Intimidate,' Jianping said. 'To intimidate people.'

'Did you see what happened to Guodong?' Mila asked Dimitri quietly, wiping her eyes.

'Only at the beginning.'

'They hit him. I saw him go down.'

Jianping was scrolling through the pictures on her phone. 'I didn't catch that,' she murmured in a mildly disappointed tone.

It began to rain as they drove on, lightly at first, then in a steady relentless downpour. The wipers swished and thumped across the fractured windscreen. The fields on either side glistened under the rain and the dwarf trees seemed to be reaching out their hands now in twisted supplication to the menacing clouds.

'What about Lai-king?' Mila asked as they reached the main road again. 'Shouldn't we try to contact her?' Her voice was dull and heavy. Dimitri glanced at her. Her reddened eyes seemed to be staring at something in the past, far away beyond him.

He took out his phone and touched the keys. Still no answer. 'What do we do now?'

Yiming didn't reply, leaning sideways to see through the windscreen. Jianping was still examining the pictures on her phone. 'Not much good,' she murmured, disappointed again. 'Maybe some of the villagers have better ones.'

'Jianping, what do we do now?'

'Wait till tomorrow,' she said composedly. 'See what happens.'

'Jianping, my friend was just beaten in that demonstration and all you can say is–'

'We can't do anything till we know more,' Yiming said sharply. 'Maybe they won't do anything, maybe they've already let him go.'

'In that case I'll phone him.'

But of course Guodong didn't answer either.

*

They scarcely spoke on the long journey back until they reached Shanghai. Every few minutes Dimitri twisted round to see if they were being followed. No, no flashing light, no screaming siren. Not yet, anyway. Perhaps the police had been too busy with the villagers. Guodong's face burned faintly in his mind like a flickering candle.

'Thanks for coming,' Jianping said calmly as they got out. 'We'll stay in touch.'

Dimitri turned away with a curt goodbye. The car drove off at once.

'Well, now Guodong's in a real mess,' he muttered as they walked back towards the hotel. 'And those two don't seem to give a toss.'

'Try phoning again,' Mila said tonelessly. 'How are your eyes?'

'Still smarting, but a bit better now.'

Outside the hotel, both San-san and Dimitri tried to call several times. First Guodong, then Lai-king.

No answer.

'Should we go round to Lai-king?' Dimitri wondered in a subdued voice.

San-san glanced at her watch uncertainly.

'Wait till she answers,' Mila said as she gazed, unseeingly, it seemed, across the grey river, glowing dully under the setting sun. 'If they wanted to see us, either of them, they'd answer their phones.'

'Perhaps they can't answer?' San-san suggested, imagining them each in a separate cell in some grim detention centre or prison.

Mila nodded. 'Probably not. But in that case, going round wouldn't help, would it? It might only make things worse.'

For them or for us? Dimitri wondered. Guodong's round, honest face still glimmered in his mind, guilelessly protesting before that flurry of sticks and stones. 'Better see what develops tomorrow, I suppose.' *So those two were right,* he thought, recalling their self-assured words in the car.

'Well,' San-san sighed, glancing at her watch again. 'I'd better be going back, then.' Her eyes were still sore.

'Stay and have something to eat first,' Dimitri said. But the invitation was half-hearted.

She shook her head. 'I have to practise for tomorrow's concert.' She held out her hand for a taxi. 'If I can read the score,' she added as the cab drew up beside her.

20

Back in their comfortable room, Dimitri phoned Guodong and Lai-king yet again. Still no answer. 'Perhaps they've both been arrested?' he said. He imagined handcuffs, barred windows, glaring lights.

Mila didn't reply. She was lying on the bed, staring up at the ceiling.

'What d'you think?'

Still she didn't answer. It was as though she hadn't heard.

'Mila?'

She shook her head slowly, still staring unfocussedly up at the ceiling. Outside, a ship's horn lowed on the river like a desolate cow, long and deep. 'I am thinking,' she said at last.

He waited.

'Remembering.'

Still he waited.

'Guodong saw me, just before they hit him. Our eyes met, I mean. I saw the look in them. It reminded me of . . .'

And still he waited.

She glanced at him, then back at the ceiling, or through it, rather, to another time, another place. 'Of my *laojiao*.'

Her labour camp, Dimitri thought. As other people spoke of *their* school, *their* university.

'Remember Father Ignatius?' she went on in that level detached voice of hers.

Yes, he remembered. It was almost the only thing she'd ever told him about her time in her *laojiao*. He remembered her telling him thirty years or so ago, on another night in another hotel, that old Portuguese hotel in Macau. He nodded. 'The priest you . . . ?'

'Denounced, yes,' she said abstractedly, as though speaking of another person, someone she barely knew.

'You told them he was secretly reciting the mass or something?'

She nodded.

'And they let you out earlier for good behaviour?'

'And they knew it all along. They knew he was reciting it. They just wanted to see if my attitude' – she smiled, a tight bitter smile – 'my *attitude* had changed.'

'If they knew it all along,' he began tentatively, 'you didn't really do him any harm–'

'There was a struggle meeting next day,' she interrupted. 'We all had to shout slogans at him. And our eyes met once, I felt him looking at me. Just for a second. It wasn't accusing, he didn't know I'd said anything. At least, I don't think he did. But it was like the look in Guodong's eyes today in that village. A kind of helpless puzzled disbelief, like . . .' – she stirred – 'like a dog might look before its master shoots it. Then they pushed his head down and took him off to the punishment cell.'

'But they didn't shoot him,' he reminded her. 'In the end he got released and ended up in Macau.'

'Yes, but that didn't make me feel any better about it. It still doesn't. Perhaps, after all, he did know I'd told them. Or guessed somehow.'

'So many bad things happened then,' he began again. 'You shouldn't blame yourself too–'

'Oh, I know that wasn't the worst.' Now at last she turned to look at him – or was she glaring? – with wide strained eyes. 'You don't know what people will do to survive,' she said quietly, yet fiercely. 'You don't know!'

No, he didn't know, not in the way she did. He kicked off his shoes, lay down beside her, took her hand in his. It lay there, still and light as a bird. 'Well, anyway, you certainly didn't do Guodong any harm–'

'But he looked at me just like Father Ignatius did.' She smiled ruefully, brushing his consolation away like a fly while she still lingered in a past he could never share.

A pale light slid into the room, slanting across the ceiling from the street lamps outside. Her eyes glistened. He watched her for some time as the twilight faded.

'Why do you keep all these things locked away, Mila?' he asked eventually.

'Just how I am.' She shrugged. 'Better to forget than remember.'

But she did remember, she remembered all right. Only she didn't tell.

Then she stirred and propped herself up on her elbow to look down at him, her eyes wide and serious. 'I shouldn't have told you that, should I? When you are – when you've been ill?'

'I haven't *been* ill, I still am. And some day I'm going to–'

'Shh!' she placed her finger on his lips. 'Not yet,' she smiled, her voice pleading. 'Please, not yet.'

'Anyway, I wish you'd tell me more . . .'

She smiled, shaking her head as if he'd asked her for an impossible gift. Then she lay down again and took his hand, gazing away out of the window. They watched the autumnal dusk slowly flooding the room, each remembering Guodong, that drab ordinary village, those sullen villagers, those stern police lines, that burst of violence like a sudden yet inevitable storm. Mila saw Guodong's helpless gaze beneath the raised baton and remembered Father Ignatius. Dimitri recalled that woman calmly lifting her hair before the storm broke. And the plop of the canisters, the billowing fog of the tear gas.

⋆

It wasn't until it was completely dark that he reached for his phone and called Guodong's number yet again. Unobtainable. He tried Lai-king once more. Still no answer. He left a voice message for her to call back any time, unsure whether that would help or harm her.

⋆

While he drifted into an uneasy sleep beside Mila, she lay awake still, reliving the past the present had revived. She gazed out of the window and saw no stars, no moon, only the bowed head of Father Ignatius, the gaunt cowed faces of her fellow-prisoners, the cold blank expressions of the guards who herded them all to work . . .

And then, as the lamplight from some passing truck glided across the ceiling, she saw herself in the crowded Hong Qiao station after she'd been released, climbing into a train full of jubilant Red Guards shouting and singing while, rucksack on her knees, she shrunk between two old women and pretended to be asleep – how else would she have made it to Guangzhou? The train was festooned with red flags and portraits of Mao, the railway officials as cowed by the mindless fervour of the young zealots as the inmates in her *laojiao* had been by their guards. Yes, that was China then, millions of mindless zealots. She'd never trusted idealists ever since. Like that pair that had lured Guodong into that demonstration – she was sure they had. Couldn't they realise they might be wrong?

How many hours did she spend on that rumbling train? She remembered the waving flags of some other Red Guard faction as the train pulled in at last to Guangzhou South station . . . How many times had those flags waved in her mind?

From Guangzhou down to Shenzhen was easy, she spoke Cantonese. Now she saw the face of that woman who sold her the old patched tyre, pumped it full of air for her and guided her through the sleeping village that August night. Was she still there in Shenzhen? Shenzhen – now a mega-city? No, of course not, she must be dead by now, she was quite old even then. Her cropped grey hair, her crooked teeth, her shabby old Mao jacket – why should she remember all that? She closed her eyes – the lids were still sore. And then she was back on the shore, sliding as noiselessly as she could into the dark, dirty water. *'Sharks only feed early in the morning,'* the old woman had assured her, as if that meant night was safe – or was it to warn her she must reach land before dawn? Her back didn't hurt when she swam, but she'd never swum that far before. And somewhere behind her she heard shouts, and then the deep sharp crack of gunfire biting the night. There was a man in the village whose job it was to collect the bodies of the escapees the soldiers shot, the old woman had said. Quite matter-of-factly, as though talking about a rubbish collector, not thinking that it might deter her. And it hadn't. Not that, not the sharks . . .

Her limbs tiring, resting wearily on the tyre. Ahead, far ahead, the glimmering lights of Hong Kong, appearing and disappearing as the waves rose and fell. The dawn breaking as she neared land, her stomach clenching at every fleeting shadow in the water that might have been a shark . . .

It was full daylight when at last she reached the shore. Ngau Hom Sha, she recognised it as her feet touched the safety of the deserted beach – she'd been there on a school trip years before. The glistening black tyre was losing air by then, bubbles oozing out round the edges of the patches.

She threw it back into the sea and trudged up the wet, then the dry, sand, towards Deep Bay Road. How leaden her legs felt. When she looked back, the tyre was lying glistening and half-deflated on the beach, like a stranded porpoise dying.

It took her some time to find a call-box. Would Dimitri still be there? Still have the same number? Would he still want her? She saw her numbed finger pulling the disc round again and again, heard it whirring back into place, heard the *burr burr* of the distant phone . . .

21

Mila was in the shower when the hotel phone rang the next morning.

'Dimitri?' The voice was heavy, expressionless.

'Lai-king, is that you?'

'Guodong's been arrested again.'

He nodded as if she could see him.

'He went back to his village.'

I know, he was about to say. We were there. But he stopped himself in time. Who knew who might be listening? 'What happened?' he asked instead.

'I don't know. They told me he'd been arrested, that's all. I just got your message.'

'Where were you, Lai-king? I kept phoning you last night.'

'They kept me overnight.' Her voice was so toneless, he wondered if she might be drugged. 'When they found out where Guodong had gone.'

'Look, shall we . . . can we come and see you? Or would you rather . . . ?'

'I don't know. I suppose so.'

'This morning? Is that all right?'

He thought he could hear her breathing, but she didn't answer.

'Lai-king? How about this morning?'

Still she didn't answer.

'Lai-king? Are you still there? Lai-king?'

He sensed she was, but the breathing silence lengthened and lengthened and at last he laid the phone down gently in its cradle – gently, as if she wouldn't hear that sharp final click.

Mila was standing by the bathroom door in her dressing-gown, a towel tied like a turban round her newly washed hair. 'Lai-king?'

He nodded.

'What did she say?'

'Just that Guodong's been arrested again.'

She unwound the towel and shook out her hair. 'Well, that was clear yesterday,' she said slowly.

'I didn't say we were there at the village, in case they'd bugged her phone.'

She nodded.

'I asked if we should call on her.'

'What did she say to that?'

'She didn't. At first she sort of said yes, then she just stopped talking.'

Mila considered. 'Well, I suppose we can't just leave her there,' she said slowly, reluctantly perhaps. 'All alone.'

'I'll phone her back.'

Mila returned to the bathroom and contemplated her face in the steam-misted mirror. She wiped the glass clear with the edge of the towel, though tears of condensed steam still trickled down its glistening surface – and felt a shadow of that fear she felt all those years ago when she heard the crowd baying, the fear that next time they would bay for her.

'She's not answering,' Dimitri called out. 'Where are my pills?'

'On that little table by the window.'

A minute later she heard him talking on the phone. She started brushing her long, dark, dyed hair. Soon the grey would be showing at the roots she saw in the mirror. One day, sooner or later, she would be a widow. Her back was hurting again. She sat down on the edge of the gleaming bath and let her body sag into the shape of its age.

'I just called San-san.' Dimitri came in. 'She's got a rehearsal this morning. I didn't say anything about Lai-king. Better we just go by ourselves. It might mess things up for her here, if she got too mixed up in this business. I didn't mention yesterday either. Nor did she. She seemed to understand it's better not to talk about it on the phone.'

'Yes.' She stood up, straightened her back. Erect and poised again.

'But look what someone's sent me,' Dimitri was saying, holding out his phone. 'Just keep scrolling.'

There were six or seven pictures on the screen, blurred and badly focussed, images of men and women shouting, of wild young men with sticks, of a man being hit, falling and clutching his head. Then Guodong, kneeling with raised hands as a policeman seemed about to strike him. Mila grimaced, imagining the baton thudding on his skull. She handed the phone back to him. '*Someone* sent them? It must have been Jianping. Or her friend.'

'Well, not directly,' he shrugged. 'It's some email address I've never heard of. Fake, presumably.'

'Delete them.'

'You think so?'

'Just delete them, Dimitri. *Delete* them!'

*

A man was sitting on a stool outside the apartment. He surveyed them with expressionless eyes as Dimitri pressed the bell.

No answer.

He pressed again, listened to the distant ring, aware all the time of the man's unwavering scrutiny. Mila glanced at

Dimitri, then turned to the man. 'Is Mrs Yu in?' she asked curtly.

The man considered her for a second or two, then shrugged indifferently, almost contemptuously.

'Yes, like hell he doesn't know,' Dimitri muttered, gazing at the thick dumb wood of the door.

But then there was a click and the door opened on its chain. Lai-king's face appeared in the slit between door and jamb, eyes large and strained, cheeks drawn. She stared at them a moment as if she didn't know them, then, with an anxious glance towards the man still sitting there watching, unfastened the chain and let them in. She shut the door at once, sliding the chain back into its slot.

'How are you, Lai-king?'

She didn't answer, looking at them as though she was too tired to speak, then gestured to some chairs. 'I don't know what to do,' she said, at last, staring down at the floor. 'They're sending him to a labour camp.'

'Are you sure?'

'Of course I'm sure. They told me they would.'

'That doesn't mean . . .' Dimitri hesitated, glancing round the room. For a moment he imagined Guodong walking in as he might have done if this hadn't happened, greeting them with his usual jovial smile. 'I mean, doesn't some sort of committee have to decide to send him there? They can't just–'

'Committees are just rubber stamps.'

'How can we help?' Mila asked quietly.

'Help? He might be there for years,' she said tonelessly. 'What about his medicines? It'll probably kill him.'

'Can't you find a lawyer?' Dimitri asked.

'And what about our daughter? Will they let her come here now?' Her voice suddenly rose and trembled. 'Will they let me out to see her?' She slumped into a chair and began to cry. She cried silently, hunched shoulders shaking, her face pressed into her hands.

Mila laid her arm round her shoulder, but Lai-king only shook her head.

'Maybe a lawyer–' Dimitri began again.

'Lawyer? Lawyer?' Lai-king moaned through her fingers. 'What difference will that make? They can do what they like with you here.'

It was cold in the apartment. Outside, the sky was grey and heavy with unshed rain. Guodong's computer stood unopened on his desk. Dimitri recognised some of the scrolls hanging on the walls. He imagined Guodong in some harsh labour camp – God knew how harsh, but harsh enough – stuck there without trial on the say-so of some low-level officials. 'We'll try and do something in Hong Kong,' he said. 'Make it known in the press, at least . . .'

'No!' Lai-king raised her head. 'That'll only make matters worse. They might let him out sooner if we don't make trouble for them.'

'But–'

Sitting beside Lai-king, Mila frowned up at him, briefly shaking her head.

'All right, maybe we should just wait and see, for now anyway,' he conceded. Well, Mila knew what it was like. If she thought they shouldn't insist, she was probably right. He was out of his depth here, floundering. And all the time he kept seeing that blurred picture of Guodong cowering beneath the policeman's raised baton.

'Have you eaten yet?' Mila asked.

'No, I couldn't eat now. I've got to write to my daughter.'

'Shall I make some tea? Coffee?'

'No . . . no, it's all right.' Lai-king stood up suddenly, wanting them gone. 'I'll call you.'

'We'll think of something,' Dimitri tried to encourage her as he embraced her at the door.

Lai-king twitched a smile but shook her head.

The man outside was talking quietly into his phone, surveying them with that same dispassionately assessing stare while they waited for the lift.

'Are we still going to San-san's concert?' Dimitri asked as they reached the street.

'I suppose so.' Mila raised her hand for a taxi, but it drove past. Then another and another. At last one drew up beside them.

'So there's nothing we can do for Lai-king? Or Guodong?' he asked as they settled into their seats.

Mila hesitated. 'Maybe ask those two youngsters?' she suggested as the taxi drove away towards the Bund. 'I imagine they'll be there tonight.'

'Them!'

She shrugged. 'They probably know more about it than we do.'

'Well, since they got Guodong into it, maybe they'll do something to get him out. But frankly I don't believe they will. Or can.'

Mila was looking at her phone. 'No more pictures from them, anyway. Or whoever sent them. There's an SMS from San-san.' She showed him the screen. *c u 2nite. starts at 7.30. tickets in ur name @ box office.*

*

There was Haydn, Mozart and a modern Chinese composer. But Dimitri's mind wandered in every piece, wandered off like a restless ghost to Lai-king's anguished face, to Guodong cowering beneath that upraised baton. Where was he now? Was he hurt? How could they help him? *Could* they at all? Every question faded in an answerless fog. In the interval they looked for Jianping or Yiming, but couldn't see them.

*

'I don't know,' San-san said afterwards as she loosened her bow. 'I left tickets for them, but apparently they didn't pick them up.' She glanced out through the curtains at the rows of empty red seats in the auditorium, as if after all they might yet come late. 'Perhaps they've been arrested too?' She laughed, a short brittle laugh.

'Perhaps we'll be next,' Dimitri smiled, then, seeing Mila's lips tighten, remembered that man outside Lai-king's apartment, his cool deliberate stare.

San-san was closing her violin case, imagining Alex waiting at the airport and herself not on the plane. She didn't believe it, and yet the image stayed. Of course nothing like that was going to happen. Not to them, not now. It wasn't like the sixties or seventies. Or was it, after all? 'Did you get those pictures on your phone?' she asked quietly.

'Yes. Delete them if you haven't already.'

San-san nodded. 'Apparently they were on the internet this morning, but they've been taken down already.'

'How did you know?'

San-san glanced across the room at several people talking and laughing with the rest of the quartet. A tall young woman was showing them an erhu, drawing the bow across the strings. It made a haunting, plaintive sound. 'Over there,' San-san murmured.

Dimitri looked back, remembering Lai-king's haunted face. He watched San-san's slim fingers fastening the clips on her case. 'I suppose they're taking you out to dinner?' he asked casually as an older man passed behind them.

San-san nodded. She was still imagining Alex waiting there in the arrival hall, waiting until the others came out with their instruments but without her. Imagining Derek – would it be Derek? Yes, Derek as the first violinist – taking Alex aside, and then the children's faces as Alex told them.

Mila approached. 'When are you leaving, San-san?'

'Tomorrow.' San-san pushed the images away, out into the dark. 'Back for the weekend. What about you?'

'We're booked for Monday,' Dimitri began. Again he saw Guodong's unbelieving face below that raised baton. He glanced round. There was no one near them now. 'It doesn't feel good leaving Lai-king all alone, but what can we do for her or Guodong here? In Hong Kong we might be able to do something. Not much, but–'

'Except that Lai-king said she doesn't want us to,' Mila reminded him firmly.

That's what Mila always says, San-san thought. *It's her leitmotif.* And then those images she'd pushed away began crawling back into her mind.

22

'She's still not answering.'

Mila looked at him across the table. 'Have you tried her mobile?'

He nodded. 'Should we go round again?'

'If she wanted us to, she'd answer the phone.'

'Unless she couldn't.'

'In which case going round might make things worse for her. For them.'

'But we can't just leave without–'

'Dimitri' – she turned and held his eyes with hers – 'we don't know whether that would be good for her or bad. Who knows what that man there yesterday is reporting to the police? All we do know is that she doesn't answer. Perhaps that *is* her answer.'

He sighed. 'Yesterday you said we ought to go.'

'Yes, we saw her yesterday and . . .' She let a shrug speak for her.

'So you think we should just leave without a word? No, we have to go round, try again. Maybe she'll change her mind?'

Again she didn't answer. *And if they detained Dimitri,* she was thinking, *what then?* She remembered her *laojiao*, Father Ignatius, the bullying and punishments. Were they still like that? She didn't know.

Half a cup of coffee later, his phone rang. 'Ah!'

But it was Jianping. 'Good morning,' she said in English. 'How are you?'

‘All right.’ He paused, refusing to return her greeting. ‘I suppose you’ve heard the news?’ he asked coolly.

‘About yesterday? Yes.’

He glanced at Mila as he spoke. ‘Lai-king doesn’t answer her phone.’

‘I know. Perhaps we can meet?’

‘Why, exactly?’ His voice cold, hostile.

‘Well . . .’ Even her assurance could wobble. ‘They’re your friends as well, aren’t they?’

‘Have you got any ideas?’

‘Ideas?’

‘About how to help them?’

‘Well, some, yes.’

‘All right, then, let’s meet.’ *This morning*? he mouthed to Mila, raising his eyebrows.

She shrugged and nodded.

‘How about this morning?’

‘Yes, this morning.’

‘Where?’

‘Where we met the other day? We’ll pick you up there at twelve, at the same place, is that all right?’

Mila looked round the restaurant, at foreign tourists and local Chinese, at an American couple examining the menu, at two svelte Shanghainese women parading their D&G and Gucci. And thought of Guodong in a grubby grey uniform in a *laojiao*, of Lai-king immured in her empty home.

‘She was speaking English,’ Dimitri said as he laid his phone down on the crisply starched table-cloth.

‘I heard. Probably better.’

‘Well,’ he fingered the toast crumbs that had fallen like dark seeds on a snowy plain, pressing them into his fingers and dropping them onto his plate. ‘I wonder what they’ll have to say.’

'So long as they don't make things difficult for us.' She imagined stone-faced policemen at their hotel door.

*

Jianping was waiting there just as she'd said, standing beside a different car this time. Glancing up and down the street, she waved and opened the door. Yiming was hunched over the wheel, the engine running. As soon as they got in, he drove off. 'We can have lunch somewhere,' he said. Leaving the Bund, he drove into Hong Qiao district, on and on into ever smaller streets. All four were silent in the car until: 'The villagers are still more angry now,' Jianping said.

'Some were hurt,' Yiming added.

'So was Guodong,' Mila said. 'By the look of it.'

'Where is he?' Dimitri asked.

'He is probably being sent to a *laojiao* . . .' Yiming turned into a still smaller street, lined with older houses and shops. How was it the developers hadn't levelled that yet, Dimitri wondered, and built another mall? '. . . We don't know which one exactly,' Yiming was saying. 'I think they won't decide officially till tomorrow. But . . .' He raised his hand from the steering wheel and let it eloquently fall.

'How long would he be in for?' Dimitri asked. 'If they do decide?'

Jianping shrugged. 'It is up to them. Unless . . .'

'Unless something happens.' Yiming pulled up outside a simple tea-house, its entrance almost hidden by busy market stalls cheek by jowl along the pavement. 'Shall we go in here?'

It was crowded and noisy, but they found an empty table at the rear and sat down on simple wooden stools. Dimitri looked round. The customers seemed to be workers, all men, speaking in some dialect he couldn't understand. Several turned to stare at them.

'Migrants from the countryside,' Jianping said. 'They don't see many foreigners.'

As Yiming was ordering rice and dumplings: 'Lai-king is very worried,' Mila said abruptly in English.

'It's all right,' Jianping said. 'They won't understand you here anyway.' But she too spoke English now. 'We are trying to find a lawyer, but it's difficult because Guodong is, well, almost like a foreigner, coming from Hong Kong.'

'Besides,' Yiming said slowly, feeling for words, 'it is a small thing for them.'

'Not for Guodong and Lai-king,' Dimitri said curtly. 'Not small for them at all.'

Yiming poured the tea before he answered. 'There was a woman a few months ago, she protested when her daughter was . . .' He hesitated, searching for the English word.

'She was kidnapped and forced to be a prostitute,' Jianping continued for him. 'She was very young, ten or eleven. The mother protested because the sentence was too lenient, so they sent her to a labour camp.'

'Weren't two of the men sentenced to death?'

'Oh, you have heard about this?' Yiming asked.

'Our press is still free.'

'For now,' Mila said.

'The death sentence doesn't sound very lenient to me,' Dimitri went on, his voice still cold.

'But she thought other people were involved,' Jianping said. 'And they weren't punished because they had some connections. It was a big thing here, to be sent to a labour camp just for protesting.'

'Isn't that what's just happened to Guodong?' Mila asked sharply.

'But his daughter has not been . . . kid nabbed and made to work as a prostitute,' Yiming said patiently. 'That is what made everyone angry.'

'Kid*napped*,' Jianping corrected him.

Yiming smiled apologetically, leaning back as the dumplings arrived. He waited till the waitress had left before continuing. 'And the police didn't want to know. So there was a big fuss on the internet. That is why she was released, there was such a big fuss on the internet. That's what the government is afraid of, the internet.'

'And Guodong's case wouldn't make everyone angry?'

Jianping and Yiming glanced at each other, then both shook their heads regretfully. 'Not big enough,' Yiming said, pushing his owlish glasses higher.

'So if it's hard to find a lawyer and he doesn't have a kidnapped daughter, what can be done to help him – and Lai-king?'

Jianping glanced at Yiming again. 'We thought if – when – they send him to a labour camp, perhaps you can make some noise in Hong Kong?'

'Noise?' Mila repeated, her tone at once incredulous and derisive.

'Tell the press, the TV?'

'The trouble is, Lai-king doesn't want that,' Dimitri said. 'She thinks it would make things worse for him. And herself.'

'And she's probably right,' Mila added.

'Besides, it wouldn't have much effect anyway,' Dimitri went on. 'Just a one-day small item in the news.'

They sipped their tea in an awkward silence that lengthened and lengthened. The two naive young idealists seemed for once uncertain of themselves. All around them, men's voices shouted and laughed, grumbled and quarrelled.

'Perhaps there will be another demonstration in the village,' Jianping said at last, 'which will make people notice. Something big. Then people will sit up. And we will send you some more pictures. For the press.'

'Thanks.' Dimitri's voice hardened. He placed his chopsticks together across the bowl, still full of rice and a half-eaten dumpling. 'I'm sure they'll be fascinating.'

They were silent again, avoiding each other's eyes. Dimitri glanced at Mila, eyebrows raised. She nodded. She'd barely touched her dumpling. 'Well, we'd better be going back to the hotel,' he said coldly. 'Thanks for lunch. I suppose you'll be in Hong Kong again soon, Jianping?'

'Sorry? Oh, yes,' she said vaguely.

'No, don't bother,' Dimitri said when Yiming offered to drive them back. 'We'll take a taxi.'

Watching them leave, Yiming and Jianping leant close across the table and began talking in low voices.

*

'Do you know this area?' Dimitri asked Mila as they walked back along the noisy crowded street.

She shook her head. 'Those two scare me,' she said slowly.

'Well, it was you who said we should ask them.' He remembered her calling Jianping a 'poor girl' when he was 'interrogating' her in Hong Kong all those months ago.

'Any port in a storm. Isn't that the English expression?' She raised her hand at the crossing as a taxi passed.

'No, let's walk a bit.'

She shook her head. 'You look tired.'

'You *think* I look tired.'

She took his arm and drew him towards the waiting taxi. 'If I think you do, you do.'

'Actually I am a bit,' he admitted as he settled back into the seat. 'Poor Guodong.'

'Poor Lai-king.'

'Why the hell did those two have to get them mixed up in all this?'

'It wasn't just them. He started it with his petition. After all, it's his ancestral village.'

'Years and years ago. I don't suppose he'd been there more than once or twice in the last twenty years. But if Lai-king is right, those two got him involved all over again. Why?'

'I suppose they think they're reforming China. Like the students in Tiananmen did.'

'A funny way to go about it.'

'Some people would say that about Tiananmen too.'

The taxi stopped, blocked by traffic. Mila gazed out of the window at a street vendor pushing his barrow loaded with large cabbages, straining against its weight. He was an old man with grey hair and a gaunt face. 'I suppose every way is funny,' she said abstractedly. 'Unless it works.'

'That's not what you said when we saw that demonstration in Hong Kong.'

'No . . .' she admitted thoughtfully. 'Conflicted.' Then she nodded at the street beside them. 'Look.'

Two young urban control officers had stopped the old man and were shouting at him. People on the pavement paused as they passed, some staying to watch, while most turned and walked on. In a small tea-house, heads swivelled, then swivelled back after only a cursory glance. Now a cabbage fell off the old man's cart as he dropped the handles. One of the officers kicked it contemptuously away into the gutter.

'No licence, I suppose,' Dimitri said. 'What will they do with him?'

Mila asked the driver, who was also watching, in Shanghainese. The driver gave a brief, humourless laugh. 'Confiscate his cabbages and send him back into the countryside,' she translated.

'Without a trial, I imagine?' Dimitri asked, in Mandarin now.

The taxi driver gave another humourless laugh.

The old man stood there, head bowed, abject and docile, while the other officer spoke into his phone.

'Well, at least you can see what those two young idealists are on about, can't you?' Mila said quietly. 'And Guodong?'

'Oh yes,' he muttered. 'You can see that all right.' *But then,* he thought, *that kind of thing can happen anywhere, not just in China. As Frankam said.*

The car in front of them moved at last and the taxi jerked forward, then drove smoothly on. Dimitri gazed out at heavily laden trucks flowing the other way, like barges on a sluggish river.

'It will be quite a relief to be back in Hong Kong,' Mila said slowly, almost as though she thought it might be difficult to get there. 'Do you still want to call on Lai-king again? Before we leave? We won't have much time.'

They were approaching the Bund, its long wide promenade bustling with tourists, Chinese and foreign, all blissfully ignorant of what went on in some remote provincial village. As ignorant and indifferent as that cargo ship Dimitri was watching now, steaming calmly down towards the tranquil sea. And if they did know, would they care?

'Dimitri? Do you still want to call on Lai-king?'

He stirred at last and nodded. 'You don't have to come with me, though.'

'No?' Her eyelids fluttered. 'Just sit in the hotel and wait for you to come back?' She leant forward and gave the driver the Yus' address. 'Might as well go now. Try phoning her first.'

But still there was no answer.

23

The taxi stopped opposite the gleaming mall and a new passenger waited, his hand already proprietary on the door while Dimitri paid. They stood a moment gazing at the entrance to Guodong's building as though doubtful it was the right address. 'Well,' Dimitri breathed, and they climbed the steps. Inside the lobby, an elderly woman with a large shopping bag emerged from the lift. Her eyes, lingering curiously on them, seemed to drag her head round as she passed.

They watched the floor indicator flashing as the lift whirred up, quivering faintly. The doors slid open and they stepped out. The same man sat on the same stool, scrolling on his phone screen. Mila nodded faintly, but the man's face remained as expressionless as a block of wood while he watched them pause once more at Guodong's door. Dimitri pushed the button beside the Yus' name. As they listened to a faint peal and then a lengthening silence behind the door, the man began speaking quietly into his phone, his hand almost covering his mouth.

After half a minute, Dimitri pushed the button again, glancing at Mila with raised eyebrows. The same deep silence followed the faint peal far behind the door, a silence that felt like a listening silence. Gazing at the door, he thought he saw the light change behind the spy-hole. Or was he mistaken? He listened for some sound behind the thick dumb wood, but heard nothing. He nodded towards the man, who was watching them now, his arms folded.

Mila turned. 'Is Mrs Yu in?' she asked in Shanghainese.

The man's eyelids flickered.

'Mrs Yu?' she repeated more loudly.

'I can speak English,' the man said tonelessly, gazing, not at her, but at Dimitri. 'One, two, three, four . . .'

Dimitri glanced uneasily at Mila, his eyes puzzled.

'. . . five, six, seven, eight . . .'

'Is he mad?' Dimitri whispered.

'. . . nine, ten, eleven, twelve–'

'Let's go!' Mila murmured urgently.

'. . . thirteen, fourteen, fifteen–'

The lift bell tinged behind them, its doors smoothly parted and two men stepped out. *Stone-faced,* Mila had time to think as her stomach quietly lurched.

The man on the stool stood up. The older of the two men nodded. The younger flashed a card at Dimitri which he had no time to read. 'Security,' the man said in English. 'Your passport, please.' Turning to Mila: 'Identity card,' he said brusquely in Chinese.

'Passport,' Mila answered quietly, reaching into her shoulder bag. 'British.'

The man considered her coldly a moment before taking both their passports and slowly turning the pages. 'You were born in China.' He glanced up at Mila again. 'So you are still a Chinese citizen. Remember that.'

While he slowly turned the pages, the older man walked to the window and looked down at the street, then turned and gazed thoughtfully at them, folding his arms and leaning against the wall.

'Anything wrong?' Dimitri asked expressionlessly in Mandarin while the younger man scrutinised their Chinese visas.

The man didn't answer until, satisfied, he closed the passports and looked up. 'Ah, so you speak Chinese?' Now he did too. 'What are you doing here?'

'Visiting friends.'

'Which friends?'

Dimitri nodded at the closed, silent door. 'Their name is Yu.'

'What is this?' Mila asked, an uncertain tremor in her voice. 'What's this about?'

The younger man ignored her, while the older crossed his legs and inclined his head, almost, Dimitri fleetingly thought, as if he was lounging at the back of a theatre and the curtain had just risen.

The younger man nodded. 'You called here yesterday.'

'Yes.'

'Did you know Yu Guodong had been arrested?'

While Dimitri hesitated: 'We phoned his wife,' Mila answered quickly for him. 'She told us he'd been arrested, so we went to see her.'

Still the man ignored her, looking only at Dimitri. 'Do you know why he was arrested?'

'Some trouble in his home village, his wife said. A demonstration or something . . .'

Dimitri imagined himself walking on a single plank over a deep ravine. One misstep and–

'An illegal gathering,' the man corrected him. 'And you offered to help her?'

The older man leant forward slightly, as though the play was reaching its crisis.

'Yes. But she said no.'

The younger man nodded. 'What kind of help?'

Dimitri shrugged. 'We didn't get that far.'

'There are foreign elements in Hong Kong who want to instigate trouble here.' He paused, looked from Dimitri to Mila, then back again. 'Do you know anything about that?'

Dimitri shook his head.

'No?' He sounded unconvinced. 'Have you ever been to the so-called Tiananmen vigil in Hong Kong?'

Dimitri hesitated, glanced at Mila. 'Hundreds of thousands of people have.'

'Have *you* been?' The man's voice stiffened.

'Yes.'

The man turned to Mila. 'And you?'

Her face had grown tense and pale. She nodded, licking her lips. 'I went with my husband.' It was as if her voice had turned pale too.

The man turned back to Dimitri. 'Do you not know that those demonstrations are supported by foreign elements hostile to China?'

Why do they all speak in slabs of jargon? Dimitri thought as he answered. 'I don't think they are–'

The older man held up his hand, uncrossing his legs and pushing himself off the wall. 'It would be dangerous for you to interfere with matters that don't concern you,' he said slowly, letting each word sink separately in.

'My friend's situation concerns us. Isn't that normal?'

'Your friend is a Chinese citizen, being dealt with under Chinese law. That does not concern you.'

'I just want to know what's happened to him–'

'You will find out in due course. Meanwhile I advise you not to call here any more. You could get yourselves into serious trouble if you meddle in internal Chinese affairs. When do you plan to return to Hong Kong?'

'Tomorrow,' Mila said in the same pale voice.

'Yes,' he nodded as though he knew already. 'I strongly advise you' – his eyes holding Dimitri's, his voice even slower and more deliberate now – 'not to do anything that might cause you to miss your flight–'

He paused as his phone chimed, listened and quietly answered. Putting his phone away, he nodded to his junior colleague, who handed their passports back to Dimitri. 'Nothing that might make you miss your flight,' the older man repeated.

The younger man turned to push the lift button. The play was over.

Both men watched till they had stepped inside and the doors closed upon them.

Dimitri looked at Mila. Her face was still tense. 'Well–' he began uncertainly, but she frowned and shook her head, laying her finger on her lips.

He didn't speak again until they were out on the street, and then it was only to say, 'Let's walk a bit. I don't want to hang about here where they can see us waiting for a taxi.' They walked silently, alone with their thoughts. Dimitri dwelt on the faces of the two men, the bell pealing in the Yus' deserted apartment. Or was it not deserted, after all? That glimmer of light behind the spy-hole – was Lai-king hiding inside, willing them to go away? Mila kept seeing the older man's thoughtful stare, calmly assessing her as a cat might a mouse before it pounced.

'I wonder if they knew we went to the village?' Dimitri asked at last.

Mila shrugged. 'Ask San-san if they questioned her. Not like that,' she added quickly as he took out his phone. 'Just ask if everything's all right. You know, without giving anything away. She'll understand.'

'She's already left, hasn't she?'

Mila glanced at her watch. 'I don't think so. Not yet.'

Now he imagined San-san being questioned, halted at immigration or taken off the plane like that woman when they arrived.

But San-san responded almost at once. 'We're just boarding,' she said. Her voice sounded light and pleased.

'Everything all right?'

'Yes, fine.'

'Okay. Have a good trip.'

He turned to Mila. 'So maybe they don't know we went to the village?'

'Yet,' she said.

They had nearly reached the Bund. He raised his hand for a taxi. Mila gave the hotel's name in Shanghainese. They sat there silent, unseeing, as the old colonial buildings slipped past, their minds turned inward. Almost like prisoners, Dimitri thought, after being sentenced. He imagined the taxi as a van, driving them to prison.

'So I suppose you were right,' he said slowly at last as the taxi waited at the traffic lights before the hotel. 'We shouldn't have gone.'

Mila stirred, as though waking from sleep. 'Who knows?' she said.

*

'Someone's been in the room,' she said tensely.

'What d'you mean?' but he knew very well from her tone what she meant.

'Look, your case is on top of mine now. I left mine on top.'

'You sure?'

'I'm positive.'

'The maid?' Dimitri began.

She shook her head decisively. 'It was cleaned before we left, don't you remember? While we were at breakfast.' Now she slid the wardrobe doors open. 'And look! Your clothes are all mixed up with mine. That's not how we hung them up. Someone's been going through our things.'

'Are you sure?'

'Of course I'm sure!' She pointed at his jacket hanging between her black skirt and her red silk blouse. 'We never left them like that! And my case was on top of yours, I tell you. I know it was!'

He scanned his clothes and shook his head. 'Looks all right to me.' Or did it? Had he really left that jacket there, not with the rest of his things?

Now she had pulled the cover back from the bed. 'Just look! That's not how I left it, my night-dress was under the pillow!'

'Are you really sure?'

'Of course I'm sure!' Now she was opening the dressing-table drawers, one after the other. 'Look in your wardrobe drawer.'

He opened it, frowned and shrugged. Had he left that shirt on top or under? 'I don't know–' he began.

'Well I do! They've been through our things.' She sat down on the bed, gazing empty-eyed across the room. *It's all right,* she kept telling herself, *it's all right. They won't stop you from leaving . . .* But the restless butterflies of fear still fluttered in her stomach.

24

The traffic was so bad along Caine Road that Dimitri got off the bus at Old Bailey and walked down to Wyndham Street. Then Wyndham was clogged too, so he decided to go overground through the malls on his way to Central station. That way you didn't have to dodge through the crowds or wait at the traffic lights, sucking in all the carcinogenic car fumes. If you started near the junction of Wyndham Street with Queen's Road, you could pass through one mall after another until you descended into Statue Square and the station entrance without touching a road.

On the other hand, he realised too late, you couldn't avoid the syrupy Christmas carols oozing out of loudspeakers wherever you went. Still oozing, even though Christmas was over and in two days a new year would have begun. The same music, or something like it, was oozing in the Shanghai malls, he remembered, a good month before Christmas, and probably in every damn mall in the world except Saudi Arabia. A tourist landing in the malls here wouldn't know whether they were in Shanghai or Hong Kong. Except here the government wasn't all-powerful. Yet. That's why he'd had that persistent unease in Shanghai, ever since that demonstration in Guodong's village, even more after that encounter with the security police at Lai-king's door. That persistent feeling they might be stopped at any time, right down till the moment they were belted up on the plane. They'd both felt it, Mila and himself, a wary tenseness until the plane soared and a quiet tide of relief flooded through them as the tarmac slipped further and further away. And

San-san must have felt it too, even though she'd had no brush with the police. He knew she did, he saw it in her eyes after that concert. What then must Lai-king be feeling? And Guodong? Was there really nothing they could do for them now? It was as if he was watching them from a distance, a distance he could not bridge, while a relentless heavy hand pressed them slowly down.

Then, perhaps because of that particular slush, *I'm Dreaming of a White Christmas* drooling through the speakers, or perhaps because he was near where that café used to be, Dimitri remembered that other Christmas, forty, no, forty-three years before. Mila, sitting opposite him at the small, round glass table, telling him she was going back to Shanghai in the middle of the Cultural Revolution. After the trial, after the inquest, when everything was as dark as it could be and then became darker still. *But she came back,* he reminded himself, *she came back.* Yet his mind wouldn't let the desolating memory go – the half-empty coffee cup, her slim pale fingers toying with the spoon, the curve of her cheek, and sweep of her hair . . . What had become of that coffee shop? He looked round. Surely it was over there, where they were selling mobile phones now? Why had they destroyed it, destroyed a part of his past, a part of his life?

The memory was still clinging to his mind as he went down from Princes Building into Statue Square and saw the familiar tall fountains wavering and splashing in the December light just as they'd splashed and wavered then, nearly half a century ago. Some things remained, then. Some things remained.

He walked to the escalator and down into the underground station. Yes, his steps were shorter now and so was his breath. Young men and women walked past him with a quicker, firmer stride. But he was still in the clear, still in the clear.

Walking along the passageway towards the trains, he felt a hand laid lightly on his shoulder and knew before he turned that it was Elena's.

There she was, in narrow black trousers and a light blue jacket, her eyes radiant with pleased surprise. 'Where are you off to? You're looking great.' A tall Eurasian-looking man was standing half a step behind her.

'Ah Wong. Christmas visit. Bit late I'm afraid, but . . .' He glanced at the man.

'Oh, this is Kevin.' Elena turned with a casual gesture.

The man bowed faintly.

'My father,' Elena explained to Kevin. 'Off to see our old *amah*.'

'Right,' Kevin said respectfully. 'Your old *amah*.'

'Hello, Kevin.' Dimitri shook Kevin's hand, then turned to Elena. 'So where are you both off to?'

'Lunch in that new Italian place on Hollywood Road.'

'Ah,' he said vaguely. *Hollywood Road*, he recited inwardly, *Queen's Road, Chater Gardens, Wyndham Street* – the legacy of empire. You could tell the history of Hong Kong by reeling off those names.

'Never heard of it, have you?' Elena was laughing. 'We'll take you there some time.'

'Great.' He glanced at his watch. 'Well . . .'

'Yes, we'd better be going too, or they won't keep our table. Tell Ah Wong I'll phone her next week, will you? And we're seeing you on New Year's Eve, aren't we? Say hi to Mila.'

Kevin raised his hand and smiled goodbye.

After a few steps, Dimitri looked back. Elena was holding Kevin's arm, leaning affectionately towards him as she talked. Where had she found him? How long would it last? And where did she get that effervescent *joie de vivre* from, which nothing could dampen? Surely not from her depressive mother. Nor from him, come to that. He was too much of a sceptic. He walked on through the hurrying crowd and waited at the platform. And how was it that with all that zest, in all that rush of life, she still found time to phone Ah Wong and chat with her, sometimes call on her in her tiny room and take her out for dim sum? At first it was Alex, the son, who was Ah Wong's favourite. But after their mother's death it was Elena, perhaps because she was younger and more dependent on her then.

Elena had turned too, pulling Kevin's arm, as they neared the station exit. She nodded at Dimitri walking away towards the Tsuen Wan train platform. 'Think I look like him?' she asked.

Kevin considered, shrugged, shook his head. 'I wouldn't have known he was your dad.'

'No, apparently I look more like my mother. That's what Ah Wong – our *amah* – used to say anyway. And d'you know what else she said once–' She stopped, shook her head and turned back to the escalator. 'Never mind. Come on, I'm starving.'

'Your mother was jealous,' Ah Wong had said. That was the word, jealous.

'Jealous?' she'd asked. *'Who of?'*

But Ah Wong had pressed her lips into a thin tight line and shaken her head. So Elena had taken the last dumpling with the chopsticks and placed it in Ah Wong's bowl. She knew Ah Wong wouldn't say any more. And perhaps she didn't want her to.

⋆

The train arrived, the glass doors smoothly parted and Dimitri sat down near the door. It was easy to find a place, the train started there. So he was spared the embarrassment – no, the humiliation – of being offered some young person's seat.

Under the harbour and a hundred ships, then under Kowloon and a million people, then the change to the East Rail and out into the open country of the New Territories. Except the open country had been driven back by the new towns, where a million more people lived in forty-storey cement blocks like the tall trees of one concrete plantation after another. And yet behind them the hills still rose, green and untrodden beneath the pollution-hazed sky. To think there might be people still living there who were children when the last tiger was shot in Hong Kong!

As the train rolled smoothly on towards the border, Dimitri saw more and more mainlanders getting on. He could tell them by their loud voices, their strange accents and their heavy cases, full probably of baby milk powder bought in Hong Kong, since they didn't trust their own. He got out at Fanling, two stops before the border at Lok Ma Chau, and another memory speared him – that border post at Lok Ma Chau forty-three years ago, when China was a closed land of labouring peasants and wild Red Guards. He'd stood on top of the hill by the police post and watched Mila cross into the vast green countryside of China, thinking it was the last he'd ever see of her, that solitary slender figure leaning slightly against the weight of her suitcase, passing from the British post with its Union Jack into the Chinese with its red flag. Where there were empty fields and barbed wire fences before, there were now railway lines and hectic towns. Only the memory remained. *But she came back, she came back*, that voice whispered inside his head. He smiled with relief as if he'd only just realised it. Yes, she came back. She came back.

He walked from the station to the government housing

estate where Ah Wong lived. He was the only *gwei lo* for miles around. People looked at him, wondering what a foreign devil was doing there, thinking perhaps he was a missionary – there were always Mormons around, although he hardly looked like one of that young, neat, sure-of-themselves band. But these people were busy living their own lives and their curiosity was short-lived. Their questioning glances strayed and quickly faded. Past the steep steps up to the Taoist temple, past the middle school, past the drab parade of shops, into the narrow green space from which Ah Wong's tenement block rose, grey and bleak. Beside it was another block, the ground floor a nursing home, where Ah Wong said she would one day go to die. He'd long ago bought her a place for her ashes in the temple. She'd been restless till she knew she had her own little compartment where her urn would be laid, one slot beside another in a blank wall. Like post office boxes in the GPO, each with a name and a stern photo placed on the door. She'd shown him her little niche with the pride another might have had showing their brand new luxury apartment.

A woman with two schoolchildren was opening the back entrance to Ah Wong's block and he followed her in, along the naked narrow corridor to the lift hall. The two children, humping their heavy satchels, stared at him in silent curiosity as they waited for the lift while their mother gazed politely away at the flickering floor-indicator. The people at the desk used to ask for his ID whenever he came, but now they knew him and only smiled a brief welcome. The lift came; he stepped in after the two children, who watched him press the first floor button then looked at each other inquiringly while their mother still behaved as though they were alone. No wonder the kids looked; they knew that only old women lived on that floor.

He got out and walked along the bare cement corridor,

past heavy metal doors with metal gratings pulled across them. Just like a jail, he imagined, and thought at once of Guodong in his labour camp. How was he bearing it, how was Lai-king? They hadn't heard, and Lai-king never answered emails or the phone.

Ah Wong's door was open a little and through the grating he heard her television blaring. She never had a television while she worked for him, claiming it was bad for the eyes. They'd been damaged by the sun in her childhood, she often said, when she had to squat on the beach all day long, splitting oyster shells. Perhaps that was why she always looked at you through half-closed lids, as though squinting in bright sunlight. But when she came there, she'd accepted his offer of a small portable set – anything else would have been too large – and now she never turned it off, day or night, until she went to bed. He paused to watch her. She was in the doorway of her room, bending over a kettle she'd placed on an electric ring. How slowly she moved now, how stiff she'd become.

Something alerted her and she straightened up, rubbing her back as she turned towards him. 'Ah, master!' she exclaimed. 'I was just making coffee for you.'

It took her some time to pull the grate open and he noticed again how worn and knobbly her knuckles had become. 'How are you, Ah Wong?' He glanced at the two closed doors next to hers. 'Still nobody else here?'

She shook her head. 'No one come in since they die. More better that way. The last ones too much talky-talky.'

He remembered how the two old women used to peer at him whenever he visited Ah Wong, how one plied her with questions about him, assuming he didn't understand Cantonese. Was that why Ah Wong often insisted on speaking pidgin to him, so they wouldn't understand? The talkative one said she had a son in America, he remembered, and thought he was going to come and take her there. But one year passed and then another and no son ever came. Then, a few years ago, she died. He'd hardly known the other old woman, who Ah Wong said was crazy. And last year she died too. No wonder Ah Wong preferred being alone with the sole use of the bare communal kitchen and toilet.

Now she was busy pouring boiling water onto a heaped spoonful of instant coffee in a large yellow plastic beaker, then laying out some chocolate biscuits on a petal-shaped plastic plate. That was her ritual, unchanged for fifteen years since she'd moved into this cell with its TV, refrigerator and two-tiered bunk bed. There was no more room; you could just squeeze between the bed and the refrigerator to get to the window, which was veiled with a cheap flimsy curtain. All she owned in the world lay on the top bunk of the bed, packed into plastic bags, where she also kept presents for Alex and Elena's children, the nearest thing she had to grandchildren.

He sat down on the edge of the bed and sipped the coffee. On top of the TV were photos of Ah Wong with the children as they grew up. And one of herself as a young girl when she first came to Hong Kong from the mainland soon after the Japanese war, illiterate, hardly older than San-san's daughter Cathy was now. All she'd done since then was cook, wash and clean for other people. Yet that had been better, far better, than how her sisters who stayed behind had fared on the mainland. Till now, at least. Ah Wong hadn't known civil war, starvation, the hysterical cruelties of the Cultural Revolution. To her family she became the rich sister who'd made good abroad.

'Very beautiful,' he said, nodding at the photo.

'*Mah mah dei*,' she answered, in Cantonese now, wrinkling her nose as she shook her head. *So-so.*

He reached across to the photo and, as he took it,

stopped short. Helen gazed at him from behind it. There she was in a faded snap, the edges curled, standing by the kitchen door in the red cheongsam she wore that evening she killed herself. He gazed at her numbly, aware of Ah Wong's sharp intake of breath beside him. 'Sorry, master,' she murmured.

After some seconds: 'How did you get it?' he asked brittly. 'Did Missy . . . ?'

Ah Wong nodded. 'She told me to give it to the children, the day she . . . But I thought she looked too sad.'

He nodded. There was a faint smile on Helen's face, but a lake of sadness filled her eyes; it was a goodbye smile.

'Alex and Elena were very sad,' Ah Wong went on. 'After it happened. Very unhappy.'

'I know.' Still gazing at Helen, behind his eyes he saw the two children clinging to Ah Wong at the funeral. When he glanced round at her, it seemed there was a gleam of reproach in her eyes. She, who had never really liked Helen, who had resented her irritable temper – she was blaming him for her death? *And why not?* he thought a second later. Didn't he blame himself? But had she known about Mila then? Could she have possibly known why Helen killed herself? Was that why she was always so cool towards Mila? He didn't want to know. Some truths should not be spoken. Some wounds should not be probed.

Ah Wong took the photo of herself gently out of his hands and placed it back over Helen's. It was like closing a book. Or a tomb.

They sat there silent for several minutes. That wasn't unusual. But the reason for it was. Helen seemed to gaze at him still with forlorn eyes from behind Ah Wong's photo, to speak to him through Ah Wong's silence, speak the words she'd written at the bottom of that lethal note. *If you can be happy with her, it gives me one more reason to go away . . .*

He forced himself to look away, to glance round the tiny room, even surreptitiously at Ah Wong's deeply lined yet serene face.

She used to talk readily, but over the years she'd become more and more withdrawn, as though the waters of life were failing in her, flowing ever more slowly. If he brought presents for her, she gave them away to that niece of hers, Suk-yee, who'd managed to slip into Hong Kong all those years ago. How many mainlanders made that journey? How many perished trying? Far more, he guessed, than those who died at about the same time trying to escape from East Germany. But, unlike the Germans, there'd never be any museum, any plaque for them. Some truths are just too inconvenient – the same Party was ruling China now as then. Yes, Suk-yee, young and pretty then. What would she be like now?

But what was he doing, sitting there thinking of Suk-yee when Helen was gazing at him still through Ah Wong's photo – Helen, in her last moments of life? Trying to forget, of course. Yes, some wounds really were too deep to probe.

Ah Wong sat passive on her little stool a few feet away from him, her hands clasped on her knees. Every now and then, he felt, rather than saw, her glance at him, waiting. At last he stirred, and, as if it was just another ordinary visit, brought out pictures of the grandchildren. She smiled. 'Like Elena,' she said of Tara, holding the photos close to her eyes. 'Like Alex,' of Michael. While she placed them on the TV, he slipped a red envelope full of banknotes under her pillow. Before, whenever she saw him doing that, she would refuse and insist he take it back. But lately she'd stopped watching for it and they seemed to have come to a tacit arrangement that if she didn't see it, she would keep it – to give to Suk-yee, he suspected, or use it to buy presents for Alex and Elena's children.

When she turned back from the TV, she asked, 'Are you better, master?'

'Much better,' he nodded. 'How are you?'

'Old lady now.' She shrugged. 'Go home soon.'

And so they were back on their customary course, as though no revelatory or reproachful gust of wind had blown them off it.

'Elena said she's going to phone you next week.'

She smiled again. 'Elena's a good girl.'

But there was something on her mind, he sensed. She was unusually silent, even for her. Something other than Helen – *that* had happened only after he'd accidentally unveiled her photo.

'How's Suk-yee?' he asked as the silence lengthened.

'So-so.' She hesitated. 'Her son died.'

'What!?'

'In the ferry crash.'

'That collision in October? Why didn't you tell us?'

She shrugged. 'You weren't well.'

'But that was months ago!'

She shrugged again.

How much had Elena told her, about his illness, he wondered. 'I'm so sorry.' And he was. A son dying, that was the worst in China. An image slipped into his mind – the Mothers of Tiananmen, that small band of mothers who'd lost their only sons in the massacre and had spent the rest of their lives fruitlessly seeking an explanation, and being locked in their homes on every anniversary. Yes, their only sons. What about their daughters? But of course if they had a son, they wouldn't have a daughter – they were only allowed one child.

'How is Suk-yee?' he asked a moment later.

Ah Wong shook her head.

'And her husband?' But did she have a husband, he suddenly wondered. It was so long since he'd seen her.

'No husband now. He got other one wife.'

'When?'

'Long time.' Her lips pursed. 'Suk-yee more better without him.' Then she leant forward, looking at him more closely with narrowed eyes. 'You really all right, master?'

'Yes, really.' He felt his doubts and pushed them aside.

*

After that there wasn't much more to say. Ah Wong kept her life to herself and only occasionally let him glimpse it. It had always been that way. He'd known her almost half his life and still he didn't know much more about her than when she first began to work for Helen. Wong was her family name. They should have called her by her personal name, but Helen had called her Ah Wong because she couldn't remember that Chinese 'said their names backwards', as she'd impatiently put it when reminded that the family name came first, before the personal names. For a moment he saw Helen's face again in that photo, hidden now behind young Ah Wong's, the clouded eyes he'd once found beautiful, the faint sad smile bidding farewell. 'Like Hungarians,' he'd told her, but it hadn't helped. And so Ah Wong it had stayed. And Ah Wong had never told him about that photo, hadn't even told him much later of her nephew's recent death, because she thought he was too ill to be bothered with it, or perhaps because she thought in his state it would be unlucky to mention it. He would never know; that part of her was still as hidden as on the day he first met her.

Ah Wong accompanied him to the door when he left. He looked back at her standing by the half-open metal grate and saw, behind her on the TV, that picture of her as a young girl on the threshold of her life. That photo, behind which stood Helen's on the threshold of her death.

She must come to his funeral, he thought, unless he went to hers first. Walking back past the Taoist temple, he recalled the empty niche in the wall, waiting for Ah Wong's ashes. He must remember to tell them – Mila, Alex, all of them – tell them she must come to his funeral. But of course Elena would make sure she came. She would know he wanted her to. So would Mila, even if Ah Wong did treat her as the number two wife, inferior to the first. And now, perhaps, he knew why.

*

Waiting for the train at Fanling Station, he tried ringing Lai-king once more.

Still no answer. What had happened there? Perhaps they should have tried to do something, after all, something to make Guodong's case public? But then he saw Lai-king's harassed face, heard her anxious voice telling them not to, and recalled those two security officers outside her door. And, as the train arrived, moving smoothly along the platform, he remembered those two young activists regretfully saying Guodong's case wasn't big enough. He found a seat by a window and, looking out towards the still-green hills, saw only Helen's farewell smile, then Guodong cowering beneath that welter of sticks and stones, that menacing upraised baton.

25

She felt that familiar sudden twisting curl in her stomach when the woman officer invited her to come and drink tea. It was the same one as before, the one with a mole on her cheek. Her voice was quite friendly, but Lai-king knew 'drinking tea' with the police meant a warning of some sort – a warning at the very least. That was why she'd never answered the phone when Dimitri called, or San-san – and still less when those two young troublemakers did. She hadn't even opened her laptop, which stood as resolutely closed as Guodong's, both garnering the dust because she hadn't the heart to clean the place now. Why, then, did they want to see her? What had she done wrong? Or was it Guodong? Her heart staggered as she suddenly imagined them handing her his death certificate and, in a plain brown cardboard box, his ashes.

At the station, the woman nodded to the uniformed officers at the entrance and led her back to a small room with blank walls. A slightly older man was sitting behind a desk, reading a document. He glanced up at her and nodded to the empty chair facing him while the woman drew up a chair beside the desk.

'I suppose you know why we've asked you here?' the man began as Lai-king sat down. The woman reached for a tall red Thermos and poured water – not tea – into a cup, then pushed it along the desk towards her.

She shook her head, fingering the handle of the cup.

'Really? But you know why your husband's been sent to a *laojiao*?'

'I had nothing to do with that.'

They both looked at her for some time, as if waiting for her to go on. At last: 'So you had nothing to do with it,' the man repeated dubiously. 'Really?'

She shook her head again. *Careful,* she told herself. *Be careful.*

Then the woman began. 'Didn't you know he was going back to the village, though? Going back to cause trouble?'

'He didn't tell me. He just left a note after he'd gone.'

'You should have told us,' the man said.

Lai-king gazed down into the cup. It was January, cold and damp. She could see the water was cooling, there wasn't any steam. 'I thought you knew already,' she said, her voice low and heavy. She felt something stirring in her, a timid resistance to them, a dull resentment of their power.

The man leant back in his chair and took a cigarette pack out of the top pocket of his jacket. Zhonghua, she saw, the most expensive soft pack too. He drew a cigarette out, rolled it to and fro between his finger and thumb, placed it between his lips and, feeling in his side pocket, drew out a lighter. Holding it up, he contemplated it, head on one side, as though it was a piece of precious jade. At last his thumb pressed down. On the second click the flame flared. Very deliberately he lit the cigarette and gazed meditatively at the lighter's steady flame before snapping it shut. Leaning still further back in his chair, he exhaled a long funnel of blue-grey smoke up towards the ceiling, which, Lai-king noticed, was smudged and grey. 'Who do you think put him up to it?' he asked the ceiling. 'Any idea?'

Lai-king wondered if they were recording everything she said, and somehow that increased her helpless resentment. She was a mouse and they were cats, patting her with their sheathed claws.

Those two young people! she wanted to blurt out. *They got him into all this!* But that timid sullen resentment held her back. And anyway, she thought a moment later, would it help Guodong if she did tell them?

'Any idea?' the man repeated, leaning forward suddenly on the desk and looking her in the eyes. And at the same time the woman leant forward expectantly too.

Dumbly she gazed down at her hands, clasped in her lap now, and slowly shook her head.

The man negligently took up the file lying on the desk, casually turned the pages, then stopped and slowly read. 'Those two people from Hong Kong' – he looked up at her – 'the ones who called on you after your husband was arrested. Called twice. You know who I mean? The foreigner with a Chinese wife?'

Lai-king nodded.

'Did you know they went to the village when that illegal gathering took place? With two Chinese students and that musician from Hong Kong?'

She shook her head.

'But you do know those students, don't you?' the woman asked, while the man frowned down at the paper now as if he found it hard to decipher their names.

'Know?' Lai-king watched the smoke curling up from the cigarette between the man's fingers, at the ash still clinging precariously to the tip. 'I've met them three or four times.'

'Three or four times,' the man said doubtfully. 'Is that all?'

Lai-king shrugged. 'I didn't count.'

'But you know the . . .' – he bent over the desk, frowning down as he pulled the file closer – 'the Johnston family? You know them very well, don't you?'

Lai-king gazed down into the tepid water and decided to sip some before she answered. 'Yes.' She licked her lips. 'We knew them in Hong Kong.'

'Hong Kong,' the man said, looking up at her at last. 'You lived there for twenty-five years, didn't you?'

'My husband did. I was born there.' And as she spoke, she saw the old building of her Girls College in her head – *In Faith Go Forward* – then the university with its quiet tree-lined paths and the lily pond where they sometimes used to have tutorials in the spring. She felt hot tears searing her eyes. How had it all come to this?

'Right,' the man nodded. His eyebrows arched then drew together in a frown as he pored over the file. 'So you must know there are Western people there who are trying to subvert our system?'

'I don't know about that.'

'Really?' he asked sceptically again. 'After all those years living there? And one of those students,' – he glanced down at the paper – 'Jianping, is studying there, isn't she?'

'I believe so.'

'Believe?' He glanced up sharply. 'You *know* so, don't you?'

Lai-king imagined a cat with its claws out now, sharp and curved. 'She said she was, I know that.'

'Right.' The man nodded. 'So you know that.' He drew on his cigarette and closed his eyes while he breathed the smoke out. 'So what else do you know?'

Lai-king hesitated, gazing down blankly at her hands in her lap. What else did she know? What did they want?

'We'd like to know more about those two students, Mrs Yu,' the woman said suavely when Lai-king still didn't answer. 'We want to know if they've been . . .' Her voice trailed uncertainly.

'Contaminated,' the man said. 'Contaminated by Western agents, the agents who are trying to subvert our system, our government.'

'You see, if you were able to help us, Mrs Yu,' the woman

went on when the man nodded to her, 'it might help to reduce the time your husband spends in the *laojiao*.'

Now Lai-king glanced sharply at her. The woman was smiling almost sympathetically. 'You know conditions are rather, well, uncomfortable there, aren't they? For someone like your husband, who isn't used to hard work – manual work, I mean?'

Lai-king felt the words thudding into her like little leaden bullets, one after the other. For a moment she imagined herself being shot, her body crumpling and sagging.

'And he has a heart condition, too, doesn't he?' the woman went on softly.

Lai-king nodded slowly, gazing down again at her hands, the fingers moving restlessly now, twining and untwining. She felt their eyes on her, calm and certain. Purring cats regarding their helpless quivering mouse, stretching their claws out, retracting them, stretching them out again. 'I'd like to see him,' she said in a low pleading voice at last, without looking up. 'I'd like to see my husband.' She heard her voice quaver, felt the hot smart of tears again behind her eyes. 'Don't I have the right?'

'I expect that could be arranged,' the man said. He looked all over the desk as though searching for something, then with a shrug tapped the ash off his cigarette onto the floor. '*If* people are co-operative.'

'I'm sure your daughter would like to see him too, wouldn't she?' the woman added in that same suave, friendly tone. 'If he was out of the *laojiao* when she came? She'll want to come again, won't she?'

'Yes,' Lai-king said. 'If she gets a visa.'

'Have you ever thought about joining your daughter in the States?' the man asked abruptly. 'You and your husband, when he's released? Keep him out of harm's way? You wouldn't want him to go back into a *laojiao*, would you?'

'I thought the Party said they're going to abolish the *laojiao*?' Lai-king looked up, almost challenging him.

The man was considering the new ash growing on his cigarette, like someone watching a caterpillar slowly emerging from its chrysalis. 'There'll always be somewhere to put troublemakers,' he said ruminatively. 'Whatever it's called.'

Lai-king stared down at the half-empty cup in front of her. There was a little chip in the rim, she noticed absently, while *always somewhere to put troublemakers* echoed dully in her head.

'Here, sign this,' the man said abruptly, sliding a sheet of paper across the desk.

26

Dimitri turned in his chair as the door latch clicked behind him.

'I met San-san in town,' Mila said, unbuttoning her coat. 'She said Jianping's here. Apparently she wants to meet us. To talk about Guodong again. What have you been doing all morning?'

'Nothing much. Watching the sea.' But thinking now of Guodong in some grim labour camp. What could Jianping possibly have to say about that? An apology, perhaps? Some hope. He turned back to gaze out over the balcony at the grey cold surface of the sea; at a black and white ferry heading to Lamma Island, curled lip of creamed wave at its bow, churned white foam spreading, slowly fading, in its wake. Heading for the harbour where Ah Wong's niece's son had drowned in that collision four months ago. 'Did San-san tell her Lai-king has started talking to us at last?'

'I don't know.' In a week it would be Chinese New Year: the year of the snake. Then the year of the horse. How many more years would they see together? Who knew, he was still in the clear. Yet she imagined herself coming in one day to an empty flat, still and empty. 'Funny place, Hong Kong,' she said, hanging up her coat. 'Two New Years, one after the other, Western and Chinese.'

'Best of both worlds,' Dimitri answered. 'The people in between. But speaking of the Western New Year, I was thinking just now of the English martyrs.'

'Martyrs?' She laughed. 'What's that got to do with the Western New Year?'

'Oh, nothing really. It's just that I was reminded of them last New Year's Eve, when we all went up the hill to watch the fireworks . . .' For a moment he saw them again, the children running ahead with Elena, afraid they might miss the start. Mila with Alex, himself with San-san, who was afraid the last slope might be too steep for him. He heard the ships in the harbour once more, blaring out their cacophonous greetings on the stroke of midnight as the glittering, banging fireworks display began.

'Martyrs to the noise?' Mila smiled, sitting beside him.

He shook his head. The ferry was gone behind the headland now. The slate-grey sea was as still and empty as the slate-grey sky above it. 'No, when we got to the top, Michael asked me where the old Queen Elizabeth liner sank, and I pointed it out to him, more or less, and told him how it burned for three days.'

'Ah,' Mila nodded. 'I remember when that happened. We were driving down to the university . . .'

Dimitri was still gazing out at the sea. '. . . And I said it reminded me of the English martyrs being burned at the stake by Mary Tudor.'

'And I had no idea who they were.'

'Right. Remember who they were now?'

'Er . . . Hugo Someone?'

'Hugh Latimer and Nicholas Ridley. Queen Mary was Catholic and they were Protestant. Since they wouldn't conform, she had them burned alive. Remember I told you what Latimer said to Ridley as they were both being chained to the stake?'

'Something about a candle?'

Dimitri nodded, closed his eyes and waited for the words to come. *'Be of good comfort, Master Ridley. We shall this day light such a candle as I trust shall never be put out.'*

She smiled. Yes, she remembered it all. She had started

teaching again, they were married, Alex and Elena had accepted her . . .

'And you said there'd been millions of martyrs in China just recently,' Dimitri was saying, 'but their candles seemed to have been put out pretty quickly . . . Remember?'

'Yes. I remember.' For some seconds she was silent, watching the past. That sense of safety at last, of hope, of contentment. A contentment always shadowed, however, by the thought that Dimitri's first wife killed herself because of her. *'It wasn't your fault,'* he kept telling her. *'Something like that was bound to happen, she was always threatening it.'* Yes, perhaps. But it happened as it did because of that anonymous letter, because of her.

'Why did that liner remind you of those English martyrs?' she asked at last with a faint returning smile. 'Even if it was the biggest liner in the world?'

'Don't know. Perhaps it was just the royal name?'

'And the flames, I suppose,' she said slowly. 'And the flames.'

*

It wasn't just Jianping, it was her friend as well, Yiming. There they sat in the corner of that old tea-house off Hollywood Road, a steaming pot of tea already on the table. They rose and bowed politely as San-san, Mila and Dimitri approached. '*Nie hao*?' Yiming said.

So they were to speak Mandarin.

'Thank you for coming,' he added gravely as he shook their hands.

'How are your studies?' San-san asked Jianping as Yiming poured tea for them. Dimitri glanced round at the dark panelled walls, the long scrolls hanging down, the heavy lanterns suspended from the high ceiling.

'Good,' Jianping smiled. Yiming nudged his glasses higher up his nose.

They sipped their tea.

'Something to eat?' Yiming asked. 'Dim sum?'

They shook their heads. It was already afternoon, after all, too late for dim sum.

'Any news about Guodong?' Dimitri asked as the silence lengthened.

Jianping glanced at Yiming. 'Yes, good news. We've found a lawyer who is willing to help.'

'Really?' Dimitri looked at them both with surprised respect. 'That is good.'

'Only,' she added slowly, 'Lai-king says no, not yet.'

'So she's talking to you too, now?'

Jianping smiled. 'You sound surprised?'

'I am a bit, yes.' He thought of Lai-king that morning in Shanghai, the day after that violent village demonstration. Her wide, strained eyes and drawn cheeks.

Yiming nudged those heavy black glasses up again – why didn't he get a pair that fit? – and blinked like a sleepy owl. 'If only she would let this lawyer work on his case . . . It will take some time to get any result.'

'And the *laojiao* he's been sent to,' Jianping added. 'It isn't very good.'

Mila placed her cup down on its delicate porcelain saucer. 'But you know why Lai-king doesn't want a lawyer, don't you?'

Jianping shrugged. 'She's afraid it might make things worse for Guodong.' She smiled, almost dismissively. 'She thinks you cannot fight the system.'

'And you think you can?' Mila's tone was sharper.

'If we don't try,' Yiming said, 'how will we find out?'

They looked away from each other. Their cups quietly chinked.

San-san broke the uneasy silence. 'So that's good news about the lawyer, but it doesn't help if Lai-king won't–'

'Couldn't you talk to her?' Jianping interrupted. 'She trusts you. Couldn't you persuade her to change her mind?'

'But suppose she's right?' Mila asked. 'Suppose that did make things worse for Guodong? Medicines stopped, food parcels held back, no visits . . . Punishment cell?'

'So you know about all that?' Yiming's owlish eyes widened behind his thick lenses.

'Oh yes, I know.' Her mouth set firm. Then she relented. 'A long time ago now.'

'That is what we're trying to change,' Jianping said.

'At whose cost?' San-san asked, lowering her eyelids.

Jianping looked down at her cup. 'We all take risks,' she said quietly. Her fingers curled and then uncurled round the cup's handle. For a moment Dimitri imagined she was fighting back tears. So she wasn't always so sure of herself?

'The people in the village are refusing to move off their land,' Yiming said with a glance at Jianping. 'There will be more trouble. It is not like here in Hong Kong.'

'It's not that perfect here,' Dimitri said drily.

'But people cannot have their land just taken from them by officials?'

'Not yet, anyway.'

'Some people on the mainland look at Hong Kong and ask why it can't be like that there.'

'And some people in Hong Kong look at the mainland and ask if – or when – it's going to be like that here. That's why they have second passports, those that can get them. And demonstrations.'

'So it is worth fighting for,' Yiming concluded with a faintly triumphant smile. 'And here people can demonstrate. That is what we want on the mainland.'

'Yes,' San-san said. 'But not at the cost of others' lives instead of your own.'

'Not instead of, no,' Yiming answered quietly. He looked down at the golden-coloured tea in his cup.

Now Jianping gazed at all three of them, that unnerving determination returned to her eyes. 'Will you do something for your friend? If this lawyer we've found works for him, will you help to make his case known here? Here and outside, if you can?'

San-san, Mila and Dimitri all looked at each other.

'Well, yes, of course,' San-san said.

'If Lai-king agrees,' Mila added with a cautionary glance at San-san.

'Or Guodong,' Dimitri added. 'Though I don't know how we'd find that out.'

'We might be able to,' Yiming said.

'Do you think they'll let you see him?'

'There are ways of finding out.' Yiming smiled, a sly, mysterious sort of smile.

'And will you try to persuade Lai-king?' Jianping persisted.

'I'm not sure about persuading,' Dimitri said. 'But we'll talk to her, certainly. It's a question of what's best for Guodong.'

'Not just Guodong,' Jianping said. 'There are others too. The villagers want their land back. That's what it's all about. If it doesn't work with the lawyer, we have to try something else. To make people notice.'

They pondered what that might mean while Yiming poured more tea for them, leaving the lid off the pot for the waiter to refill it.

'So what are you doing here, Yiming?' San-san asked as the abstracted silence lengthened. 'Just visiting or . . . ?'

Yiming smiled as he nudged those oversized glasses higher up his nose once more. 'Buying books we aren't allowed to buy on the mainland.'

'I hope you get them through customs,' Mila warned.

Yiming smiled his mysterious smile again.

Now Dimitri turned to Jianping. 'You know, you sometimes remind me of what was said about one of the student leaders in Tiananmen.'

Jianping tilted her head, smiled and waited. Dimitri noticed Yiming's eyes alertly watching him too. The others turned to him as well, sensing the keen edge in his voice.

'She gave an interview to an American journalist, I think it was, shortly before the massacre. According to the interview, she seemed to be saying she felt bad she couldn't tell the students in the square that what she was actually hoping for was bloodshed. You know, only through bloodshed could the revolution get started, that kind of thing?'

Jianping nodded, as if yes, she did know.

'But unfortunately – she was reported as saying, I don't know if it was true – unfortunately she herself couldn't stay for the bloodshed because, of course' – he raised an ironic eyebrow – 'her situation was different. She was a leader, too important to die just then. I don't know if it was distorted or not, but that's how it was reported.'

Jianping's eyelids fluttered. 'And what happened to her?'

He held her gaze. 'People here in Hong Kong helped her to escape. Eventually she settled in America and became a fervent Christian.'

'Ah yes,' Jianping said, her eyes clearing as she remembered. After some seconds, she smiled, still steadily meeting his gaze. 'I do not think I will become a Christian.'

'No? Nor do I. Although you are from Zhejiang, aren't you?

Jianping nodded.

'There are quite a lot of Christians there, aren't there?'

She smiled, but didn't answer.

Yiming's phone chimed on the table. He looked down at it, frowned, then with an apologetic smile, rose to go outside. Talking earnestly, he walked a few paces up and down the narrow street, where two young backpacker tourists, a man and a woman, were dubiously picking over the knickknacks laid out on a canopied stall in front of an old antique shop.

The others watched him through the window in uncertain silence as he gesticulated while he talked.

'Tiananmen,' Jianping said quietly, her eyes on Yiming. 'My father was killed there.'

'Tiananmen?' San-san stared at her.

Jianping nodded.

Mila frowned. 'But you weren't born then, surely?'

'Yes, seven months before.' She was still watching Yiming as, listening intently to whoever was calling, he glanced alertly up and down the street.

'Was your father a student, then?' Dimitri asked, as incredulous as Mila and San-san.

She shook her head. 'A worker.' Her eyes stayed with Yiming, who was coming back to them now, pushing the glass door open. 'You know, many more workers died than students. Apparently, he was one of those trying to stop the tanks.' She shrugged. 'My family never told me. They used to just say he died soon after I was born. Then, the first time I was leaving for Hong Kong, my mother did tell me.' She smiled wryly. 'I suppose she thought I might not come back. So that's why I started finding out about it here.'

'I'm afraid we have to go,' Yiming said, exchanging swift, meaningful glances with Jianping as he returned to the table. He raised his hand for the bill.

'No, it's all right,' Dimitri said in a subdued, almost contrite tone. 'Our turn to pay. You're our guests here in Hong Kong. We'll talk to Lai-king, of course, see what we can do.'

27

'Hello? Lai-king?'

'Yes. Dimitri.' Her voice, as usual, tired and expressionless.

'How are you?'

'Okay. About the same.'

'Any news about Guodong?'

'No.'

'Can't you even see him? They're supposed to allow visitors, aren't they?'

'Well, I think I'll be able to see him soon. Perhaps.'

'Actually, I wanted to ask you again if you wouldn't like to have a lawyer work on his case?'

'Not really, Dimitri. Not yet anyway.'

'Only we saw those two students here the other day–'

'Where? In Hong Kong?' At last her voice rose above that blank level tone. 'What are they doing there?'

'They said they've found a lawyer who's willing to work on the case, if Guodong agrees. Or you do?'

'I don't think Guodong wants one, Dimitri. Not yet anyway.'

'Are you sure? Shouldn't you ask him?'

'I don't think he wants one.' Her voice definite now. 'Which lawyer, actually?'

'I don't know his name. Someone who's willing to help him, that's all.'

'Could you find out his name please? Then I could think about it.'

'I suppose so. I'll ask them.'

'Who? Jianping and . . . ?'

'Yes.'

'What are they doing in Hong Kong? Are they seeing people there?'

'I don't know. Jianping's a postgraduate here.'

'Yes.'

'I don't know about Yiming. I suppose they see people here, yes,' Dimitri said warily. 'Why?'

After a pause. 'Don't know. I just wondered.' Her tone changed. 'Dimitri, someone's at the door. I'd better go now. Tell me the name of the lawyer if you find out, won't you?'

*

'And that was that,' Dimitri said a month later. 'She still doesn't want us to do anything. I asked her again last week. So Guodong goes on languishing in some *laojiao*.' As he laid his chopsticks down on the silver rest, carved like a doll-sized Chinese pillow, he recalled that this was the very restaurant where they'd held Guodong's farewell dinner ten or so years ago. He looked round the room. Yes, it might even be the same round table, the same waiter serving them.

'She doesn't want Guodong to get hurt,' Elena said. 'I don't blame her.'

'He may be getting hurt anyway,' Mila said.

'How long is he in for? Or is that up to them?'

'Eighteen months,' Dimitri said. 'But they can lengthen it if he doesn't "behave".'

'There you are, then. A lawyer couldn't get him out anyway, could he?'

'Who knows?' Dimitri shrugged. 'Jianping says they're still working on it. I spoke to her last week. But she wasn't very hopeful . . .'

The others were silent. Why did he have to bring that up today, Dimitri reproached himself, when no one can do anything about it?

Alex was snapping his chopsticks together like the jaws of a hungry crocodile. 'Did you hear about the Occupy Central movement?' he asked Elena's new boyfriend.

'Occupy Central?' Kevin repeated uncertainly. 'You mean Occupy Wall Street?'

Well, he'd only been here a few months, Dimitri thought. On the other hand, a manager in an American bank, surely he ought to know about it? And with a Taiwanese mother and GI father, too?

'No, here in Hong Kong,' Alex was saying.

'Oh, right.' Kevin's face cleared. 'Occupy *Central*, right.'

'They want to occupy Central next year, if they can't get to choose their leader democratically. You know, anyone can stand and everyone can vote, like in America.'

'They're hoping to get ten thousand people,' Elena told him. 'Civil disobedience kind of thing.'

Kevin nodded. 'Crazy.'

'Why?' San-san asked, mildly surprised.

'He's working there, in Central,' Elena laughed. 'He doesn't want people messing up his workplace.'

'No.' He shook his head as he took a piece of fish neatly with his chopsticks. 'But it's unrealistic, isn't it? I mean, is Beijing really going to say okay guys, go ahead and elect your own leader in Hong Kong, while we stick with the Party deciding everything here? Maybe if you could tow Hong Kong a few hundred miles out to sea and tie up near Taiwan, but . . .' He shrugged, dipping the fish in some thick dark soya sauce.

'So what will happen?' San-san asked. 'If they do get ten thousand people in Central?'

He held the fish over his rice. 'I guess the police will move in.'

'Suppose people get hurt?' Alex asked. 'How will that look in the world's press?'

'Will they care?'

'Well, suppose half a million went there?' Dimitri speculated. 'It's happened before.'

Kevin shrugged again, raising his chopsticks. 'Another Tiananmen?' He popped the fish into his mouth. Then, after a moment's reflective chewing: 'Or they'll slowly smother it?' he added. 'Or just wait for it to fizzle out?'

Tiananmen, Dimitri thought, remembering that sea of candles flickering at last year's vigil. *We shall this day light such a candle as I trust shall never be put out.* The words slipped into his head as he leant back for the *fo gei* to place more dishes on the table. Beggar's chicken, he saw. And lion's head.

'But what if they did the same in Beijing, Shanghai, Guangzhou?' Elena asked.

'They won't,' Mila said. Kevin nodded as he scooped up rice from his bowl.

'But they did in a way a couple of years ago,' San-san reminded her. 'Remember the Jasmine Revolution?'

'A few hundred people at most.' Mila's eyelids drooped. 'And it all faded away in a week.'

Yes, she was right, Dimitri thought. A few people arranging on their smart-phones to protest by strolling together at a certain time in a certain place in a few cities. He recalled seeing a photo of some of them, outside McDonald's in Beijing of all places, on a bleak cold February day – you could hardly tell the protesters from the merely idle onlookers. Or the plain-clothes police, for that matter. It was almost pathetic – no, it *was* pathetic, an anaemic ghost of a protest. But still, the government was rattled enough to snuff it out at once. There were probably ten times as many police there as protesters. No wonder Jianping and Yiming preferred online demonstrations to physical ones.

'But there is another movement,' Alex said, frowning as he tried to recall the name. 'New Citizens' Movement, I think they call it . . .'

Kevin's eyebrows rose to form two sceptical arches. He fingered his crisp white napkin.

'. . . A group of lawyers and academics, asking for more civil rights and that kind of thing. I believe they even demanded a few weeks ago that top government officials disclose their wealth. I wonder what will happen to them?'

'Guess if they get anywhere – you know, like attract attention – they'll get quietly squashed.' Kevin slowly closed his fist round his napkin. 'Like this.'

The napkin grew gradually smaller, crushed and crumpled beneath his tightening grip.

'But what would happen if thousands of people did all protest one day in Chinese cities like they do here?' Elena persisted. 'You know, a sort of real Chinese Spring like the Arab Spring, marching through the streets, filling the squares?'

'Bloodshed and chaos.' Mila laid her chopsticks deliberately down. 'Like Tiananmen.'

Her tone was so decided that for several seconds no one spoke, covering the silence by eating. Chopsticks clicked, tea was poured. Then Elena asked, her voice small and deflated like a pricked balloon, 'But it's got to change sooner or later, Mila, hasn't it?'

Mila granted her a smile as wan as winter sunshine. 'Everything changes sooner or later, Elena. But sooner might be fifty years. And later . . .' She shrugged.

It was just after the Ching Ming Spring festival. The hillside cemetery near Dimitri's and Mila's apartment had teemed like an anthill all day that week as descendants visited their ancestors and swept their graves. They lit incense sticks, kowtowed and laid food on the graves. Some burned paper replicas of banknotes for the dead to use in their afterlife. Would Ah Wong's niece Suk-yee visit her aunt's blank little box in the temple wall one day and make offerings for her? And did all those dutiful relatives, who usually avoided cemeteries like the plague, did they really believe they were somehow helping their ancestors? They didn't ask themselves; they just did it because they always had. Was that what it was like on the mainland with their government? They would go on obeying the Party or the Emperor or whoever – and what exactly was the difference anyway – because they always had? Or because, when they hadn't, as Mila said, they'd had bloodshed and chaos?

He turned to San-san. 'When's your next concert in China?'

She smiled a little wryly. 'We don't know, we haven't been asked yet. They were quite keen when we were in Shanghai, but, well, it seems to have gone cold now.'

'Maybe they've been warned off?' Dimitri suggested.

San-san shrugged. 'We've got an offer from Kuala Lumpur next month, and maybe something in Taiwan.'

And so they talked of other things and forgot China and, for a time, Guodong and Lai-king. *I am still in the clear,* Dimitri thought. *Still in remission.* That close dark horizon that had ringed him round nearly a year ago was gradually widening in sunlight before his eyes, stretching further and further into the distance. True, there was a little smudge not far off in the clear bright sky, a little smudge that every day grew a fraction larger – his next check-up. But that was still a long month away.

28

The rubber plant looked thirsty, he thought, despite April's humidity. And so did the ferns surrounding it. He uncurled the green hose from its hook on the wall and turned the tap. The dried earth swallowed the water greedily down, hissing gratefully as it darkened with its quenching moisture. He glanced up at the clouded sky. No stars tonight, then.

The balcony door glided open behind him.

'Dimitri?' Mila's voice was subdued, he realised a second later.

'Yes?'

'Elena just phoned.'

'Yes?' he turned.

'Apparently . . . Ah Wong's had a stroke.'

'Oh Christ!' He felt his body grow suddenly heavier. 'When? How is she?'

'Yesterday. She's all right, Elena said.'

'All right?' He saw Ah Wong waving him goodbye at the door of her bare little room, and, on the television behind her, that black and white snapshot of her as a fresh young girl. And behind that, Helen in her red cheongsam. ready to die . . .

'Remember her niece?'

'Suk-yee,' he nodded. The last time he saw her, years and years ago, she was embracing that young man in the shadows outside the kitchen one summer evening, and the languorous look she gave him as they drew apart was more provocative than embarrassed. The young man looked like a triad member, he remembered.

'Well, she phoned Elena,' Mila was saying. 'They had an arrangement she would apparently, if ever anything happened to Ah Wong.'

'Where is she? Ah Wong?'

'In hospital in Fanling. She's got some paralysis down the left side, but Elena says it's getting better.'

'Elena saw her? Yesterday? With the ballet and everything?'

Mila nodded. 'You're going to drown those plants.'

But of course Elena would, he thought as he turned off the tap. The large grey vase was almost overflowing now. It was strange, he thought as he watched the water slowly drain away into the sodden earth; it was strange, he felt as much resigned as sad. It was what you should expect to happen at a certain age. Even to yourself. Although your own case was one you never really resigned yourself to, try as you might. 'I'll go and see her tomorrow.'

Mila knew he would go alone; it would be what Ah Wong wanted.

*

He lost the way driving to the hospital and visiting hour was nearly over when he arrived. The receptionist sent him to Ward 4C. It was a large ward full of old men and women lying propped on their pillows. Some had oxygen masks over gaunt faces. All had tubes linking them to monitors or sneaking coyly out beneath their sheets down under the bed. An old man in the corner lay flat on his back, staring up at the ceiling, repeatedly calling someone's name. *Is that how you will end too?* a voice asked in Dimitri's head as he walked down between the beds. Well, if it was how he would end, it needn't be soon. If his next check-up in two weeks' time was okay, future check-ups would be less frequent. And why shouldn't it be okay?

Most of the patients were alone, but four or five had visitors. Those without visitors lay there motionless, apart from their glinting hooded eyes that followed him as he walked down between the beds, searching for Ah Wong. And the visitors, glancing round at him, stared a moment before turning back. Foreign devils weren't expected here. He began to think he must be in the wrong ward – he'd nearly reached the end – when a middle-aged woman with a teenage girl smiled at him. '*Sitau*,' she said, *Master*, and he knew her at once from her husky voice, even before she moved aside to reveal Ah Wong sitting up in the bed behind her.

'Suk-yee!' Now he could see the girl she'd been beneath the set features of her older face, the girl with the sultry pout and alluring eyes of thirty years ago. And turning to the young girl, he saw the same face not yet fully formed, but with intelligent eyes that surveyed him frankly before politely, demurely almost, looking down. 'Your daughter?' he asked.

Suk-yee nodded. 'Mei-li. She's still at school, she can speak English.' She turned to the girl and gestured.

'Good afternoon,' Mei-li said in precise, practised English.

'She clever girl,' Ah Wong declared from the bed.

'Ah Wong, how are you?' He'd expected to find one half of her face sagging, her voice slurred. But no, he saw with a surge of relief, she seemed unchanged since he last saw her when he gave her *lai see* for Chinese New Year. Except, he noticed now, her hair was untidy, sparse and straggly. How had she disguised that the last time he saw her only a couple of months ago? He remembered the sleek black queue she once had, hanging thick and glossy down her crisp white tunic.

'Sorry, master.' She glanced round the large ward, taking

in the patients, the visitors, the nurses, then smiled a wry apology. 'No can make coffee for you here.'

'I didn't come for coffee, Ah Wong!' he laughed. 'I came to see you. How are you now?'

'Not bad,' she said. 'More better now.' She was speaking English, he realised, as much to show how clever Suk-yee's daughter was as to ensure that no one nearby would understand what they were saying. But Suk-yee didn't understand English either, so he reverted to Cantonese. 'How long will you have to stay here, Ah Wong?'

She raised one frail hand from the bed and he saw the other was strangely limp and still. 'Maybe one, two week more,' she persisted in English.

He glanced at Suk-yee. Her eyes were blank.

'The doctor says perhaps two weeks she can go,' Mei-li said quietly. Her glance flitted towards Ah Wong then back to him. 'She must have physical . . .' Her eyes dimmed a moment as she searched for the word.

'Physiotherapy?'

She nodded.

'Your English is very good.'

'Oh no.' She smiled and shook her head.

'How much longer will you be in school, Mei-li?'

'This year I finish. I must earn money, now that–' She stopped short.

My God, how could he have forgotten? Her brother had been drowned in that ferry collision last year! That must be why she would have to leave school and earn money. He turned to Suk-yee. 'I was so sorry to hear about your son,' he said in Cantonese.

She smiled briefly, inclining her head.

'Government pay money maybe,' Ah Wong said from the bed. 'Government pay money, Mei-li stay school.'

He turned back to Mei-li. 'What do you want to do? If you stay in school?'

The girl glanced away wistfully into a dream of the future. 'Maybe study abroad,' she said at last.

And if she didn't stay in school, he wondered, what then? But it was Ah Wong he'd come to visit and he was late. He stepped closer to her. 'Will you be able to go back to your room when you leave here?' he asked. 'Or . . . ?'

Again she raised only her right hand. The left stayed limp on the sheet. 'Doctor no say.'

He tried to tell her he was sure she would, while Ah Wong only nodded – out of politeness, it seemed.

*

After a few more minutes, nurses entered with trays of medicines. Visiting hour was over. He took Ah Wong's small, worn hand, a thing he'd never done before, the hand that lay inert on the bed. It lay just as inert in his, as still and cold as a stone. 'I'll phone the doctor,' he promised her. 'And find out how things are. And I'll come back with Elena and Alex.' For a moment he stroked it, the hand that had washed his shirts and cooked his meals and fed and comforted his children. But he saw she was embarrassed by such a display and, with a half-apologetic smile, he laid the limp hand down again. She smiled goodbye. For a moment her face seemed almost like a child's, so small and, yes, serene. He imagined her as a child on her village beach, splitting oysters under a burning sun.

As always, there had been too little to say. If there had been more time, the silences would only have lengthened and lengthened. Had Ah Wong, who used to be so talkative, grown so used to solitude now that she preferred it to company, even when she lay in hospital, recovering from a stroke? Perhaps it would be different when he came with Alex and Elena.

He turned away, but: 'Master?' Ah Wong called softly.

She was reaching with her good arm for the bedside table, wincing as she struggled to pull the drawer open. Grunting with the strain of it, she felt inside, her worn fingers scrabbling till they found a grey-white card. When, with a sigh, she took it out and turned it over, he saw it was that faded photo of Helen she'd kept so long hidden in her room.

'More better you keep it, master,' she said quietly, as though she didn't want to be heard.

He slid it silently into his shirt pocket. 'Thank you, Ah Wong.' He didn't know what else to say.

Suk-yee was waiting with her daughter at the foot of the bed, ready to leave. Yes, she had come, he thought. Despite their very different lives, the bond with her aunt had survived. Well, of course, she was Chinese. Family still meant something – everything, even.

At the entrance to the ward he turned back. Ah Wong was still watching them from her pillow, still serenely smiling. She raised her good hand and let it fall.

'Where are you going now?' he asked Suk-yee as they walked out into the warm night.

'Train to Kowloon.'

'I'll take you to the station.' He nodded towards the car park. 'You live in Kowloon?'

She held up her hand, smiling. 'Two rooms. It was better before. Now everything's too expensive. We had three rooms before, we can't afford that now.'

'Before there were three of us,' Mei-li reminded her mother.

'Four,' Suk-yee said curtly. Mei-li blushed, looked away.

Four, he thought. The husband that was now off with

another woman. Should he mention that? Well, she herself had opened the door.

'Four?' he repeated.

'My husband was no good,' she said matter-of-factly, as though she was discussing a piece of furniture she had now discarded.

'That must be hard for you, though?'

'Before was better,' Suk-yee said decidedly.

'When your husband and son were–'

Suk-yee shook her head. 'Before the mainlanders took over. Now everything's too expensive. Not enough work, not enough money.'

He wondered if she'd only said that because she thought it would please him, a foreign devil. He smiled. 'You were a mainlander yourself.'

She shook her head again, as though that was irrelevant. 'Before, I had work,' she repeated. 'Now no work.'

He thought of her slipping across the border to escape the dreary life of a desperately poor communist village, before China's rulers forsook Marx for Mammon and proclaimed that greed was good. Had she ever regretted coming here? The Hong Kong Dream didn't always end happily any more than the American Dream did. And the Chinese Dream?

'What do *you* think?' he asked Mei-li as he released the car doors' locks.

Mei-li shrugged. 'I don't know,' she said reluctantly. 'I don't know what it was like before. I am too young.'

When they reached the station, he exchanged phone numbers with Suk-yee, so they could talk in case anything happened to Ah Wong. They waved their hands and murmured '*Baai-baai.*' He watched them walk into the entrance. There was still something about Suk-yee's hip-swaying gait that reminded him of the sultrily seductive girl she'd been twenty, no, thirty, years ago. Mei-li, though, walking a little apart, had only an air of settled, earnest purpose. At the last moment, before they were swallowed in the station's crowded maw, they both looked round, smiled and briefly waved again.

He smiled back, raised his hand and waited for a bent old woman to push a barrow loaded with used cardboard cartons slowly, very slowly, across the road. Then he eased the car out into the clogged current of rush-hour traffic.

Well, he thought, as he drove out of the town, Ah Wong hadn't looked bad at all, except for that limp left hand. After some phsyio she should be fine. Yes, they were lucky; they'd both survived one shock of age. Why had she given him that photo now, though? It nestled neatly against his chest, over his heart, as though to console or absolve him. '*It wasn't your fault,*' he imagined Helen saying. *'It was nobody's fault – or everyone's.'* He settled the car onto the highway and switched on the radio. By some miracle they were playing an old recording of Kathleen Ferrier singing Handel – he knew her voice at once. *Art thou troubled? Music will calm thee . . .*

The waning moon was leaning over the hills of Kowloon, over the dark jutting mass of Amah Rock. The stars glittered faint and far behind it. Amah Rock, that outcrop that resembled a woman with a child on her back . . . It summoned that old memory of Ah Wong again, that memory of her carrying four-year-old Elena on her back and turning her head to smile indulgently at her excited cries. Then, twenty years later, the memory of how she looked back at Elena for a long moment on the day she finally left their home for good, trudging down the hill to the bus stop with all her earthly possessions in heavy plastic bags dangling from each hand, a black umbrella tucked tight under her arm. It was the only time he ever saw her close to tears.

The memories stayed with him as, borne along on the tranquil flood tide of that peerless voice – *Art thou weary?* – he reached at last the haven of those final fading tones. *Rest shall be thine. Rest shall be thine.*

29

It is a warm sunny spring day. The stunted trees are all green now with fresh new leaves. The fields are blooming and birds swoop over them, twittering and singing. A few water buffalo graze peacefully by a hedge where tangled yellow wild flowers grow.

But at the edge of the straggling village a crowd is gathered, surly and grim. They are waving placards and shouting slogans. Facing them are rows of sternly silent police in riot gear, several trucks, police vans with barred windows, an ambulance and a bulldozer. A loud-hailer warns the villagers in harsh mechanical tones. The villagers shout back, punching the air. They will not budge.

Then at a signal, the bulldozer lumbers slowly, relentlessly, forward. Villagers stand or sit in front of it, but are pulled away by the police who outnumber them. There is shouting, fighting, clubbing. Men and women are being hustled into the waiting vans. Now the bulldozer is approaching the first house, a two-storey concrete building with dull red tiles all round its upper floor. On the flat roof behind the tiles stand three men and a tall woman. The men are hurling stones at the bulldozer. The woman stands alone, one foot placed casually on a ledge, for all the world as though she's tranquilly waiting for someone, or perhaps merely resting there. Now and then she calmly pulls her long hair back from her face and stretches faintly, gazing down at the angry scene below as though it cannot possibly concern her.

Then one of the men approaches and hands her a jerry can. Is that what she's been waiting for? Once more she pulls back her hair, then negligently, as though taking a shower, she pours the contents of the can over her body. The man returns to the other side of the roof and hurls more stones, while the woman resumes her careless pose. By now it's clear she is standing there deliberately, so that she will be clearly seen. Some of the villagers below are taking pictures with their phones.

Ladders are placed unsteadily against the roof, but the men push them aside, still hurling stones at the police and the bulldozer. The loud-hailer warns again in its harsh, toneless voice. A siren wails in the distance, coming nearer. The woman strikes a match, and with a graceful gesture places it to her side. In a moment, flames burst into bloom all over her, reaching far above her head. She stands suddenly rigid as a candle for two or three seconds, then collapses behind the tiled wall. The men take no notice; they are busy struggling now with helmeted policemen who have managed to scale the wall. As more policemen reach the roof, the men are clubbed and subdued, but smoke and flames still blossom from where the woman fell.

One policeman has a fire extinguisher. He points it at the flames and douses them. Then he stoops, disappears behind the wall and, a few seconds later, rises with the woman limp in his arms. She droops there, one arm hanging down, her head lolling back, while ambulance-men now scramble up the precarious ladders. Her body seems very light in the policeman's arms. It is covered now in a shroud of white foam, but beneath the shroud her charred flesh is visible, her clothes and long black hair all burnt away.

30

'Switch your phone on,' Mila said tensely as Dimitri poured his last cup of coffee at breakfast.

'Why?'

She was frowning as she peered at something on her own phone. 'Just switch it on!'

The only message was from Jianping, with the two words *please help* on it. Then came a video. 'Jesus!' he breathed as he gazed at the film, unfocussed, shaky and blurred, from the first sight of the young woman standing there, through to the shrivelled end. He played it again, dwelling on her drawing back her long black hair, on the sudden explosion of flame, her limp body in the policeman's arms, cradled there like Christ in Michelangelo's Pietà.

At last he looked up. 'I think I remember her,' he said slowly, heavily. 'I noticed her in the crowd that day in the village. I thought then she seemed so . . . so detached from it all.'

Mila was silent for some seconds. 'What do we do now?' she asked quietly.

He shook his head. 'I suppose they want us to send it to the papers and so on. Post it on YouTube.'

'It's probably on Sina Weibo already. And all the other sites in China.'

'Yes, but for how long? The censors will remove it, there are two million of them.' While he was speaking, his phone rang.

'Have you seen it?' San-san's voice asked, small and awed.

'Yes, just now.'

'It's horrible!'

'Yes.' He was trying to imagine what being set on fire would feel like. He remembered how much it hurt when he burnt his finger on a match a few days ago. What would it be like to have that sudden scorching pain all over your body?

'It's on Sina Weibo and Renren. And WeChat. A friend in the Conservatory phoned me a few minutes ago. More than fifty thousand tweets, she said.' Now Alex's voice sounded in the background. 'It's on the BBC too, Alex says. And Al Jazeera.'

Looking up from her phone, Mila said: 'It's on YouTube already.'

'Such a candle as I trust will never be put out,' Dimitri murmured slowly, seeing the flames again, the woman collapsing behind that dull, red-tiled wall.

'Sorry?' San-san said.

'Nothing.' He was gazing down at his pills on the table, rolling the red one to and fro under his fingertip. 'I wonder why they chose a woman, though?'

'Chose?' San-san said.

'Well, it looked as though it was planned, not a spur of the moment thing.' Jianping's and Yiming's faces wavered at the back of his mind like images on rippling water.

'It must have been planned,' Mila said across the table. 'They had everything ready.'

He nodded. 'So why a woman and not a man?'

'I don't know,' San-san said, her voice shaky. 'It was horrible, anyway.'

'We should phone Lai-king,' Mila said.

'Yes, it was horrible, all right,' Dimitri said, wondering if that particular woman was the only one prepared to sacrifice herself. Was that why? Or did they draw lots? Or, being a woman, was she considered just more . . . expendable?

'San-san, I think I should phone Lai-king,' he went on. 'See what she thinks about it. Maybe it will help Guodong. Draw attention to the whole situation, I mean.'

'Maybe, yes.' She sounded doubtful.

'I'll call you back later, all right?'

'Well,' he sighed as he put the phone down, 'as usual, it seems we can't do much to help. It's all happened already.'

Mila was gazing away over the open balcony to the sea. A huge freighter was moving slowly past several smaller vessels, a whale among porpoises. 'I wonder if Jianping and Yiming had anything to do with it?' She laid her phone down, slowly shaking her head. She was thinking of that tea-house in Shanghai. *A big fuss on the internet* – wasn't that what they said? *That was what the Government was afraid of*? Something like that.

'They must have had *something* to do with it.' Dimitri nodded. 'The question is, how much?' He watched his forefinger rolling the blue pill to and fro now while behind his eyes he saw that woman pulling back her long black hair before she set herself alight. As though she wanted to save it from the flames.

*

'Oh God, how awful,' Lai-king said. 'No, I didn't know, I never look at the internet any more.'

'It's awful, but . . . well, it might help Guodong. Push the authorities to look at what's been going on, I mean.' How callous he sounded. But still, it was true.

'Might it?' She paused and then: 'Were those two mixed up in it?'

'Jianping and Yiming?' He hesitated. Who was listening in? What would happen if he said all he knew? 'I really don't know,' he said cautiously, 'I've no idea. Why don't you go online and see if it's still there?'

'All right.' But her voice was dead again and he knew she wouldn't. 'Where are they? Do you know?'

'Who? Jianping and . . . ? I really don't know,' he said more firmly. Why was she asking? 'Have you had any more thoughts about a lawyer for Guodong?'

'No, not really.'

'Well . . .'

'Yes . . .'

'Let us know if anything develops. About Guodong, I mean.'

'Yes.'

*

'So what do we do now?' Mila asked as Dimitri laid the phone slowly down.

He shook his head and shrugged. 'Wait and see, I suppose. If it's already in the media, we can't do much to help.' What else could they do? No, he could phone Jianping.

But Jianping didn't answer. He sat there several minutes with the phone in his hand, seeing that woman calmly taking out the match, calmly striking it, calmly setting it to her side, then standing suddenly rigid as a candle, sheathed in brilliant flames.

31

'Well, you're still clear,' Chan said, laying the scan report down on his desk. He leant back in his chair, smiling, a smile more authentic than that usual professional smile, which was probably the same whether it accompanied good news or bad. 'You may be bucking the trend.'

Dimitri felt all his muscles loosening. He too smiled, shaking his head in grateful wonder. 'Still in remission, then?'

'Still in remission,' Chan nodded. 'And maybe' – he held up his hand for caution – '*maybe* you'll stay that way indefinitely.'

'So I might make medical history?' Dimitri asked.

'You already have.' Chan leant back, smiling a little more broadly. 'And you didn't want to have the chemo, remember?'

'Well, I still don't know how long I'll last, though, do I?'

'Do any of us?' He turned to his computer and, still smiling, started to type. 'There are a few cases where you get a sudden relapse, but . . . I wouldn't worry about that just now.'

Dimitri felt slightly giddy as he stood up, giddy with relief. 'Well, thanks.'

'Not at all. How's Yu Guodong, by the way? Didn't you go to see him recently? In Shanghai?'

'Guodong?' *Didn't Chan know what had happened to him? Or had he forgotten*? 'Er, yes,' he said uncertainly. 'Yes, I did.'

'Quite a place it is now, so they say. My daughter was there last year.'

So they were talking of ordinary things as if there'd never been anything else, as if death had been overcome and they all might live forever, an endless procession of ordinary days and ordinary untroubled nights.

He left the bland consulting rooms where other people awaited their fate and breathed in the canned air of the lift lobby as though it was an upland meadow fresh with the scent of flowers. Why was it like this every time, every stay of execution? Did we really cling so desperately to life? Yes, we did. But not that young woman in the village. Something Xiuling, that was her name. She died two days later, the media said. So she was still alive when they first saw that shaky video on their phones. What was she suffering, how conscious was she? Were her family there when she died, or locked away in prison? The video of her burning had gone viral, but whether through sympathy and outrage or just the ghoulish excitement of a real-life horror film, who could tell? Probably both. In China of course, all mention of the village had been censored. But she must have achieved something. He'd caught it that morning on the radio – apparently there was some investigation going on there now at provincial level. But what would the upshot be? Some cosmetic face-saving formula or a real concession? And how would it affect Guodong?

He reached for his phone and called Mila. This time he'd refused to let her come with him. A quirk of his condition – he'd dreamt of Chan's consulting room the night before, of Chan gravely considering a sheet of paper covered with numbers, regretfully shaking his head. And he'd obscurely thought perhaps it wouldn't happen if this time she didn't come along. Or was it again his dread of being pitied? Well, anyway, he'd been wrong, wrong, wrong. Mila answered at once. So she'd been waiting. Of course she had. 'It's still okay,' he said.

'I knew it would be,' she answered. But the relief swelling in her voice told him she hadn't, she'd only prayed and hoped. Prayed? Who was there to pray to? Whoever atheists in foxholes prayed to, he supposed.

He walked out into the humid warmth of Statue Square. There were the green gardens and the green trees; there were the clear fountains, still splashing innocently in the brilliant sunlight. As though spring could only lead to summer, dawn to noon, winter would never come and night never fall.

But then he thought of that young woman again, who apparently for the sake of others had made herself a blazing torch. Over her once flaming body night's long shadow had already fallen.

32

Guodong dared not look up when the truck stopped at the gates, in case the guard said no, there'd been a mistake, and he'd be hauled out, cuffed, taken to a punishment cell.

But they were waved through. As the closing gates receded, he glanced across at the man opposite; their eyes met and both of them tentatively, shyly, smiled. Had he 'changed his attitude', too, Guodong wondered, vowed to be a good citizen now? Was that why he was being released? Re-education Through Labour? Re-education? Hours of hard labour in the fields, and more hours if you didn't meet your quota. And then there were the punishments, the beatings, food parcels and medicines withheld.

Memories drifted alongside his thoughts. That man in the next bunk, his face bruised and bloody, lying there all night without moving or speaking; that cheerful boyish guard with the electric baton, grinning in anticipation, as though it was all just a prank. Just finished his service in the army, someone had said. They were the worst.

He closed his eyes. Better not to think about it. But where had they learnt to treat people like that? Was there a school for it? Tests and examinations? Someone whispered once that's what they did in Masanjia – trained people to do that, to be cruel. But Masanjia was hundreds of miles away, up in Liaoning. And someone else said it was just a women's *laojiao* there, nothing else . . .

When he opened his eyes, the *laojiao* was growing smaller; he could scarcely make out the barred windows or the detachment of prisoners being marched to work, a guard cycling alongside them. Then the truck turned onto the main road, accelerated with a spurt of dense black diesel exhaust and the camp was gone. There was nothing now but wide open fields and the wide open sky. He dared to think it at last: he really might be going home.

*

It wasn't till he was walking along the familiar streets of Shanghai – that seemed now to belong to another time – it wasn't till then that he really believed he was free. He was short of breath and his head throbbed, yet he took the longer way along the Bund. The trees blossomed, people chattered gaily as they walked past, the ferry chugged its leisurely path across the slow-flowing river, the towers of Pudong soared bright and glistening through the haze on the other bank. Yes, he was free, and yet he felt he was a ghost among the living, a being they could not see, even when they stepped out of his way. Because they saw only his shape. What had happened had changed his substance. Now he would always be opaque to them. And how would it be, he wondered with a stab of anxiety, how would it be with Lai-king? Would he be a stranger to her as well, and she to him? Was that why he was taking the long way home? Yes, he realised. He was scared of their coming meeting. No, not scared, shy. As if they were strangers.

A burly policeman standing at the entrance to the building eyed him as he approached and then demanded to see his papers. 'Re-education Through Labour,' he said, frowning as he read Guodong's documents. 'One of the last. And did you get re-educated?'

'I got labour,' Guodong answered in a low expressionless voice, looking away from the man's amused scrutiny.

The officer glanced at him sharply now, searching his averted face for any sign of mockery. 'All right, then,' he said at last, handing the documents back. 'On your way.'

*

He rang the bell and waited, his head bowed, staring at his unpolished shoes. *She isn't there*, he thought, listening for some sound behind the door. *She isn't there!* And he felt suddenly as hollow as the rooms inside must be. He rang again. Perhaps she'd gone away, back to Hong Kong, to America? His heart beat unsteadily, fear fluttered like a disturbed bird in his stomach. Would he ever see her again? Then he heard the lock click back in its slot. The door opened on its chain and Lai-king peered cautiously out through the crack. Her eyes widened. 'It's you?' she said hesitantly. And then: 'It's you!'

'Yes, it's me.'

She was trembling as she unhooked the chain and opened the door.

He stepped inside.

She leant back against the door to close it. 'Are you all right?'

He nodded.

'I was afraid I might never see you again.'

'So was I.'

They stood there, constrained by the weight of what each of them knew but could not tell. 'You're so thin,' she murmured. 'Are you hungry?'

He nodded. 'A cup of Oolong first?'

She smiled at last, a quivering, apologetic smile. 'I only have Pouchong.'

'Pouchong, Oolong' – he smiled himself now, remembering – 'whatever.'

She switched the kettle on in the kitchen, reached into the top shelf to get out the best teacups, which they usually used only for visitors.

When she came back, he was sitting at his desk, gazing at his closed computer, at the scrolls on the walls, familiar yet strange; as though they belonged to someone else now and he was only visiting.

'You know, we might be able to visit Fung-ying now,' Lai-king began.

'Really?' He looked up. 'D'you think so?'

'They said we might, after you'd been released.'

'Who said?'

The kettle whistled in the kitchen. She went to make the tea. Better not tell him what the police had said, she thought. Not yet, anyway.

'Did you hear what happened in the village?' she asked now as she brought in the tray.

He didn't answer. He was still gazing at his closed computer, but seeing only the tiger bench in its dull black surface. Yes, 'the tiger bench', they called it in the *laojiao.* Hog-tied to that bench for hours at a time. He could feel the cuffs tightening round his legs again, feel the exquisite agony beginning to return. Feel the spurt of terror when the cell door slammed open and the guards came in. Especially that young one with his boyish grin.

'You haven't heard about that woman?' she asked.

Still he didn't answer, until her words reached him at last like faint sounds from a distant shore and slowly loosened memory's tenacious hold. He turned to her. 'I've heard nothing. Nothing at all,' he said listlessly. Then, suddenly alert. 'What woman?'

Her phone chimed somewhere and she went in search of it. *What woman?* he thought. And was afraid he knew.

He heard Lai-king's voice, in the kitchen, wary as she answered.

'It's Dimitri,' she said, coming back. 'Apparently, it's in the papers in Hong Kong.' She passed him the phone.

33

'At last we meet,' Guodong said as Dimitri opened the door. He was as smiling and as open-armed as ever. Yet, as they embraced, Dimitri felt he had shrunk a little into his skin. And yes, even his voice was smaller. *Is that how he sees me?* he wondered fleetingly as they separated. For her part, Lai-king smiled uncertainly, unsure whether to embrace him or not. But then she did, briefly. 'How are you?' she asked, stepping swiftly back as though embarrassed by the touch of their bodies through their clothes. 'Are you better?' And she too seemed somehow diminished.

'Oh, I'm fine now. How are *you* both?' Dimitri said. But Mila came to greet them before they could answer.

'How long are you staying?' Mila asked when they were all seated with drinks in their hands. The bamboo blind on the balcony was swaying faintly in the breeze, filtering the evening sunlight. Splinters of shadow and light drifted across the room and over their faces.

'Only two days this time,' Guodong said apologetically, as if really he owed it to them to stay longer. He glanced at Lai-king sitting uncomfortably, perched on the edge of her chair, eyes darting warily from one to the other. 'Fung-ying's waiting for us in the States. And–'

'She was very worried about us,' Lai-king said abruptly, looking down now at her orange juice.

'We all were.' Dimitri smiled wryly. 'Anyway, you're here now, so . . .'

They raised their glasses and drank.

'Yes,' Guodong sighed as he put his wine down carefully

on the table beside him. 'We're here now, because Xiuling's dead.'

'The woman who set herself on fire?' Mila asked. 'Did you know her, then?' She saw the flames bursting into bloom again, saw the woman suddenly collapsing behind that low wall on the roof.

He nodded. 'A little, yes.'

'I didn't know that,' Lai-king said. She sounded almost aggrieved. 'You never told me!'

'No. No, I never told you . . .' Guodong said abstractedly. 'She used to live near our old house before she got married.' He took up his glass in both his small pale hands and gazed contemplatively into it, swirling the wine gently round and round. Perhaps he saw Xiuling as a girl playing in the fields, or leading a water buffalo. 'That's why I went to the village that day. Jianping said they were talking about a suicide or something if the officials didn't . . . And I thought, anything but that. I thought I could persuade them–'

'So *that's* why you went?' Lai-king stared at him, shaking her head. 'Now I know.'

In the strained, almost hurt pause that followed: 'I wondered where your house was,' Dimitri said, 'when we were there.'

'Oh, a bit outside the village.' Guodong shrugged. 'You know, a bit bigger, a bit more money then . . . Not that it did us much good. My father was branded a landlord for a time, despite being a supporter of the communists at first. Xiuling's family lived nearby, in a smaller place of course . . . Anyway' – his eyebrows rose – 'I don't suppose I'd be here now if she hadn't . . . hadn't done that. I'd still be in that labour camp.'

'What was it like?' Dimitri asked when, again, no one spoke. 'Was it very bad?'

Guodong frowned, still gazing into the little whirlpool

of wine, red as blood, in his shiny glass. 'Ask Mila, Dimitri. She knows, she's been there too. I don't suppose they've changed much over the years.'

'Is that a new scroll over there?' Lai-king interrupted, her voice high with feigned interest.

They craned their necks to look at the calligraphy. 'No.' Dimitri turned back. 'It used to hang in my room in the university. A student did it years ago. It's rather good, isn't it?'

'Interesting,' she murmured. 'Unusual.' And looked uneasily down now at the floor.

Guodong tipped his head back and drained his glass. Dimitri refilled it. The bottle's neck clinked against the glass as he poured. That and the liquid music of the wine were the only sounds. 'Sometimes I dream I'm still there, in the *laojiao*.' Guodong was gazing into the wine again, as if that was where his memories were stored. 'And I'm lying there expecting the guards to come in. Especially one of them.'

They all waited, but he didn't go on. Dimitri glanced at Mila. Her eyes had lost their focus. She too was remembering.

'And then I wake up.'

'It passes,' Mila said quietly. 'In the end.' *No, it doesn't,* she thought. *It only fades, it's always there.*

At last Guodong looked up. 'But what about you, Dimitri? You're looking really well.'

'Yes, I'm okay now.' He sipped his wine and passed the nuts round, peanuts and cashews. Thank God, his hair had grown back at last, though it was thinner, more fragile than before. 'How long will you stay in the States?'

Guodong and Lai-king glanced at each other. 'We're not sure,' Lai-king said slowly. 'Maybe we won't go back at all.'

'You don't feel very safe,' Guodong explained, still

gazing into his glass, 'once that's happened to you. On the other hand . . .' He sighed and shrugged.

'And he has his book to finish,' Lai-king murmured again. 'It might be easier in America. The libraries, I mean . . .' *Have you ever thought about joining your daughter in the States?* She heard that man's voice in her head. *You and your husband? Keep him out of harm's way?* She saw the mole on the woman's cheek again and her really quite pleasant smile.

'Ah yes, my book,' Guodong was saying wistfully, as though it belonged to an immensely distant and barely recoverable past. 'Fung-ying wants us to stay in the States, of course, but that feels a bit like running away . . . Anyway, we'll see, we'll see.'

'So you'll miss the Tiananmen vigil here,' Dimitri said, remembering how they used to go together.

Again Guodong glanced at Lai-king before he answered. And then she spoke for him. 'We wouldn't want *them* to know we went there. Not after what's happened already.'

'Well, not this year, anyway,' Guodong added, as if he felt a little guilty. 'Especially not if we go back to Shanghai.' He glanced at Lai-king yet again. Her lips tightened faintly.

'D'you think they would know?' Dimitri asked.

Guodong shrugged.

'It isn't worth the risk,' Lai-king said quietly.

'Well, they certainly do seem to be tightening the screws in Beijing,' Dimitri said. 'Did you hear about Document 9?'

'We don't hear anything.' Guodong smiled wryly. 'Document 9?'

'It's a high-level directive the Party's sent out to all the cadres, warning against the perils of Western ideas like democracy.'

'Ah,' Guodong said absently. He gazed down into his glass, swirling the wine gently round and round.

Dimitri wasn't sure if Guodong was listening or not, but he went on. 'Apparently, universities have been banned from discussing a whole list of topics. Civil rights, press freedom, rule of law. And what they call "historical mistakes of the Party". Not to speak of democracy, of course. Or Tiananmen. Seven sensitive topics, all together.'

'People are calling it the "Seven Don'ts",' Mila added.

'Seven?' Guodong repeated. He was still gazing into his glass as if it was something in that pool of wine that really absorbed him.

Mila guessed what it was. Something that happened in the *laojiao*, something he was trying to forget. *No, it won't ever go away*, she told him in her mind. *Just be grateful if it dims with time.* She went out onto the balcony and raised the blind. The dying sun glowed in the western sky. When she came back in, no one was talking. 'By the way' – she settled back in her chair and raised her glass – 'did you ever hear from Jianping or Yiming again?'

Guodong shook his head, looking up at last. 'And I didn't think it would be safe to call them.'

'No, I suppose not,' Dimitri said. 'We tried to reach Jianping after . . . after it all happened. But she never answered us. And now her number's not available – I mean it's not a valid number, it says.'

Guodong frowned. 'That's strange.'

'Or perhaps it isn't,' Mila breathed quietly, glancing away out over the balcony. Her eyes took in the shadowed leaves of the rubber plant while in her mind she saw those two young activists in that tea-house, the last time they met. '*We all take risks.*'

'She's probably got a new phone,' Lai-king suggested, gazing down at her feet. Her subdued tone told them she didn't believe it.

When no one else spoke: 'Well,' Dimitri said, glancing

at the carriage clock on the bookcase, from where two junk gods gazed impassively past them all. 'Shall we go and eat now? I've booked a table at that restaurant on Queens Road, remember?'

'Just like old times, eh?' Guodong said with a faint echo of his old joviality.

⋆

After the meal, Dimitri drove them back to their hotel. 'The life's gone out of them, hasn't it?' he said sadly as he drove away down the wide avenue and on towards Central.

Mila nodded. 'It's as if they'd been hollowed out.'

The malls and cinemas were just closing as he drove on, the last customers queueing at bus stops or waiting for trams. Dimitri glanced at a clanking tram, at tired heads nodding, at two foreign tourists standing in the front on the top deck as they snapped the towered lights of Central. One of them, a young girl, was taking selfies, stretching her arm out through the open window. 'Still, perhaps they'll recover over in the States. I wonder if they'll go back to Shanghai, though?'

He was driving near the waterfront now, past that place where everything happened forty years ago. Cranes were looming like huge gibbets over the sentenced buildings and a wrecker's ball stood like an executioner before their vacant broken-window eyes. He sensed Mila looking at him.

'Never forget, do you?' she murmured.

He smiled, shaking his head. 'The scenery may change, but . . .'

'The play remains?'

'As long as we do, anyway.'

34

The balcony doors rolled quietly open behind him.

'What are you doing out here?' Mila exclaimed. 'The mosquitoes will eat you alive.'

'Looking at the stars.' Dimitri was leaning on the silvery balcony rail, gazing up at the night. 'You don't get a clear sky that often any more. I got an email from Guodong, by the way.'

'Oh? How are they?' Mila struck a match and held it to the tip of the green mosquito coil, then slotted it onto its flimsy metal stand.

'They've been in Disneyland with their grandchildren, apparently.' Dimitri smiled. 'He said it was almost as bad as being in a *laojiao*.'

'Must be very bad in that case.'

'But he did say he'd started looking at his *Anthology of World Poetry* again.'

'Well, they seem to have recovered over there, then. D'you think they'll go back to Shanghai?'

'Not if Lai-king has her way–' He pointed suddenly. 'See that?'

'What?'

'Over there. A shooting star.'

'Missed it.' Now she stood beside him, leaning on the rail, hands clasped. Dimitri thought of that other balcony all those years ago, of her leaning on the rail just like that, of how she turned when he spoke to her, how she smiled . . .

'You spend a lot of time looking at the stars these days?'

'These nights, you mean. Yes. It takes you away from the mess of the world, reminds you how small we are, how transient.'

'How insignificant?'

'Not necessarily. Shorter songs are sometimes best.'

'But does anyone listen to them out there?'

Dimitri shrugged.

She was gazing up at the sky, darkened by Earth's shadow, glittering with stars. 'I wonder why there are so many stars?' she mused. 'It seems almost extravagant.'

'The real wonder is why there's anything at all. Why isn't there nothing? God, it's hot tonight.'

'It's going to rain soon, the forecast says.'

'I suppose that might stop people going to the vigil.'

'Us?'

'No, not us. But I guess we can be sure Jianping won't be there this time. Or Yiming. Those two remind me of Tankman. Except that Tankman didn't get involved in someone burning herself alive – if they were involved.'

Mila thought of Tankman, that man caught by the camera the day after the Tiananmen massacre. That ordinary-looking man in dark trousers and a white shirt, stepping in front of a column of tanks and stopping the first one in its tracks, dodging this way and that to confront it each time it tried to drive round him. She remembered the man haranguing the crew, even clambering onto the hull and shouting down at them through the hatch. Yes, she remembered Tankman, she remembered watching him on the TV, Alex and Elena too, clustered round the set, transfixed and awed. And then they watched him being hustled off, who knew whether by plain-clothes police or friends or onlookers, never to be seen or heard of again. Yes, Tankman.

'Maybe he's still alive somewhere,' Dimitri was saying.

'Maybe they killed him. We'll never know. The same for those two, Jianping and Yiming. Except there was a Western cameraman filming Tankman and the whole world got to know about him, whereas those two – they'll always be invisible.'

'I wonder how many more there are like them in China?' Mila murmured, the image of that ordinary, slightly tubby, man in his white shirt and dark trousers still hovering behind her eyes. *Not very many*, she thought.

'Who knows? Oh, by the way, Guodong wanted me to look up that poem by what's-his-name – Faiz. He wants to include it in his anthology, but he forgot it in Shanghai.' Dimitri drew back the balcony doors and went to the bookshelf.

Mila broke off the smouldering tip of the mosquito coil and left it to die among the ashes in that old cracked saucer where it stood. She watched the glow slowly dimming, the smoke thinning and fading, like an animal dying, she thought, then followed Dimitri into the room, drawing the doors smoothly shut behind her. The air-conditioning welcomed her in its cool, sterile embrace.

Dimitri had the book out of the shelf already and stood leafing through the pages. She watched him stop and read. 'I heard a recording of this once,' he murmured. 'Sometimes I wish I'd learnt Urdu. Too late now. But it's pretty good in English anyway.' He stood there reading the poem to himself while Mila sat down and watched his lips forming the words she could not hear.

Your heart will ease, the pain will cease.

The day will dawn, the season change.

Do not grieve. Do not grieve.

'Can't I hear it?' she asked. 'Read it aloud.'

He looked at her sitting there still and upright, her

ankles crossed, her arms folded, eyes wide and expectant, as though waiting for the curtain to be raised at the theatre. 'Tomorrow,' he said, closing the book. 'Too tired now. Let's go to bed.'

35

June 4th 2013

'My appointment with Chan,' Dimitri said, driving slowly up the ramp to the City Hall car park.

He felt her glancing at him. It was as if the air moved in the car. 'It isn't next week. It was yesterday.'

'I know,' Mila said softly.

'You know?'

'He phoned me this morning.'

'He had no right to–' he began, then sighed and shrugged. No point in getting angry now. But now he knew why she'd been so silent all the way down from home. He swung the car round on the top floor and found a space looking out over the harbour. 'Well, it's metastasised again,' he said brittly, staring out over the grey swollen sea. 'It sometimes happens like that, Chan said, though he was surprised.' He saw Chan's face, grave yet detached, his hand stroking back the lock of grey hair that was forever falling over his forehead. 'Anyway, it's . . . very aggressive, apparently. There's nothing more they can do except palliative care.' He heard his voice quiver as he spoke. When he turned the ignition key, the engine's quiet throbbing ceased like a failing heart.

Out of the corner of his eye he saw her nodding. 'I know, Dimitri.' She laid her hand on his knee. 'He told me everything.'

'Why didn't you say?'

'I knew you'd tell me when you wanted to.'

He let his hand fall onto hers as he gazed out over the piers at a ferry crossing towards Kowloon. How many times had he travelled on one of those ferries? But that was like her, to wait until he spoke. Would she have waited a week? A month? Yes, she would. She was unfathomably aware of all he felt, every atom of his being. 'Don't tell the others yet. Not tonight.'

Her hand gently pressed his knee in acquiescence. They sat there watching the ferry all the way till it berthed. There was a heavy, sullen swell from the west. The ferry wallowed in it till it reached the calm of the far jetty. The sky above the harbour loured with fold upon fold of dark grey cloud, gravid with rain, but he knew the sun must be setting over Sunset Peak on Lantau. *Fast falls the eventide.* A memory pierced him: climbing up that peak one summer with the children, a snake slithering away under his feet. And then the trek back past Perfect Pool, where they'd stayed for a swim on the way down to Tung Chung; now a town of dense high-rise buildings, but then just a fishing village. When was it, exactly? Just before Mila came back? All those memories, that made up his life – all soon to die and burn away. He sighed. 'Well, let's get tonight over with and then see . . .'

Again, that gentle pressure on his knee. Mila too was gazing out over the harbour, seeing nothing but the address of the hospice Chan had given her; the address, the phone number, the person to contact. She would call them tomorrow, she thought. Yes, tomorrow. Not today. She would push all that away until tomorrow. But it wouldn't be pushed away; it stayed there in her mind while her eyes surveyed the darkening harbour, inattentively registering the budding lights beyond that enchanted the approaching night. Should he die in the hospice or at home? She saw her father's dead face and then imagined Dimitri's. She foresaw the last wasting of muscles, the slow atrophy of the brain. She foresaw the soiled sheets, the helplessness, the long, wearing hours of waiting, even praying, for release. Yes, there would come a time when she was glad it was all over. She thought of the funeral, although she had no idea how it would or should be and could not ask him. She thought of the elephants she'd seen in some TV documentary, standing mournfully round the bones of a dead calf, laying their trunks gently on them in a last sad caress. Did they bellow their grief out across the lonely plain? She couldn't remember.

*

It was growing oppressively hot in the car, now the air-conditioner had died. 'Well, shall we go?' Dimitri turned to her, smiling a consoling sort of smile, as though it was she that was going to leave the world, not him.

'Let's take a taxi.' Mila's voice quavered faintly. She forced a smile in return.

'I'm not that far gone yet,' he said drily. 'I've still got a month or two. Taxis are refrigerated cells. Solitary confinement. We'll take the ding-ding as usual, while we can. There's life on a tram.' *Life*? He smiled grimly at himself. *Life*? 'Besides, a taxi won't be much quicker, this time of day.'

She took two umbrellas from the back seat. 'It's going to rain.'

*

It was one of the new trams. The turnstile entrance had been replaced by gates, but the steep winding staircase – which he insisted on climbing, hauling himself up step by step – was just as it was fifty years ago. Upstairs, the plastic seats had what looked like mahogany backs – though presumably they were really plastic too. The bell clanged, the tram jolted forward. A young couple offered them their seats and this time he murmured thanks and sat down beside Mila. Yes, he was tired, and there was a pain shooting up his back although he'd taken the prescribed dose of morphine. Would he last out the memorial vigil? He must, this time was definitely his last.

If there was life on the tram, he scarcely noticed it now. Sitting silent beside her – oh, the comfort of her warm body close to his – he merely glanced at the passengers. Schoolchildren toting heavy satchels as usual, two bent old men with sticks, women huddled over bulging shopping bags, Filipina maids chattering, young office-workers intent on their phones . . . Then he let the crowded noisy streets slowly unfurl before his eyes while behind them he foresaw the final unfurling of his life: the hospice bed, the calm, sympathetic, yet ultimately uninvolved, nurses. Mila, Alex, San-san and Elena all around him as he faded away. Not their children, though, he thought. That was no sight for children, he must remember to tell Mila that. Maybe it would be better to take an overdose and end it sooner? But then, whatever he wrote in a farewell note, they would always blame themselves, think they'd somehow failed him. No, he'd have to stick it out. And Mila – how would it be for her? That was the worst of it. How would she go on alone? They'd been together so long, their lives so intertwined, and all she'd have left of him would be her memories, memories fading like wilting flowers. He stared out with still, unfocussed eyes. The streets unfurled, blurred by the swiftly falling dusk, which was deepened by the rain-clouds overhead. His eyelids were growing heavy with a weariness beyond fatigue. He let them droop and close.

*

Once more he felt the gentle pressure of Mila's hand. They were there already. And the rain was coming. Yet the crowds were coming too as they always did, the streets leading to the park just as thronged, as people moved slowly forward, young and old, towards the vigil. He saw two policemen standing by a barrier, and another busy on his phone. But no beetle-like vans patiently lurking, no squads in riot gear. Or if there were, they kept well out of sight. The tram emptied as usual at the stop. Climbing awkwardly down the stairs, Dimitri saw only five people left on the top deck, and they looked almost sheepish.

His phone chimed as they walked slowly in the crowd towards the entrance. 'We're by the west gate,' San-san said. 'I hope the rain won't spoil it.'

And then he saw her, with Alex and Elena and the children too, beneath that Flame of the Forest tree where he always met Mila. That was new, bringing the children. 'Indoctrinating the young?' he asked Alex lightly, as though there was no shadow looming over him, heralding the long deep night.

Alex shook his head. 'They wanted to come, see what it's like.'

'Where's Kevin?' he asked Elena.

She wrinkled her nose. 'Not his kind of thing.' She hesitated. 'Besides,' she added with a shrug, 'Tara didn't get on with him.'

Tara smiled, an impish smile, and tossed her head to flick back her hair.

Taking their candles, they found a place as usual far from the stage. Yes, despite the impending rain, the park was full, and still people were pressing in. 'Someone was supposed to come from China,' San-san murmured. 'His son was killed during the massacre. But apparently the Beijing police "advised" him' – her eyebrows formed a brief ironic arch – 'not to.'

The speeches began.

They held their candles up under the menacing clouds. How many candles were glowing there tonight beneath the rain? Fifty thousand? A hundred? A jagged lightning flash of pain shot down his back again. Next year would be the twenty-fifth anniversary of the massacre. If only he could be there to see that. Surely the memorial would be bigger than ever? More demands for an accounting? For justice, for democracy, the right to choose their own government? Especially here, where freedom still existed. And how many candles were there hidden in China now – few or many? *Such a candle as will never be put out* . . . Jianping and Yiming, had their candles been snuffed, or were they hiding somewhere, waiting to be lit another time? He would never know. But then it didn't matter to him any more. Perhaps in the cool indifference of the universe nothing really mattered, everything would pass and be forgotten.

The erhu began its mournful melody, the drum its deep solemn beat. They all stood silent while the victims' names were called out one by one. Then 'Vindicate June 4th!' they chanted. 'Never give up!'

And now, as they sat down again, the rainstorm arrived, whipped on by the gusting wind. Umbrellas opened like glistening parachutes, but they were useless against a storm like that. The wind battered their taut canopies, or slapped them aside, sending the rain slanting beneath them, bombarding them with sharp little pellets. Many people were scrambling for shelter, yet the candles' wavering flames still glowed, a field of bright flowers in a dark and stormy plain.

Now they began to sing that anthem again, the one they sang every year. Would they sing it next year and the year after? Would their candles still glow, or would they lie somewhere broken and extinguished? *We shall this day light such a candle* . . . Would that Chinese spring ever blossom again, that premature spring that withered in Beijing twenty-four years ago? Could it be there, on those rain-swamped fields, where its blighted flowers had always been remembered, that they revived and bloomed once more? Or would this be their graveyard where they would finally be swept up, buried and forgotten?

*

Mila touched his arm. 'We'd better go, the children are getting soaked.' But it was him she was looking at. San-san and Alex both held out their hands as he started to rise; this time he succumbed and, wincing, let Alex pull him gently to his feet. As people made way for them to pass he sucked in a painful breath to blow out his candle.

But then he saw that girl again, the girl he saw last year, the one who offered him her seat on the tram. She was wearing a light transparent raincoat with a hood now, but he knew her at once, sitting there straight-backed and calm, like Mila when she was young. Her face was streaked with rain and a damp strand of hair hung glistening down over her forehead. As she glanced up at him and smiled her recognition, a blob of rain fell into her plastic cone. Her candle sputtered, then went out. Cupping his hand round its still flickering flame, he bent cautiously down and gave her his.

'*Dojeh!*' She looked up at him in pleased surprise. *Thank you!*

Another jagged flash of pain seared his spine, but he smiled back as he slowly, painfully, straightened. So it did matter, after all, it did matter that his candle would burn a little longer on this lonely planet, spinning slowly to its inevitable end in some remote corner of the universe. Perhaps nothing mattered more? He imagined a million such humble candles, glowing faintly even in the darkest corners of the earth.

The girl was regarding him still, her eyes glimmering faintly as they took in Mila and the others waiting behind him.

'*Joigin*,' he smiled. *Goodbye.*

'*Joigin.*' She raised her hand. Her slender fingers fluttered a delicate farewell.

Mila's eyes had widened, luminous with concern. Her hair was moist. Tears of rain trickled down her cheeks. 'Are you all right?' she asked softly, so the others wouldn't hear.

'Yes.' He gazed round one last time at the myriad flickering flames still bravely challenging the empire of the night, then turned to leave. 'Yes, I'm all right.'

36

Mila left the treacly Christmas carols oozing behind her in the mall and, hoisting her bag higher on her shoulder, walked through the twilight past the splashing fountains of Statue Square.

'Excuse me!' A girl ran after her. 'Excuse me!'

She turned.

'You just dropped this.' The girl was holding out an unstamped airmail envelope, stiff with a card fitted snugly inside.

'Oh. Thank you.' *Mr and Mrs Yu, Huangpu, Shanghai.*

As Mila slipped it back into her bag, the girl looked closer, hesitated, then asked: 'Weren't you at the Tiananmen vigil in June? With . . . with a . . . ?'

Mila smiled. The girl didn't want to say *gwei lo*, but it was on her tongue. 'With my husband? Yes.'

'I thought so. He gave me his candle.'

'Ah yes. I remember.' *That girl in the rain*, she thought. *Dimitri said she was like me when I was young. Dimitri, Dimitri.*

The girl smiled. 'Are you going to the vigil next year?'

'I expect *I* will. My husband . . . I'm afraid not any more.'

'Oh.' The girl's expression changed, her smile fading, her eyes swiftly shadowed. She'd understood at once. 'I'm so sorry. I . . . I thought he didn't look very well.'

Mila smiled, inclining her head. She was almost used to it by now.

‘I kept that candle,’ the girl murmured awkwardly. ‘I’ve still got it somewhere in my . . .’ Her voice faltered, stalled.

‘I’m sure he’d have appreciated that,’ Mila said slowly and precisely. She glanced away from the girl’s shy, sympathetic gaze, away at the nearest fountain, its clear water splashing as it always had. *The waters of life*, she thought. *The waters of life*. ‘But unfortunately he . . . his other candle went out in October.’ She smiled again, briefly, wistfully.

‘Yes.’ The girl nodded. ‘I’m so sorry,’ she repeated, standing there still, uneasy and uncertain. Then, with an effort: ‘I expect there’ll be more people than ever there next year,’ she said at last. ‘The twenty-fifth anniversary, I mean?’

‘Yes, I expect– I hope so.’ *But the year after that*? Mila wondered. *And the year after that*? ‘Perhaps I’ll see you there?’ Raising her hand, she smiled goodbye and walked on towards the post office and the City Hall car park, where, in its space overlooking the darkening harbour, the grey Honda was waiting empty in the dusk.

Epilogue

On June 4th 2014, one of the largest ever candlelight vigils was held in Hong Kong to commemorate the twenty-fifth anniversary of the Tiananmen massacre.

On July 1st, the anniversary of Hong Kong's return to China, tens of thousands marched in the wind and rain, demanding full democracy. When the Chinese and Hong Kong governments rejected their demands, the movement Occupy Central called on people to occupy sites in the city's financial district. Many thousands of students and young people joined the protest and soon became the largest group of demonstrators. The demonstrators were mostly peaceful, cheerful and well-organised. Students completed their assignments on improvised desks, first aid centres and cleaning teams were set up, notices were posted apologising for inconveniencing people who worked in the vicinity.

When the police used tear gas and pepper spray in an attempt to dislodge them, the demonstrators unfurled umbrellas to protect themselves and still more people joined them. From then on the movement was known as the Umbrella Revolution.

As the weeks passed and winter approached, the number of demonstrators gradually dwindled to the hundreds, who, after seventy-nine days of protest, resolved to pursue their campaign by other means and left their encampments.

As their barricades were being dismantled, a few scattered banners were found:

We will be back.

The text on page 1 is an extract from a BBC news report by the journalist Kate Adie CBE, first broadcast in 1989.

CHRISTOPHER NEW is the author of the *New York Times* bestselling novel *Shanghai*, part of his critically acclaimed China Coast trilogy. Born in the UK, educated at Oxford and Princeton Universities, and for many years resident in Hong Kong, he is a former Head of the Philosophy Department at Hong Kong University. He has written a number of highly praised novels set in Asia, the Middle East and Europe.

CHRISTOPHER NEW is the author of the
New York Times bestselling novel *Shanghai*
[illegible] and the critically acclaimed China Coast trilogy.
Born in the UK, educated at Oxford and Pennsylvania
Universities, and for many years resident in Hong Kong,
he was also Head of the Philosophy Department at
Hong Kong University. He has written a number
of highly praised novels set in Asia,
the Middle East and Europe.